Temptation had never been so hard to resist

What was it about a wet naked man? Macy wondered. So much clean skin in which to bury her nose and breathe, in which to dart the tip of her tongue and taste.

"Macy?" Leo called. "Are you cooking yet?"

If he only knew, she mused. "I was thinking of bringing a couple of eggs in here and poaching them in this steam."

Leo's movements stilled and then she heard the magnetic latch click. The door eased open and Macy got her first unintentional look at his body before she jerked her gaze up to his face.

He wore a grin that was pure ego and conceit. The brief look she'd caught of his body was enough to confirm he had good reason.

Besides, at the moment, she was willing to forgive him just about anything. Water streamed down his face, dripping from spiky lashes, matting his hair to his head with a boyish charm.

The complete pictu
stepped into the sho

D1359970

Dear Reader,

I admit it. Fashion fascinates me, as do fads. Who would have thought we'd see the return of tie-dye and bell-bottoms? Or that individuality and flaunting convention could make for such eye-catching style?

I also find myself fascinated by the entrepreneurial spirit and boundless imagination (not to mention energy!) found in so many members of Generation X.

Welcome to gIRL-gEAR, the combination of my fascinations, where you'll meet a group of six twenty-something women who've launched an urban fashion empire and, because this is my fantasy, have set the retail world on fire.

All Tied Up, the first story, follows the Peter Pan adventures of Macy Webb, who wildly embraces her inner child—until she meets corporate attorney Leo Redding, who is all grown up.

If, like Chloe Zuniga, the heroine of the second story, you enjoy those sexy scenes from classic cinematic love stories, you won't want to miss *No Strings Attached*.

Finally, join Sydney Ford as she sets sail toward a romance that was *Bound to Happen!*

Enjoy!

Alison Kent

P.S. To learn more about the girls, the company and the series, visit www.girl-gear.com, where you can always find the latest in fun and games, dating tips and more!

Books by Alison Kent

HARLEQUIN TEMPTATION

ALL TIED UP

Alison Kent

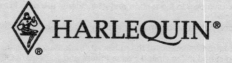

HARLEQUIN®

TORONTO • NEW YORK • LONDON
AMSTERDAM • PARIS • SYDNEY • HAMBURG
STOCKHOLM • ATHENS • TOKYO • MILAN • MADRID
PRAGUE • WARSAW • BUDAPEST • AUCKLAND

If you purchased this book without a cover you should be aware that this book is stolen property. It was reported as "unsold and destroyed" to the publisher, and neither the author nor the publisher has received any payment for this "stripped book."

ISBN 0-373-79028-7

ALL TIED UP

Copyright © 2002 by Mica Stone.

All rights reserved. Except for use in any review, the reproduction or utilization of this work in whole or in part in any form by any electronic, mechanical or other means, now known or hereafter invented, including xerography, photocopying and recording, or in any information storage or retrieval system, is forbidden without the written permission of the publisher, Harlequin Enterprises Limited, 225 Duncan Mill Road, Don Mills, Ontario, Canada M3B 3K9.

All characters in this book have no existence outside the imagination of the author and have no relation whatsoever to anyone bearing the same name or names. They are not even distantly inspired by any individual known or unknown to the author, and all incidents are pure invention.

This edition published by arrangement with Harlequin Books S.A.

® and TM are trademarks of the publisher. Trademarks indicated with ® are registered in the United States Patent and Trademark Office, the Canadian Trade Marks Office and in other countries.

Visit us at www.eHarlequin.com

Printed in U.S.A.

gIRL-gEAR
urban fashions for gIRLS who gET it!

SYDNEY FORD
Chief Executive Officer

MACY WEBB
Content Editor
www.gIRL-gEAR.com

LAUREN HOLLISTER
Design Editor
www.gIRL-gEAR.com

CHLOE ZUNIGA
Vice President

gRAFFITI gIRL   gADGET gIRL
the cosmetics line   the accessories line

MELANIE CRAINE
Vice President

gIZMO gIRL   gOODY gIRL
the technology line   the gifts line

KINSEY GRAY
Vice President

gROWL gIRL   gO gIRL
the party wear   the active wear

A big thank-you to:

Birgit Davis-Todd for your enthusiasm and your patience
Karen Solem for your encouragement and patience
Susan Sheppard for the conversation over dinner
on the River Walk—and did I mention your patience?
And to Walt, for too many things to mention but,
on this book in particular, for your patience
with my need for tiramisu and caramel lattes.

Prologue

The gIRLS behind gIRL-gEAR
by Samantha Venus for *Urban Attitude Magazine*

This month we begin a multipart series introducing the women responsible for the cultural phenomenon that is gIRL-gEAR. (And to think it all began at an Austin, Texas, Starbucks!)

Three years ago, the firm blasted onto the retail scene with urban fashion's *next best thing,* and now gIRL-gEAR has had every department store across the country scrambling to catch up. All we at *Urban Attitude* have to say is, Good Luck!

Let's meet our first gIRL...Macy Webb—a fitting choice for our initial profile, as Macy works as content editor for the Web site's discussion forums and advice columns, offering tips on dating and suggestions for singles. And let's be honest here. Do we doubt for a minute that the gIRLS whose fashion advice we've followed now for three years would steer us wrong when it comes to M-E-N? I don't think so!

Creator of gIRL gAMES and gIRL gUIDE, the site's fun and advice columns, Macy's currently organizing a trial run of her latest gIRL gAMES project—a very sexy scavenger hunt. "An after-hours, adults-only, you-find-mine-I'll-find-yours kind of contest," she says. The rules will be posted in her next column, due online at the end of the month. (www.girl-gear.com)

MACY WEBB READ the laminated copy of the magazine article tacked to the corner of her drafting board while waiting for her printer to spit out the lists she'd be needing later tonight. When she considered how far the company had come in such a short period of time... She shook her head, amazed that the firm's partners still possessed a shred of sanity, what with the out-of-control pace of the business.

The six friends who'd founded gIRL-gEAR, hadn't even met until their senior year at University of Texas, while sharing late night shifts at a new Austin Starbucks. Macy had been a psychology major. Her roommate, Lauren Hollister, had been working toward a degree in commercial art.

Sydney Ford, gIRL-gEAR's CEO, had managed the coffee shop while studying business and finance. Kinsey Gray, Melanie Craine and Chloe Zuniga, the last of the partners, had been on equally diverse career paths, from marketing to technology to fashion.

Until one fateful night following a late November football game, the six women had assumed they'd go their separate ways come commencement the following June. That night the UT Longhorns had trounced the Houston Cougars in a nearly unheard of Texas windchill of seventeen degrees.

And the teamwork involved in ordering, brewing and serving enough lattes, mochas and cappuccinos to defrost what seemed to be every single spectator, convinced business-minded Sydney that she'd be a fool not to capitalize on a sure thing.

The sure thing had launched with the explosive sparkle and flash of a Fourth of July bottle rocket. Each of the women brought her own individuality and vision to bear on the corporation's mission statement. Each brought her own field of expertise as well, putting her degree to work to expand the conceptual whole.

Macy and Lauren worked as respective editors of content and design for the interactive e-commerce Web site and mail-order catalog. Chloe headed up gRAFFITI gIRL and gADGET gIRL, the cosmetics and accessories lines.

The gift line, gOODY gIRL, and the technology line, gIZMO gIRL, were in Melanie's capable hands. Kinsey divided her time between gO gIRL and gROWL gIRL, the active-wear and party-wear divisions.

Sydney had been forced by time limitations and ever-increasing executive responsibilities to hand off the original gIRL-gEAR fashions to the firm's junior associates, who did their best to keep up with consumer demand.

Thirty-eight months after graduation and two years into incorporation, the six founding partners had revised their five-year business plan for the second time. But even if the corporation's fireworks fizzled next week, each of the women had a portfolio reflecting an investment in the future.

A good thing for all involved, but Macy didn't dwell on what might or might not happen. The way she saw things, the future was...the future. Much too far away to think about when there was so much fun to be had now....

1
_____

"I DON'T KNOW, Macy. You think we have enough food here?"

Macy Webb set a tub of tortilla chips and a trough of salsa next to the Crock-Pot of hot *chile con queso* plugged in on the kitchen bar. She added a festive tower of throwaway bowls in red, yellow, green and blue, and a stack of matching paper napkins. Eyeing the colorful layout, she smiled and, hands at black capri-covered hips, turned to answer Lauren.

"Well, there's you and me, the other girls, and Anton, of course." Lauren's boyfriend was as much a permanent fixture on game night as the gIRL-gEAR partners, who helped Macy fine-tune the ideas for her column.

"And the guys? Who did you invite this time?"

"Ray, Jess, Doug and Eric." Macy gave serious thought to the combined appetites of five in-the-prime-of-life, twenty-something men. "Hmm. Now that you mention it…"

She took in the long buffet table Lauren had pulled from the loft's office space into the dining area and covered with a brightly fringed Mexican throw.

Pico de gallo. Chopped tomatoes. Shredded lettuce. Grated cheese. Chafing dishes with pinto beans *a la charro* and sautéed onions and peppers. A metal washtub of iced Corona longnecks, and fajitas on the grill. It looked like enough, but…

"Margaritas, maybe?" she asked.

Lauren rolled her eyes, shook her head. Healthy strands of sun-streaked blond hair brushed her shoulders. "I was being facetious. We'll be eating leftovers for a week, at least."

"Not a problem." Macy pinched a tiny tomato square from the serving bowl, popped it into her mouth. "I can eat Tex-Mex morning, noon and night."

"That's because you have the metabolism of a man. I, on the other hand, have no metabolism, which means I have the hips of a woman."

"Hips, ha! You and your perfect C-cup boobs. Don't be giving me any of your metabolism crap." Macy tugged on the hem of her hot-pink T-shirt, glanced down the scooped neckline in search of cleavage. "Oh. I know. You forgot the guacamole."

Lauren stopped in the middle of setting out rows of plastic cutlery to lift a delicate brow. "Looking down your shirt makes you think of avocados?"

"If only. More like green grapes. Key limes, if I'm lucky." Macy adjusted her shirt hem and went to clear a place on the table for the platters of meat. "I owe what bustline I do have to the push-up bras Kinsey stocks. Employee discount be damned. I've invested a fortune."

"Are you sure you're getting your money's worth?" Lauren's expression was the picture of fresh-faced innocence. "I don't see any pushing up going on at the moment."

Macy stuck out her tongue. "That's because my pusher-uppers are all still wet. I've been busy with the party and didn't get my laundry done until this afternoon."

"That explains the funky-looking delicates hanging in my bathroom." Lauren headed back to the kitchen.

"My bathroom's open to the public. Yours is off the beaten path. I didn't want just anyone fondling my things." Of course, she might make an exception for the right man. The right man with the right hands and a kiss to knock her socks off.

"Then your things should be safe. No one but Anton has any reason to be in my room. And I'll make sure the only thing delicate he fondles is me," Lauren said, returning from the kitchen with her hands full of serving utensils.

"Thanks for rubbing it in. Now I only have you to worry about. You and the guacamole, which I see you have once again managed to forget." Macy waited for an explanation more reasonable than the one she knew would be coming.

"It's in the fridge." Lauren gestured over her shoulder with a tilt of her chin. "Behind the fruit trifle."

"And you left it there why?"

"I thought we just covered this? Metabolism? Hips?"

Macy considered smacking the grin from Lauren's face. But that was best-friend rule number one. No smacking allowed.

She took the serving pieces Lauren offered. "So now I have to set the table, get the guacamole from the fridge *and* grab the chicken and shrimp off the barbie?"

"Cute. Aussie Tex-Mex." Lauren reached for the platter and barbecue tongs. "I'll get the meat. The guacamole might not make it to the table if left up to me."

Grr. "Will you stop already with the food obsession? I've seen what you eat. If you ate any less I'd be worried."

"If I ate any less, I'd be a saint. Which I'm not. And you can keep your unsaintly comeback to yourself."

Macy bit back the unsaintly comeback on the tip of

her tongue. "I was only going to say that I can't believe you'd worry about calories on game night."

Lauren stepped through the sliding glass doors and out onto the balcony. She tossed her reply back into the room. "Your game nights are beginning to scare me. It's like you're a walking, talking Cosmo poll. Where do you come up with these ideas?"

A walking, talking Cosmo poll? Macy chuckled, even while recognizing the analogy to be a fairly accurate description of the ease with which she created gIRL gAMES and gIRL gUIDE, the fun and advice columns she wrote for gIRL-gEAR's Web site. Her job was child's play. She liked it that way, and planned to get away with *not* working for a living as long as she possibly could.

Meeting Lauren between the table and the balcony door, Macy took the platter of chicken from her roommate's hands. "Don't ask me where the ideas come from. They just show up. I test them, work out the kinks, write the columns. And the rest, as they say, is history."

"Well, I guess that's all good, since yesterday Sydney mentioned your two columns are still generating the most feedback for the site." Lauren headed back to the grill.

"Wow! How cool is that!" Macy left the chicken on the table and followed, wanting to hear more.

"Actually—" Lauren gestured with the tongs "—we talked about a new design for your Web pages. I think you need a logo. Maybe a caricature. Or a cartoon-type figure."

"Hmm. Cartoon is good. A takeoff on my name? A cuddly spider, maybe? Big eyes and long lashes. None of that black widow, Barbie doll, comic-book cleavage."

"Cuddly, huh? I'll see what I can do." Lauren

plucked the last of the shrimp from the grill. "Oh, and I think Sydney wants you to write an ongoing serial, too. Where readers vote on ideas or submit suggestions for each installment? Anyway, I'm going to run a few design ideas by Anton later."

"Wow, super." Macy pasted on a broad smile. "Hey, what would I do without you and Sydney to take care of me?"

"That's what best friends are for."

Macy wandered back into the loft before sarcasm got the better of her. Yes, she was excited. Yes, she was thrilled. She loved her career, after all. But success was blowing in on hurricane winds and she wasn't prepared for the storm.

It was now that mattered, now that counted. Living for and in the moment. Not worrying about the price of technology stock years down the road. She didn't want to lose a minute of today planning for the future. Why couldn't anyone see that?

Lauren stepped inside, catching the balcony door with her hip and giving a gentle shove. With food, drink and all things paper, plastic and edible in place, she lifted a brow at Macy, looked back at the table, then to Macy again.

Macy shrugged. "If you cook it, they will come?"

"You'd better hope they come soon or I see a whole lotta freezer bags in your future."

As if on cosmic cue, the buzzer signaled the approach of the loft's renovated freight elevator.

"I don't know how you manage to do that every time. But there's something about a gift horse and his mouth that I think applies here." Lauren scurried toward her rooms at the far end of the loft, her low-slung jeans topped by a billowy gauze shirt a shade lighter than the purple tube top beneath.

"Hey," Macy called. "Where're you going?"

"I need to check my stuff before Anton gets here." And, with a wiggle of her fingers, Lauren disappeared behind one of the hanging panels of hammered brass that separated her living quarters from the loft's main room.

"Stuff? What stuff? Oh, never mind. Who cares about your stinky ol' stuff, anyway?" Pouting, Macy headed for the kitchen and the guacamole. She could eat both her helping and Lauren's, return for seconds and never gain an inch or an ounce.

The only way the avocado salad would make any difference to her figure was if she scooped it directly into her bra. Sort of an edible implant. Kinky, but, hey. A girl had to do what a girl had to do if she wanted to have stuff of her own.

And anyone worth checking it for.

"THIS SHRIMP IS outstanding. Absolutely outstanding." Eric Haydon shoved another in his mouth and gave Macy a closed-lipped, shrimp-eating grin.

She added a fifth throwaway plate to the stack balanced from fingertips to elbow, added a hint of twisted wickedness to her parting shot. "Just doing what I can to fatten you up for the kill. Hansel."

Chipmunk-cheeked Eric stopped chewing. Then swallowed. "I was afraid of that."

"You know, Eric, if you weren't so easy to tease, well, I wouldn't tease you." Macy reached the kitchen alcove separated from the rest of the loft by eight floor-to-ceiling lava-lamp bubble sculptures. She dropped the discarded plates into the trash. "Tonight's game will be painless. I promise."

Longneck in hand, Eric leaned a shoulder on a turquoise figure eight. His dark-blue Henley shirt seemed hard-pressed to cover his broad shoulders, but did great things to his eyes. "I've figured something out about you, Macy Webb."

Well, that made one of them, because sooner or later she needed to figure out why he wasn't her type. "What's that? That no matter how creatively you beg, I'm not leaving gIRL-gEAR to come cook for you?"

Eric owned his own sports bar, Haydon's Half-Time, and had been after Macy for months to give up writing and editing to sling his hash instead.

Except Macy only cooked for fun, not for money. Money made work out of play, and what kind of a life was that?

"I wish. But I know you're not going anywhere." He finished his beer, tossed the empty bottle in with the plates and utensils. "Can't blame a guy for trying, though."

"I don't blame you. As the object of your culinary pursuit, I have been flattered." Macy thought for a minute, then puffed out her lower lip. "As a matter of fact, now that I think about it, I'm going to miss being wooed."

"You want woo? I'll give you woo." Eric took a step closer and slowly smiled, allowing his dimples to deepen to maximum impact. Then he leaned down and poured all that macho charm into Macy's personal space.

She leaned up into his, pulling to a halt before she actually got stupid and kissed the man. "Yeah? You and whose football team? Hmm." Eyes closed, she held up one finger. "Let me take a minute here to imagine the possibilities."

"Very funny, Macy."

"Okay. I'm done." She opened one eye, then the other, laughed out loud as Eric rolled his.

"You're sick."

"And you're gullible." She punched him in the shoulder.

"Hey." He rubbed away the damage. "You know, just for that I think I'll take one last shrimp and leave."

"You can't do that." She grabbed and ended up with a handful of loose sleeve minus the elbow she'd been aiming for. "I'm already one man short, since I don't know where Anton is."

"I knew it." Eric hung his head, his chin lowered in defeat. "This is going to be one of those games where we have to pair off into couples, isn't it?"

"And what makes you jump to that conclusion?" Besides the fact that at least fifty percent of her games were designed for interaction between the sexes, and her players knew the odds rarely changed from month to month.

"Two things. The tougher the game, the better the spread. And you have fajitas coming out the wazoo. Second thing. If you're a man short, that means couples." He held up a second finger, jabbed it at his chest to make his point. "And there is no Mrs. Eric Haydon in my future."

"No need to be so touchy, Eric. It's just a game. Not holy matrimony."

Eric braced both hands on the edge of the sink, shook his head and looked down.

Macy moved in, massaged circles on his back between his shoulder blades. "Poor baby. Your breakup with Cathy was a tough one?"

"Brutal. Totally brutal." He pushed back from the sink, stood in the center of the kitchen with his hands at his hips as if waiting for a flying tackle.

Macy didn't know whether to hug him or push him over with a feather, which she was sure would be all it would take. She did manage to bite her tongue on a chuckle.

If he wasn't such a Tarzan... Hmm. Maybe that was the problem. She never had made a very good Jane. "You know, Eric, I hate to say it...."

"Go ahead. Everyone else has."

"Okay then. I told you so. You and Cathy were totally wrong for each other."

"Well, it didn't feel so wrong when we got together." Eric rubbed the base of his neck, looked from Macy to the wildly paint-splattered kitchen floor and back again.

She just waited, one brow lifted while he stewed.

When his juices reached a simmer, he jumped from the frying pan into the fire. "Damn it, Macy. Just spit it out before you choke on your tongue."

"It didn't feel so wrong when you got together because you didn't get out of bed for a week." She punctuated her pronouncement with a sternly pointed index finger.

"Yeah, so?"

"So?" Were all men so daft? "Man cannot live by bed alone."

"Aha! Wrong. Man can. Woman cannot."

Macy was gearing up to set Eric straight when a soft female voice cut into the conversation. "Sounds to me, sugar, like you haven't met the right woman."

Both Macy and Eric turned, to find Chloe Zuniga with one hip propped on a bulbous red sculpture.

With a gorgeously full Jennifer Lopez figure, naturally highlighted platinum hair and eyes that changed color depending on her choice of contact lenses, Chloe was fantasy pinup material.

It was only when she opened her mouth that the myth was dispelled. Chloe had a voice as soft as down...and the vocabulary of a wharf rat.

Hand extended, Eric started forward. "Eric Haydon. And you would be?"

Batting ingenuous eyes that said less about her innocence and more about her understanding of artful naiveté, she dispensed a frosted pink, candy-coated smile. "Why, your wildest dream, of course."

Eric grabbed her wrist, turned his cheek and nuzzled his lips to her skin. And he did it all without breaking eye contact. "Is that a promise I should be holding you to, Chloe?"

Time to stop this conversation's downhill slide, Macy decided, stepping into the standoff before either of her guests could strip to their skivvies. "Any sign of Anton yet?"

Chloe extricated herself from Eric's hold, leaving him with a pat on the cheek. She crossed the kitchen to pull a bottle of spring water from the fridge. "He's here. Lauren sent me to tell you."

"It's about damn time."

Macy breathed a sigh of relief, which Chloe interrupted by adding, "But Doug's not coming. A bad blueprint on one of the condos, I think was the deal."

Chloe twisted the cap from her bottle and sipped. "Oh, and Kinsey just called. Her parents came into town this afternoon and insisted she join them for dinner."

Oh, good aggravating grief, Macy thought, and grimaced. The more feedback on the game, the better to gauge the column's success. "Now what am I going to do? I planned this month's game around five couples."

Eric, of course, found the news to his liking. "Looks like I'm off the matrimonial hook."

All Tied Up

Chloe slid up against Eric's side, gave him a look from beneath sultry lashes. "Speaking of a matrimonial hook, rumor has it, sugar, that Cathy cut you loose."

Eric blew out a long tolerant sigh and wrapped a brotherly arm around Chloe's shoulders. "Chloe, Chloe, Chloe. Seeing as how this is Macy's party and I'm working to be on my best behavior here, I'm going to let that one slide."

Macy wished she could slide. All the way into tomorrow, and forget tonight ever happened. "I'm not sure your behavior's going to make any difference, since it looks like Macy's party is now Macy's bust."

"Actually," Chloe began, cutting off Macy's third-person soliloquy, "five couples won't be a problem. As long as you play, too."

"Whoa. Wait. You're not off any hook yet," Macy said, but Eric had already scooted out of the kitchen. She turned to Chloe. "What do you mean, five couples? Who's my extra man?"

"Anton's not alone. He's got that lawyer with him."

The floor beneath Macy's feet became a hungry black hole. "That lawyer?"

"Uh-huh." Chloe stepped back to follow Eric into the other room. "Are you coming?"

"Yeah." Macy turned on the kitchen faucet.

Leo Redding. Here.

In her loft.

With her underthings the length of the building away.

Of all times to be without cleavage. "Let me wash my hands. Tell Lauren I'll be right there. And whatever you do, Chloe, don't let Eric escape."

Chloe leaned around a stack of bright, glossy yellow spheres to watch Eric's retreat. "He does have a cute butt. I suppose it wouldn't be so bad to play Jane to his Tarzan act.''

''His Tarzan isn't an act, Chloe. He's an alpha of the highest order. Head of the pack and all that psychobabble.''

''Such a shame. Swinging from a vine is so uncivilized. Give me a chandelier any day.'' Chloe sighed and, when Macy rolled her eyes, gave a quick flutter of her fingers. ''I know, I'm going. And I promise no one will get away.''

Macy shook her head and got back to the business of washing her hands. Chloe, the enigma. The bad girl body, the baby doll face. No wonder Eric had gotten all touchy-feely when Chloe walked into the kitchen.

Men. They all had such one-track libidos. Macy could just imagine Leo Redding's tongue lolling in Chloe's direction like some expensive... What breed of dog would an uppity attorney own, anyway?

Whatever the pedigree, because he was definitely pedigreed, he'd pant after Chloe's cute-toy-poodle personality long before he'd share his bone with Macy, the scruffy rat terrier.

She didn't care. She didn't care! Why should she care? It wasn't like he'd ever offered her more than the time of day.

Leo Redding III, Esquire, had first come into Macy's life a year ago, during changes to the corporate structure of gIRL-gEAR. Having landed the account through Anton's connection to Sydney via Lauren, Leo had drawn up the required documents for shareholding and ownership. He'd been a total automaton during the group's corporate dealings.

Sydney, who seemed his perfect female counterpart, declared him unsuitably career obsessed. Neither Kinsey nor Mel had managed to crack his focused composure. Even Chloe's cotton-candy Chloe magic had only resulted in Leo removing his pewter-colored wire-rimmed glasses to rub the bridge of his nose. She'd declared him to be a big waste of time.

Macy hadn't known him well enough to disagree. Things hadn't changed. One thing she did know was that, along with Eric Haydon, Ray Coffey and Jess Morgan—all gorging on fajitas in the loft's central room—Leo played on the same adult soccer team as Anton. The soccer team meant Macy had a jackpot of single men to draft into service on game nights.

But this was the first time Leo had come to play.

Oh, and then there was his incredibly acute sense of hearing, and matching sarcastic streak, both traits she'd happened to discover when he'd stopped by the loft with Anton one Saturday morning last fall.

The men had been on their way to a soccer game, and Anton had dropped by for Lauren. As much as Lauren loved cheering on her favorite forward, she hated pacing the sidelines alone, and had begged Macy to come along. And Macy had been tempted.

Like any healthy twenty-five-year-old female, she more than enjoyed spectating when it came to a twenty-two-man testosterone tournament. She'd said as much to Lauren. Said as well that she was glad to be a child of the new millennium, where men were equal opportunity sex objects.

And then she'd made the mistake of glancing across the loft in time to catch Leo's indulgent expression turn to one of annoyance, insult even.

Humph. Leo, obviously, still lived in the past.

But then, after Macy had dodged Lauren's bullying, walked the three to the freight elevator and reached for the switch to send the car to the ground, Leo had stepped back into the loft and done it for her.

He'd looked at her, studied her, stared down at her, making one-on-one visual contact for the first time in their brief association.

She hadn't counted on his eyes. He wore wire-rimmed glasses when working, and Macy had to admit they added a je ne sais quoi to his smoothly urbane image.

But he hadn't been wearing them that morning. He'd been wearing clear contacts, if any at all, because there was no reproducing that shade of pale, translucent, dollar-bill green.

The worry lines at the corners of his eyes had fanned out toward his temples, his expression one of a man enjoying a private, inside joke. He'd never smiled. To this day Macy didn't think she'd seen him smile.

But he had parted his lips. And she had responded in kind. His effect was like that, his appeal a powerful weapon. She might not like him much in her mind, but her body didn't share her mental morals.

Using the tip of one finger, he'd lifted her chin, made sure he had her attention, taken her frantic pulse with the stroke of his thumb. "Macy?"

She'd managed a vague, "Hmm?"

"I know about equal opportunity. I've handled a lot of cases, and won more than my share. I'm very good at what I do." His glittering eyes had promised it was no idle boast.

A true believer, she'd swayed forward a telling fraction.

And he'd backed a step away. "But without evidence of a challenge? I'm not about to waste my time."

The elevator had returned by then and he'd stepped inside. The doors had closed on his mocking expression.

He'd taken the easy way out, leaving her breathless and scrambling for a suitable retort.

Well, Macy wasn't having any of that tonight. Tonight she was forewarned, and no smooth-talking lawyer would get the best of her. Not again, no sir-ree.

Leo wanted a challenge? She'd give him a challenge.

Because when it came to playing games, she was more than very good.

She was the absolute best.

2

ABANDONING THE SANCTUARY of the kitchen, Macy returned to the loft's main room. She snatched a shred of lettuce from the floor and tossed it on a stack of plates destined for the trash. "Okay. Let's get started."

A collective groan went up and threatened to drown out the techno-pop music vibrating the wall-mounted speakers. Walking by the entertainment center, Macy turned down the volume. She hated having to shout over the music, on top of shouting over nine voices engaged in both conversation and complaint.

With the boom-boom faded to a muted thump-thump, the groans became intelligible protests. None she hadn't heard before.

"It's too late. Let's wait till next weekend."

"Hey, I'm not finished eating."

"Anyone want to head down to Karma? I think Azrael's spinning tonight."

Macy took the objections in stride and overrode each one. First to Jess. "We can't wait until next weekend. I'm on deadline." Next to Anton. "You can eat while you play. The two are not mutually exclusive."

Finally to Ray. "Karma will still be there when we're finished here for the night, and Azrael never spins before midnight." Eric she silenced with only a look. No doubt he was still recovering from Chloe.

And then there was the fifth man, the quiet one, the interloper, whom Macy dodged.

She wasn't sure why Anton had brought Leo along. Or now that he was here, why he stayed. Participation was mandatory for all who set foot inside the loft on game night.

And no matter how hard she tried, or how many times, she could not picture Leo Redding playing her game, her way. Not with all that starch in his collar. Not even on a dare.

He sat sprawled in the huge armchair upholstered in yellow-and-red plaid. But his posture was deceptive, his thoughts clearly focused elsewhere. More than likely on one of his challenging equal-opportunity cases.

Macy enjoyed a private smirk. He had no idea what sort of challenge was about to land in his lap. He'd be leaving here tonight with a new respect for fun and games. If he could actually enjoy himself with a noose around his neck.

It was Saturday night. It was party time. He wore a white dress shirt and, admittedly, a fairly fashionable tie. But it was still a tie. And it was still knotted.

His slacks were dark gray dress wool and neatly pressed, his shoes black tasseled wing tips. Tonight he wore his glasses, the rims serving to emphasize his incredible light-green eyes.

So much for her smirk, she thought, pulling, instead, a grimace. This was not a good start to the evening, noticing his every male detail when she shouldn't be noticing him as anything but a piece of data by which to measure the success of her game.

"Uh, Macy?" Lauren edged up to Macy's side, pulling her away from the gathered group, who'd long since quit paying attention. "This bunch is off in the ozone.

If you launch your game idea now, you'll be talking to the wind.''

"So I noticed." Whatever was in the air tonight could've picked a better time to blow. It wasn't like she was on deadline or anything.

Lauren twisted the cap from her bottle of water, twisted her mouth as she thought. "You've got to get their attention. I was thinking maybe...Spin the Webb?"

Macy's version of Spin the Bottle had never failed to perk up audience interest in the past. Of course, there was the small matter of who to ensnare....

"You know, Lauren, I like the way you think." Macy pushed her best friend back to the center of the group, all of whom looked more interested in sleeping off the evening's food and drink than anything she had to say.

Lauren clapped her hands. "Okay, gang. Before Macy tests her newest gIRL gAMES creation on all of us, it's time for the evening's first act. Her famous version of Spin the Bottle. Better known as Spin the Webb!''

While Macy attempted a pirouette on the toe of one clunky leather clog, Lauren frowned and patted pockets she didn't have. "Uh, Mace. I don't have anything to use for a blindfold.''

Macy twirled to a stop and did a visual search of the room. She gave serious consideration to volunteering Leo Redding's tie, but decided she might need it later for bondage, uh, leverage.

"No problem. I'll cover my eyes with my hands.''

That, of course, started another round of mouthy macho maneuvering.

"How fair is that?''

"Yeah. How do we know you won't peek?''

"Foul! Foul!''

After peering through spread fingers to stare down

both Ray and Jess, Macy turned to the last bellyacher, who was sprawled across two of the sofa's three cushions. "Watch it, Eric. Or Lauren might accidentally spin me into your lap, right on top of your shrimp."

Eric frowned. "Hey, hey. Watch out who you're calling a shrimp."

"I'm talking about the fajitas, you goober."

"Hey, hey. Watch out who you're calling a peanut."

"Pillow, please," Macy called to Sydney Ford, who'd settled into the heap of mismatched bolsters and cushions cozily stacked against the corner of the entertainment center.

Sydney chose a goldfish-shaped throw pillow, started to pass it over the back of the sofa to Macy, but changed her mind. Instead, she got to her feet and tossed not one, not two, but pillow after cushion after sham in Eric's direction.

Chloe and Melanie cheered her on, then jumped up and pitched in until all that was left visible of Eric were his feet, his knees and one hand. That hand he used to reach out and grab the rear pocket on Sydney's long narrow denim skirt. He pulled her over the back of the sofa and down.

With a yelp, she tumbled into his lap. Anton chose that moment to start up the music, a sexy, heavy-breathing number that sent Sydney into a scramble away from Eric, who'd started to bump and grind beneath the heap.

Turning to Macy, Lauren asked, "Who invited him, anyway?" And Macy could only roll her eyes.

"Attention, people." Lauren clapped her hands again. "The time has arrived for one of you to test your powers of self-preservation while our resident spider weaves her web. For those of you unfamiliar with the rules—Leo—don't despair. All you have to do is resist her demands.''

"Easy enough," said the bane of Macy's evening.

She didn't even bother acknowledging his insult. She was not about to give him an edge when she had a game to win.

"For any of you thinking of cutting out early, we have a special incentive for you to keep your butts parked exactly where they are." Lauren's announcement served its purpose. The gang perked up. "But I'll let Sydney do the honors."

Sydney, being the perfectionist she was, checked for misbehaving strands of hair and smoothed both her narrow denim skirt and burgundy silk tank before she spoke.

"A week or so ago, Macy warned me that this month's game was more involved than previous versions. So I decided to add a participation incentive."

"Incentive?" Eric stuffed an extra-large red corduroy bolster behind his head and laced his hands together in his lap. "You mean bribe, right?"

"Bribe, bonus, compensation, prize. Whatever. I think it'll be worth your time to pay attention."

"That means shut the hell up, Haydon." Egged on by jeers and wolf whistles, Ray did little more than wink and return the floor to Sydney.

Daring anyone else to interrupt, she took a deep breath. "Here's my winner-take-all deal. My father, who many of you know, has made me an offer I should refuse. But I won't."

Macy waited for reactions as the out-of-left-field comment sank in. She wasn't disappointed. Those who'd met Nolan Ford were curious, and said so. Those who hadn't still wanted to hear what the millionaire venture capitalist had to do with the evening's game.

"Nolan's going to pay us to play?" Anton made the crack while sorting through Macy's CDs.

"No," Sydney answered. "But he's selling his ketch and giving me the final week to use it. Full crew of sailors included."

"What I want to do is donate the week to the winner, who is then welcome to choose a destination, within reason, and take along as many guests as the yacht can handle."

Anton applauded. "All right, Sydney."

"Oh, my God! Are you kidding?" Melanie's eyes grew wide.

And at that, Macy leaned over and kissed Sydney's cheek. When she smiled in response, Macy wrapped an arm around the other woman's shoulders and whispered, "You don't have to do this."

Pressing her forehead to Macy's, Sydney returned the hug. "Yes. I do. You know how things are with Nolan."

Macy had more to say, but now wasn't the time. She left Sydney with another quick peck and addressed the crowd.

"Hey, people. No one is going to be sailing anywhere if I don't get my way. Anton." Macy pointed, and he pumped up the volume. "Lauren." Lauren held Macy by the shoulders and, once Macy had covered her eyes, twirled her to the rhythm of the beat.

Macy barely had time to decide what she was going to ask from Leo before she was pulled to a stop, turned to the right, then back to a stumbling, feet-tangling left.

A deep breath and...it was time.

She lifted her chin, ran her fingers into her hair, her tongue over her lips. Then, with her imagination wearing the underthings she'd failed to wash in time for her body to wear, she looked Leo Redding in the eye.

Big mistake. Big, big mistake.

She'd forgotten about his eyes. How he seemed to see more than a near stranger should see. How what he saw was intimate, private, not at all what she wanted to reveal.

With each step she took toward him, her pulse quickened.

At every bluesy note, her heart beat harder.

From the roots of her hair to the tip of her toes, her blood ran hot, raising a flush on her skin. Leo never looked away, stirring her further. Macy would swear she felt her nostrils flare.

And then she knew what she wanted. To see him smile. To *make* him smile. As much to prove that she could, that she possessed the stronger will and the necessary feminine wiles, as to add fuel to the fire of her fantasy.

Having drawn even with his widespread knees, she wedged her legs between, leaned forward and planted both hands on the flat arms of the chair. The tips of her fingers brushed the insides of his elbows. His only move was to reach up and remove his glasses.

She angled in closer, lifted one hand and touched a finger to his cheek. "I want you to do something for me."

Leo raised a brow. In the background, an anonymous hand clapped to Eric's mouth muffled a smart remark. Macy gathered her wits and her courage and climbed into Leo's long-legged lap.

"I want you to smile. Can you do that? Can you smile for me, Leo Redding?"

Moving even nearer, she twisted around and settled

her seat in the natural dip of his thighs, draped her legs over the arm of the chair, her elbow crooked around his shoulders.

He smelled wonderfully warm and male, and she snuggled up to his body, which felt...oh, he felt like nothing she'd ever known.

His legs beneath her bottom were hard. His belly at her hip was hard. The muscles across his shoulders were solid and hard beneath her forearm. Even the hand, the very large hand resting on her shins, was a study in masculine strength.

Lips parted in seductive invitation, she stroked an index finger over Leo's cheek and shivered at the prickle of evening beard. She trailed the same finger down a path to his collar, worked loose the knot on his tie.

"C'mon, Leo. I know you can smile. You've got all the right muscles." She toyed with the top button of his shirt, poking the bare tip of her finger beneath the placket to his collarbone.

Still no response. Nada. Nothing. Ignoring the murmurs of the audience, she whispered directly into his ear. "I'll make it easy on you. A quick grin and we'll call it a night."

She pulled back to look at his face, expecting a gradual capitulation. But no, he was stoic to the core. It was time to get down and dirty.

Pouting always worked for Chloe, so Macy gave it a try at the same time she lightly touched her thumb to the edge of Leo's mouth, drawing the corner upward.

No reaction. Macy held back a scream.

She plied her final weapon, running her fingertips in feathery movements over his tightly drawn lips, begging, with her mouth only inches away, "One smile. Please?"

And then she felt it. A shift. A change. A flare and a

flash in Leo's eyes, and a new sense of his body hard-ening beneath hers.

A part of her wanted to extricate herself from both his lap and a situation as awkward as any she could recall sharing with a man. A part of her wanted to wiggle, to experience and explore this private intimacy.

She managed, instead, to sit very still and avoid dis-closing to the rest of the room what was now so im-pressively, so solidly pressed to the back of her thighs.

Leo reached for her wrist, removed her motionless fingers from his lips. She blinked slowly and smiled, a smile meant for Leo only, Leo alone. She wanted him to know that, between the two of them, they'd get out of this with no bloodshed, go on to live another day.

And then the man blew the wind from her sails.

He smiled.

Not a humorless grin. Not a slight curl of his lip. Not a sneer or a snarl, but an ear-to-ear, start-my-heart-beating smile. Yet that wasn't the worst part. The best part. The worst. Because once he'd released her wrist and she'd made ready to hop up from the chair, he cupped the back of her head.

And he kissed her.

Oh, hallelujah, the man could kiss. He tasted like beer and smoky barbecue and a man aroused, and she was starving. She couldn't get enough when he teased her mouth with the tip of his tongue, rubbed his lips softly, then roughly, over hers.

It was a complicated kiss, meant for show and to prove that he was not relinquishing the win. Mentally, she fought back. Physically, she surrendered.

Desire took full advantage, reaching between her legs to remind her how long it had been, how good it could be. Oh, this wasn't supposed to happen.

She silently grimaced and broke the kiss—to cheers and applause and ear-piercing whistles. She pulled back far enough to meet Leo's gaze.

His mouth was slightly reddened and still smiling. But his eyes sparkled with fireworks that were less a celebration and more a signal of an incoming salvo.

Hey, now. She wasn't the one who'd done all the kissing, much less the one who'd started it. The seduction she'd admit to, and she was willing to be a big girl and swallow her medicine. But she would not take all of the blame.

She shoved a hand back through her hair and kept her voice low when she said, "I'd say that makes me the winner."

Leo chuckled—a sound deep in his chest that rumbled through his muscles, through his bones and into Macy's body. "The winner? You're kidding, right?"

Hmm. That wasn't what she'd expected. "Why would you think I'm kidding? I got what I wanted, didn't I? You did smile."

"No. You got what I let you have." His smile had totally vanished. "I got what *I* wanted."

Is that so, Mr. Hotshot, Esquire? "And what was it that you wanted?"

"Isn't it obvious?"

Macy's subtle shift of weight prompted a convincing surge of pressure beneath her thighs. "Yes. It is. Quite obvious, as a matter of fact."

Holding his gaze, she waited until the gleam in his own turned smug. She would never let this man have the last word—or the upper hand—again. No matter how strong the physical pull heightening every one of her senses.

With a pat delivered to the center of his chest, Macy

hopped off the hot seat. "Unfortunately, Leo, the obvious isn't...well, much of a challenge, if you know what I mean. Sorry, but I just don't think I'm interested."

Watching Leo's startled disbelief fade into grudging respect, Macy turned quickly, lest the moment be spoiled.

No sense wondering if her fleeting triumph was worth the promise of retribution she'd just seen in his eyes.

THE FAJITAS WERE HISTORY and the conversation had returned to a low drone by the time Leo Redding recovered. He didn't think he'd given up such an inappropriate hard-on his entire adult life.

And Macy Webb wasn't even his type. His reaction had to be rooted, so to speak, in that very contradiction. She wasn't what he was used to, so in effect, he was responding to the mystery of the unknown.

She had this mass of unruly hair, a dark caramel-brown color, streaked to vanilla cream on either side of her face. It was short, hitting her neck between the base of her skull and her shoulders and causing a riot around her heart-shaped face. Last year, when he'd seen her that first time in his office, he'd thought she'd been working on dreadlocks.

But tonight his fingers had slid through the strands without hitting a single snarl. The entire wild-child look was one-hundred-percent natural. He hadn't expected that, any more than he'd expected her eyes to be so clear, so golden. So compelling and candidly open.

Her weight was as substantial as a miniature marshmallow. But the soft press of her bottom had been plenty enough to get a rise out of his, uh, lap. That and the curve of her mouth. She knew how to kiss, how to use her lips. His primitive side had imagined hearing the slide of his zipper, feeling the slide of her tongue.

If she hadn't broken his hold when she did, he wasn't sure he would've had the willpower to keep his hand safely in her hair. He'd wanted to explore her body, find out exactly if quality, not quantity, was the myth he believed it to be.

He upended his Corona and drank. He never should've come here tonight. He'd spent the afternoon looking at the neighborhood condos and lofts Anton's architectural firm, Neville and Storey, had restored and designed. He and Anton had been out longer than either intended and, when Anton suggested they join the gang for fajitas, he'd agreed.

He should've gone home, but his car was parked at Anton's Galleria office, and the thought of taking a cab, only to reheat Chinese take-out or order fresh once he arrived, held little appeal. He usually didn't hang with the guys away from the soccer field. But tonight he'd thought, why not?

Emptying the longneck he'd spent the last ten minutes nursing, Leo leaned back on a tall green pillar half as wide in the center as it was on either end. His vantage point near the kitchen kept him out of the way, but gave him a very clear view of Macy's goings-on.

He'd overheard fragments of her post-kiss conversation with Lauren, and apparently his arrival had complicated her plans. He couldn't say he was overly concerned. But, after hearing that, he'd thought about skipping the rest of the evening.

He'd even pulled out his phone to dial Yellow Cab until he'd realized exactly how far out of her way Macy was going to avoid him. When he'd brushed up behind her to reach for this beer, she'd stiffened, then scurried

off to organize the game that was apparently the purpose
of the evening's get-together.

Interesting, for a woman not attracted to his...challenge.

"Don't sweat it. She always wins, you know."

Leo spared Anton a brief glance before returning to
his study of Macy. Why was everyone so sure she had
won? It wasn't as if Leo had cried uncle. "She's done
that to you?"

"Not the smile thing, but, yeah. She convinced me I
had a mosquito buzzing around my face. Her deal was
that I'd scratch this one spot at the corner of my nose.
By the time she was finished, I'd damn near clawed my
eyes out."

Leo chuckled under his breath. "She does have...
something, doesn't she?"

Shoving both hands down in his pockets, Anton nodded. "Most of that something never gets noticed until
she climbs up into your lap, if you know what I mean."

Leo knew exactly. He cleared his throat. "Yeah, well,
it's been fun, but I've got a load of work waiting at the
office. I think I'll get the hell outta here."

"Think again. Stick around here and you may get a
second chance to give Macy Webb a taste of her own
medicine."

"Isn't that what I just did?"

Anton laughed and leaned one shoulder into the same
green pillar. "I wouldn't go that far. But I gotta say,
you're the first one to shut her up using your own
mouth."

"Hmm." A murmur was all Leo could manage without Anton's comment bringing to mind the taste of
Macy's lips and tongue, the smooth edge of her teeth,
the warmth of her body in his lap.

"Yeah, Lauren was freaking out. I don't think she's ever seen Macy kiss anyone quite like that."

"Like what?" Leo absently asked, then wished he hadn't.

"The woman looked like she wanted to swallow you whole, man." Anton lifted a brow as the conversation took a turn for the prurient. "And I don't think she planned to stop with your tongue."

"Hmm." This time Leo's reticence to respond was rooted in an irritation he had no reason to feel. The kiss had been public; Anton had been a witness. The other man had every right to his curiosity.

It was Leo's strange desire to retain his privacy that gave significance to an act that had none.

None. The kiss had been nothing but part of a game.

"I gotta say, seeing Macy come unglued like that..." Anton shook his head. "That was some serious shit."

Leo's beer bottle was empty. He needed to make up his mind. Should he stay or go? He glanced toward Macy, watched her expression, the childlike enchantment as she joked with Sydney and Lauren. "She doesn't look old enough for serious."

"I think that's a big part of the problem."

"Her looks?" Leo frowned. Until tonight, until he'd seen her up close and gotten personal, he would've agreed. She'd been just another face, one he'd never noticed because he'd always gone for striking instead of subtle, obvious instead of rare.

"No, man. Not her looks. Well, yeah. I guess it is her looks." Anton shrugged off the quandary. "She's cute and all that, but she doesn't look like she's older than eighteen."

Leo nodded in agreement and forgave himself the silent lie. After all, he'd just looked into the wild child's eyes, and what he'd seen was as old as the Garden of Eden, as seductive as the serpent, as ripe as the forbidden fruit.

He made his decision. He wasn't going anywhere. Not just yet.

3

WHILE LAUREN ADJUSTED one row of track lighting to spotlight the loft's hardwood floor, Macy prepared to distribute the sheets of pink and blue paper she'd printed earlier today.

Five for the girls, five for the boys. Ten unique lists for her newest gIRL gAMES adventure.

A scavenger hunt.

An after-hours, adults-only, you-find-mine-I'll-find-yours kind of contest.

Macy was certain she'd never conceived a more brilliant idea. And if all went according to plan, this month's edition of gIRL gAMES might possibly be the best yet.

Which would mean more reader feedback. More assignments from Sydney. More input from Lauren on column design.

Hmm. Hoist with her own petard.

Well, she couldn't worry overly much at the moment. Her focus group had to first pull off this game without killing each other. And she had to remember that tumbling Leo Redding was not the point of play.

It didn't matter that his hands were the hands of her fantasy. Or that she'd never been more thoroughly kissed. Physical attraction wasn't the problem. She was still trying to decide if she liked the man. A decision that would have to wait, because it was time to get on with the evening's main game.

Careers left all of her crew, herself included, little time to party. Her column, gIRL gAMES, was meant to provide the Web site's readers with social alternatives to bars and clubs.

Yet none of her previous game ideas had offered her scavenger hunt's possibilities for girl-meets-boy, up-close-and-personal, one-on-one contact.

From a ticklish spot to an erogenous zone to a kinky fetish, the lists for the hunt included additional items equally intimate and more intense.

And the list she'd be assigning herself held a grouping of search items as random as those to be chosen by everyone else in the room.

Well, almost everyone else in the room.

Only Lauren and Anton's items had been specifically designed. Which made sense, since it was Lauren and Anton's interaction of late that had sparked the idea for the game.

As much as Macy's best friend adored her boyfriend and vice versa, elements of the seemingly perfect relationship struck Macy as anything but. And she was doing what any best friend should do under the circumstances. Butting in.

She'd put together two fiercely personal lists, the purpose of which was to put both Lauren and Anton through, well, through hell if the couple truly gave the game their all.

Macy would just have to keep her fingers crossed that she'd be forgiven the sabotage should the plan blow up in her face.

Lists in hand, she wound her way through the center of the loft. She slapped a blue list against Jess Morgan's reluctantly offered palm, then climbed over Anton's long legs, looking up to in time catch Jess unfolding his folded blue paper.

"You! Stop!" She first pinned Jess, then Anton, with the sharpest eye daggers she could throw. "Don't even think about looking until I say so."

Jess slowly closed his half-opened sheet and, holding the list behind his head in laced fingers, began to whistle.

Anton, guilty until proven innocent, his list in his lap, held up both empty hands. "Don't think about looking where? At what? I don't know what you're talking about."

"Good." Macy leaned down and dropped a kiss on the top of his head of unruly, sun-bleached curls. "I'll explain everything in a minute. And don't think that just because I have my back turned I'm not keeping an eye on you two."

With that, she moved on, scrambling over feet and furniture to reach the three women whose fate she didn't already know. Sydney tentatively accepted the pink list Macy offered. Melanie was more wary, finally choosing one of the last two sheets. Chloe scooted to the far side of the plaid chair and had to be coerced.

"Hey." Macy nudged her hip into Chloe's shoulder. "We're all in this girl business together, remember? You scratch my back, I'll scratch yours?"

Tapping the folded edge of her list on her pink-denim-clad knee, Chloe eyed Macy thoroughly from head to toe.

"Let's see. My departments are cosmetics and accessories. I don't see where you're scratching much of my anything, sugar. You have a great natural look, but it's not helping my numbers."

"For your information, Miss Cosmetics and Accessories, this natural look costs me a fortune. Your moisturizers and oils and exfoliators and cleansers do not come cheap.''

With a tilt of her head, Chloe acquiesced. "Okay. I'll give you the cosmetics. But you're still short-changing me on the accessories.''

Macy stood, stuck out her tongue. "What can I say? It's hard to accessorize perfection.''

"Before you go?'' Ignoring the groans, Macy looked back at Sydney, who held up her folded list. "We do what with this?''

"Oh, right. Just hold on to it. Don't look. I'll give instructions to everyone at the same time.''

And with that she glanced across the main room where, circled like a wagon train around the washtub of longnecks, stood the last of her three confirmed bachelors. Blowing out a long breath, she headed that way, presenting the three remaining sheets of blue paper to Eric, Leo and Ray.

"C'mon, guys. Pick a card. Any card.'' There were no takers the first time out, so she tried again. "I'm only offering three options here. That means the man brave enough to pick first has close to a fifty-fifty chance of winding up with the female partner of his choice.''

Eric backed up to sit on the arm of the sofa, lifting one brow, but making no further move. Rolling her eyes, Macy took matters into her own hands, folding one of the lists over the neckband of his shirt.

Definitely time to look for a new line of work, she thought, handing one list to Ray and, to Leo, the last.

He took his time slipping it from her fingers. Way too much time, because it was a simple piece of paper and nothing as intimate or suggestive as his slow-motion withdrawal would indicate.

It wasn't like his long strong fingers were reaching for

hers, though she hadn't yet forgotten their texture or the trail of warmth his touch left behind on her skin.

It wasn't like the paper held a private invitation, an indecent proposal, a back-alley proposition.

It wasn't like he was taking anything she hadn't offered him freely. Was there anything she wouldn't offer him freely?

She shook off the thought, found what remained of her brain. "Sorry, Leo. Looks like you're stuck with long odds."

He looked down at his hands instead of her way, folded the list and tucked the sheet of blue paper into the breast pocket of his crisp white shirt. "Guess I shouldn't have gotten my hopes up."

"Hopes up?"

"About playing with you again." This time he met her gaze, a calculated move, his eyes seeking hers and delving deep, beyond the surface of the game and into territory that was personal and intimate, a part of herself she rarely shared.

Oh, the way he looked at her. Oh, the way he said "again." A five-letter, two-syllable word that sounded like too much of a good time to turn down now that she knew how he kissed.

She heaved a regretful sigh, part sound effects, part honest bafflement over what he was making her feel. "If that's the case, you have no one to blame but yourself."

"How so?"

"This is my game, remember? I could've made sure we ended up on the same team if I'd known you were so anxious for my company."

"Not above cheating?"

"A girl's gotta do what a girl's gotta do." She

shrugged, then nodded toward the list he'd stashed away. "Good luck."

"Thanks," Leo replied. "But I can hold my own."

"Against these women?" Macy glanced briefly around the room. Leo truly had no idea who he was up against. "I wouldn't congratulate myself just yet."

She left him with a wink and then addressed the room, pulling her numbered pink list from the waistband of her capris. "Okay. Here's how this month's game works. The sheets of paper each of you hold are numbered from one to five. Inside you'll find an itemized list you'll need for the game."

"What kind of list?" asked Melanie.

"What kind of game?" asked Ray.

"Patience, my children. Patience. Now, as I'm sure you've already guessed by my not so subtle color scheme, tonight's game involves pairing all of us into five male-and-female teams.

"Okay, this is how we play." Taking a reluctant Eric's hand, she guided him to the spotlighted foyer, opened the first fold of his list and pointed to the number printed at the top.

"Two. Which means you stand in the second circle and wait for the female half of your team. Now, if I happen to have number two—" she lifted one edge of her sheet "—which I do not, you and I would be partners. I have number three, so I'll stand here in the third circle."

Anton pushed up from his usual place on the sofa. "C'mon, Macy. This spotlight business is too over the top."

A spoilsport in every bunch. "Of course it is. That's what makes this so much fun."

"Fun in whose opinion?" grumbled Eric.

Having cheated and checked his number early, Anton moved into the fifth spotlight. "So, what happens once we all pair off? Uh, team up," he corrected when Eric let out a pained, hand-to-throat choking groan. "Sorry, Eric."

Macy glanced at Eric, glared at Anton, blew out a breath to bolster her rapidly dwindling patience with the male species.

"If you two are through? Thank you. Now, on each sheet of paper is a list. A list for my gIRL gAMES... scavenger hunt!" The groans barely got off the ground before Macy hurried to squash them. "A kinky, suggestive, sexy and one-hundred-percent adult scavenger hunt."

"I'm not sure what you have in mind here, Macy, but I don't plan to visit any sex shops to find whatever it is you've come up with for these lists. I don't care how popular your columns are." That said, Sydney crossed her arms.

"Give me a little credit, Sydney. This game may be more daring than most, but sex shops? I think we can all flex our imagination beyond the obvious. After all, the brain is the body's true sex organ."

"Maybe your true sex organ," said the holder of blue number two. "Mine's a few feet lower on my body."

Macy groaned. "Only a man could made such a crass point."

"I'll show you a crass point."

Chloe diffused the ticking bomb of Macy's sanity by flashing a pink number two and moving into Eric's spotlight. "You very well may be showing me, sugar, since it looks like I have your number."

Eric all but rubbed his hands together with glee.

"Sexy and kinky in the flesh. We're either going to kick ass as a team or else..." His hand-rubbing slowed.

"Or else?" Chloe prompted.

"Or else you'll be busting my chops."

Macy felt the corners of her mouth pull into a blossoming grin. Petard or not, she was definitely brilliant. Or maybe just marginally brilliant, she amended, catching Leo Redding's eye as he watched her watch her number two couple.

Eric and Chloe were already shooting off the first round of sparks due to her cleverly designed plan. But with the match-up of the pink and blue number twos, and Anton and Lauren making up couple number five... Oh, please.

Surely she hadn't done what she'd just done. What Leo's expression was confirming she'd done. "I hope none of the rest of you have stooped so low as to cheat. And peek at your numbers before it's your turn."

"I did! I did!" Lauren practically hopped into Anton's circle, interweaving her feet and her legs with his and wrapping both arms around his neck. Anton hugged her back, and a shadow could not have slipped between the two lovers' bodies.

"This isn't Twister, you know," Macy chided. "You don't have to keep all four of your feet in the circle."

"But it's so much more fun this way." Lauren giggled, snuggling closer to the man who'd already managed to get his hands beneath the flowing fabric of her blouse.

Oh, well, Macy thought. The pair might as well enjoy the calm before the storm. She sighed, remembered Leo, sighed again. "Since no one is paying any attention to my directions, we can do this one of two ways. We either all cheat and peek, or I finish telling you how this works and we go from there.''

"I vote to cheat and peek.'' Melanie cast her ballot with one raised hand.

"I second that," said Sydney.

"Ditto," Ray chimed in.

Jess nodded. "Let's do it."

Macy turned to Leo and waited. "I suppose you share their lemming mind-set?"

"Share? No. Take advantage of? Sure." He slowly lifted his beer, took a drink, lowered the bottle, maintaining eye contact through the entire slow-motion process.

Did every move he made have to draw her gaze until she hovered on the verge of drooling? She narrowed her eyes. "Bet you don't know the difference between a lawyer and a vulture."

"A vulture can't take off his wing tips."

Eric laughed before Chloe could stop him. "Give it up, Macy. He's got you beat."

Macy ignored Eric's outburst as Leo once again downed a swallow of beer, calling her attention to his bare forearms and the elegantly expensive, chrome-cased watch fastened to his wrist with a glossy, black leather band.

Fashioned from the hide of a courtroom opponent, no doubt. "You've rolled up your sleeves, I see. Ready to sling mud?"

"Ready to get as dirty as I have to."

Grr, but he was good. Too damn good for her damn good. "Okay, then. If everyone's in agreement, let's see who ends up with whom."

"I like the end of my whom." Eric leaned down and nuzzled Chloe's nape.

She glanced back over her shoulder. "I may be standing here with my ass in your lap, but that doesn't mean you'll be ending up with anything that belongs to me."

Eric straightened and squirmed. "How long do we have to stand here anyway, Macy? I'm afraid my backup singers are in danger."

Reaching up to pat his cheek, Chloe answered, "Don't ask me to adjust your microphone, and we'll get along just fine."

For a minute, Macy felt sorry for Eric. Then her sympathies switched to Chloe. The two were proof positive of that thinly drawn line between love and hate.

Sydney chose that moment to move into circle one. And, not wanting to be the only woman left standing with the boys, Melanie stepped beneath the fourth spotlight.

Ray, Jess and Leo exchanged glances of shared male misery. Ray bit the first bullet, glanced at the number on his sheet and took his place beside Sydney.

His rugged olive-hued brawn and broad shoulders created an interesting backdrop for Sydney's classic elegance. The two made a perfect couple, and Macy felt a giddy twinge. At least until, in the next second, she registered the remaining odds.

She wouldn't think about it. She wouldn't panic. Not until she knew for sure… Okay, it was time to panic. Because as Jess stepped in beside Melanie, Leo took up his position at Macy's back.

The man whose eyes she wanted to gouge out, whose feathers she wanted to ruffle and pluck, whose clothes she wanted to strip from his body in order to learn the scent of his intimate skin, was going to be her partner.

"Okay," she said, and her voice squeaked, so she started again. "Okay. This is how this works. The first rule is that you never show your partner the items on your list. Guard it with your life.''

"Got it," Jess stated.

And Melanie, not to be outmaneuvered by her mate, added, ''That's easy.''

So far, so good. Macy opened her mouth to start again—only to have her next words cut off by Eric's loud, ''Wait a minute here. This doesn't make any sense. What's the point of working in teams if this isn't about teamwork?''

Leave it to the sports fanatic to overanalyze the rules of her game. ''What's the point of a game of chess? A game of racquetball? A one-on-one game of hoops?''

The stadium lights dawned in Eric's bright blue eyes. ''One-on-one, eh? Well, why didn't you say so earlier?''

Definitely the wrong comeback to make when surrounded by five of the six gIRL-gEAR women, starting with Macy on his left.

Her hands found a perch on her hips. ''Because you didn't stop with the smart-ass interruptions long enough for me to explain?''

Melanie chimed in next. ''Because you didn't trust a woman to come up with a game that would interest a man?''

''Because you didn't give a woman credit for having an original thought?'' Lauren. Always one to support her best friend.

And Sydney. ''Because you didn't think a woman's competitive streak could really be a mile wide?''

''Because, when it comes to sports, you don't listen to anyone who doesn't have a penis?''

The potshot volley, having begun in the third circle, continued down the line—the final salvo too close for

Eric's comfort. At Chloe's question, he took a step back and raised both hands in surrender.

"Okay, okay. I give. Macy, you're brilliant." He offered her a deferential bow. "Abso-friggin-lutely brilliant."

"And here I thought you'd never notice." She was beginning to think no one would notice. That she'd been imagining her brilliance alone all this time. The way things had been going this evening, in fact, she felt positively unbrilliant.

So, of course, Leo chose that moment to move in closer, nudging his hip to her backside, reminding her of the pickle her unbrilliance had gotten her into. Here she was, stuck playing a game of her own making with a partner more foe than friend—a petard of an entirely different nature.

His breath brushed the hairs at Macy's nape. She ignored the sensation, chalked up the contact to his proximity and not to any underhanded attempt to move his first pawn—though she did reserve the right to change her mind and retract the benefit of the doubt.

She exhaled and regained her train of thought. "Okay. Where was I?"

"Guarding our lists with our lives," he reminded her.

"Right. It's also important that once you start finding the items on your lists, you keep your findings to yourself. This is not a team effort. One-on-one, remember? The prize goes to only one of you. One of us. Whatever."

"Anyway, when we get together next month, the one who has found the most items on his or her individual list will be off sailing the Seven Seas. Or at least the Caribbean." Sensing a cheater at her back, she crushed her paper to her chest.

"Now, I don't expect it will take anyone the entire thirty days to finish. There might even be some of you who finish up tonight." She sent a pointed glance down the row toward Anton and Lauren. "But Sydney won't be awarding the prize until next month's game night."

"And I suppose we have to be present to win?"

Macy winked at Ray. "I like the way you think."

Eric had finally had enough. "Can we look now or what?"

"In a minute." The crucial moment had arrived. Her players were pumped and primed. Now not to lose them in the details. She pinched together the pads of her index finger and thumb. "Just one more little itty-bitty thing to mention."

"Uh-oh," echoed in tones from soprano to bass.

"The items on your list? The kinky, suggestive, sexy and one-hundred-percent-adult items?"

"I told you, Macy. No sex shops."

Macy was definitely going to have to introduce Sydney to the joys of a certain store she'd discovered on lower Westheimer.

"Actually, Syd, none of the things on your list could be purchased even if you wanted to buy them. Well, I suppose that's not exactly true, but I'm not going to go there."

Macy waved away the thought of offering payment to Leo Redding, and dropped the bomb. "You see, the source of every item you'll need to find to win the scavenger hunt belongs to the member of the opposite sex in your spotlight."

LEO REDDING STOOD ALONE in the first-floor hallway of Macy and Lauren's building. The light was dim, the narrow windows being set high in the old warehouse's walls, and night having long ago fallen. The row of original and restored bare-bulb fixtures cast enough of a glow to allow him to read the list he hadn't yet taken time to go over.

He had to give Macy credit. The woman had a sense of adventure like none he'd ever encountered. This scavenger hunt of hers was inventive and inspired and...he wasn't sure he could put into words what all it was.

He knew women well, was used to the sexual subterfuge engaged in by those he dated. He expected no less when he entered a relationship and discovered the unique challenges each partner offered. Sex was always an exchange of power, whether shared in a one-night stand or a when-the-mood-strikes fling.

Which was why this scavenger hunt of Macy's intrigued him. She had the competitive spirit he enjoyed in a woman. Too bad she didn't recognize the potential of that energy. Or didn't apply her ambition beyond living for the moment.

He couldn't deny the cultural phenomenon of gIRL-gEAR. He'd spent enough time on the firm's corporate structure to know that Sydney Ford and her partners had hit with uncanny accuracy on urban fashion's next best thing.

And now, reading the list of a dozen-plus personal items he'd agreed to discover about Macy Webb, he was struck with the logic that drove her individual success.

Beyond her enthusiasm for putting together the game, she knew what buttons to push to get play under way. In this case, the collective testosterone buttons of the five men in the room.

The women of gIRL-gEAR were hot. And if the rest of the guys' lists were as provocative as Leo's, he figured winning wasn't much of an issue when Macy had made the chance to score a prize in itself.

Then he wondered what was on the list of items she would be working to discover about him. He wouldn't mind if she discovered his preferred brand of long-legged briefs. He'd gladly allow her to find his only childhood scar; the skateboarding accident had required a zipper of stitches to sew up the Frankenstein gash on his hipbone.

And, while she was there with his pants down, he wouldn't object to her searching out not only the erogenous zone he shared with all men, but his other. The one women loved to discover—at least those who took the time to learn exactly what *he* liked in bed.

Okay. Here he was, standing in a darkened hallway working on a hard-on. Something had to give. Twice tonight Macy had brought him to the point of wanting to get off and she'd done nothing more than run him over with her clever little mind.

And wasn't that what made a woman worth knowing? If she knew how to flex her mental muscles, she could be guaranteed a man's appreciative attention to the rest of her body. So why was he standing here playing with himself when he could be upstairs playing with her?

Or at least seeing how many of his game points he could rack up this evening while he had her to himself, before she'd had time to recover from the party or shake off the chemistry they'd stirred. He wasn't an underhanded cheat, but neither was he above playing all odds in his favor.

Besides, he had nowhere to be tonight, and the idea of going back to the office held less appeal than it had an hour ago. Macy was alone. Lauren had left with Anton, which meant Leo was footloose as well.

He and Macy had taken turns moving their pawns all evening. She didn't have to know his return was a calculated advance on her queen. And if she learned more than he wanted her to know, well, that was a tactical risk he was willing to take.

He could afford a forfeit or two. He could afford whatever it took to beat Macy Webb at any game of her making.

Anton
and the
would
around
of her

moment

4

ANOTHER GAME NIGHT BITES the dust.

Macy pulled one bra after another from the shower rod in Lauren's bathroom, testing for dampness between her fingers and the palm of her hand. Dry enough were the ten she hooked over her forearm. The last two she moved to the towel rack.

Lauren could hardly object. She was gone for the night. Totally ignoring every best-friend rule ever written, she'd gone home with Anton, lucky dog, leaving Macy alone to deal with the leftovers of the evening's insanity.

Oh, well. Tonight the work would be welcome. In addition to the physical chores, mentally sorting through the events of the evening would keep her plenty busy until time for bed.

Should she run out of questions to ask herself about the way the scavenger hunt had unfolded, or have trouble coming up with answers, well, there were always toilets to scrub. Floors to wax. A balcony to sweep clear of cobwebs and fallen leaves.

Then there was the mural on her bedroom ceiling that needed another fish or two. A dolphin. A turtle. A mermaid to give the room a bit of oomph. If Macy reached total desperation, she'd sit down under the sea, make a list and have it ready for when her artistic best friend came home.

Anything to keep her mind off the fact that, with Lauren gone, the loft was empty. Macy was alone.

Back to the scavenger hunt, she thought, flipping off Lauren's bathroom light. How practical, really, were the game's dynamics for her readers? If not for the sailing vacation, Macy's guinea pigs would no doubt have expressed even less enthusiasm at having to devote time to an activity that came with no guarantee of, well, anything.

Strangers playing would at least be getting to know potential dates. This group was only in it for the prize, not the possibilities. The game was too long; that was it. The true challenge would be to find the items in one evening. From several members of the opposite sex. Forget the one-on-one, long-term assignment. The lists could be distributed as the guests arrived. No coupling, no teamwork.

Actually, though, now that she thought about it, she could present both options. The longer game would provide a broader field, giving players time to test their partner's boundaries. And the shorter version was the perfect arena in which to rack up rapid-fire points, boom-boom.

She liked it. Liked it a lot. A two-fer. Now to figure out how to get two columns out of one idea. Ha! As if Sydney in a million years would go for that idea. It was probably a good thing Macy wasn't a solo entrepreneur. She'd be forced to fire herself for living by the motto that all work and no play made Macy a dull girl.

The whir of the loft's elevator motor caught her off guard, and she scurried from Lauren's corner of the loft. If Lauren and Anton had already gotten into it over the game, Macy wanted to be out of her best friend's throwing range.

But when the freight car ground to a stop, when the outside gate rattled opened and the inner door followed, Lauren and Anton were the least of Macy's worries.

Because standing inside the metal cage, one long-fingered hand propped on the wall, the other braced against a lean waist, head lowered, shirt cuffs buttoned, tie snug to his throat, stood one incredibly gorgeous corporate attorney.

Leo Redding looked up, and Macy's stomach thudded to her feet. A man shouldn't be able to do to a woman what this one could do with his eyes alone. Gingerly, she retreated.

Boldly, he advanced, bringing into the room not only his uppity attitude, but an air of such style and class Macy itched to lick him, er, to muss him from his *GQ* hair to his toes shod in rich black Italian leather.

The heavy metal door rolled shut behind him. He pulled the hinged grate to a close along its metal track.

Alone. The two of them. Together on her turf.

The devil jabbed a pitchfork at her shoulder. An angel sang sweetly from the opposite side. It was so hard choosing between naughty and nice.

"Lost your way, I see," she said.

He shook his head. "Only my ride. I came here with Anton, remember?"

"And he took Lauren with him. Leaving you stranded."

What a weasely excuse. She knew what Leo wanted. The cheater. Thinking he could learn her scavenger hunt secrets if he caught her alone, with her guard down and…ten demi-cup, push-up bras hung over her arm.

Oh, good humiliating grief.

"I suppose you need to use the phone to call a cab?"

She directed a pointed glance toward the leather cellular case attached to his waist.

Shaking his head, he moved farther into the room, assessing the equipment in the entertainment center, thumbing through the selection of CDs, crossing to the balcony and sliding open the plate-glass door before he answered. "I have a phone."

"Well, then, I assume you came back for the obvious."

"The obvious?" He tossed the question absently over his shoulder.

"To get started on your scavenger hunt." She waited for a denial, but he stepped outside, giving her nothing but a very nice view of his backside, from wide shoulders to long legs and his really great ass in between.

"You've got a terrific view from here."

"You can say that again." She muttered the comment under her breath and followed. Leaning a shoulder against the wall on one side of the door frame, she kept the heels of both bare feet on the loft's hardwood floor, dipping only her toes into the balcony's shark-infested waters.

Leo finally glanced in her direction. "I'm sorry. I didn't hear what you said."

"Nothing. Just agreeing. About the view." A safe enough reply. And true.

The neighborhood itself was newly renovated, which meant ongoing construction, the noise of road work and heavy equipment filling many hours of the day. Part of the price the residents paid for being among the first to support the new downtown.

But the nights were another thing entirely. From her fourth-floor balcony, the view of the city skyline beckoned to Macy like a playground, a theme park, a child-hood never-never land waiting to be explored.

She glanced over to catch Leo still staring her way.

He'd turned his back to the railing and stood, arms crossed and relaxed. "You like it here, don't you?"

The pitch of his voice had lowered and softened, but Macy couldn't think about the change in his tone. She couldn't afford to let down her guard, or her anything, around this man. "I do. It's fun, watching the city morph and change. Everything old is new again, or however the cliché goes."

"Seems to be the way of things. I've been looking at condos in the old Rice Hotel. And Anton showed me a couple of the places near Buffalo Bayou he and Doug renovated."

Macy nodded an acknowledgment, then moved back into the loft, sensing this conversation would soon turn to the weather. Leo wasn't here for that any more than he was here to discuss the city's real-estate market.

She wanted to know why he'd come. What he wanted. If he intended to stay. Why she wanted him to do just that when she should be showing the arrogant beast to the door.

He walked out of the balcony's darkness and into her light. The stars in the night sky behind him winked with but half the sparkle in his eyes. Macy forced herself to breathe.

She couldn't let him get to her this early in the game. She had to avoid this plaguelike attraction. The man was too logical, too seriously uptight and sensible. She doubted she'd find a spontaneous bone in his body.

Then again, that depended on what one considered a bone, didn't it?

"What's the frown for?"

She glanced up at his question and frowned. "I'm not frowning."

Sliding the balcony door shut behind him, Leo responded to her denial with the bold arch of one brow.

"Okay. I'm frowning. But only because you said I was." Yes. That made a world of sense. But it was certainly better than confessing her previous ponderings.

"Then you admit to the charge. And I rest my case."

Macy once again crossed her arms, sending the clothesline of underthings swinging at her waist. "Tell me, Mr. Redding. What's the difference between a lawyer and a prostitute?"

"A prostitute won't screw you when you're dead."

She snorted. He hadn't even hesitated long enough to blink. "I suppose you've heard them all."

"It comes with knowing the territory." He took a predatory step into the room. His mouth crooked with a predatory grin. "And I'm very good at what I do."

Maybe so, but Macy Webb was no man's prey. "Yes. I remember you making that boast."

"I wondered about that. If you remembered."

"I don't forget much of anything. Unfortunately."

"Except where you keep your lingerie?"

"Funny." She glared and draped the lot over the back of the sofa. "Okay, I forgot to do my laundry until this afternoon."

"So I noticed."

"That I didn't do my laundry?"

"That you weren't wearing your laundry." At her affronted expression, he added, "When you were in my lap."

"And I guess I should be flattered?"

He shrugged one shoulder instead of answering with

a simple yes or no. "It wasn't like I went out of my way to look. Your chest *was* in my face."

"I see. So, what you're saying is that when my chest isn't in your face you don't notice it?"

"No. That's not what I said. But now that you mention it..." He let the sentence trail away.

Macy picked right up where he left off. "Mention what?"

"Victoria's Secret? I think she shared it for a reason."

He was *so* going to pay for that one. And he could start with a little scavenger hunt currency. "What about *your* secrets?"

"My secrets?"

"Sure." She plopped down on the sofa, tucked her knees to her chest, wrapped her arms around her shins. "That's why you're here, isn't it? To zip through your scavenger hunt list? Get it over with and out of the way?"

He headed for the big square chair in which he'd sat earlier this evening. She watched him walk, watched him sit, watched him square an ankle over a knee and spread out his hands on the chair arms.

"Sure. Why not? What do you want to know?" He looked at her from behind those pewter rims that framed long brown lashes and clear green eyes.

She would not be sucked in by his studly *GQ* perfection. She would not. "Just like that?"

"Just like that."

Hmm. What was wrong with this picture? And why hadn't she studied her list instead of leaving it on her desk to go over in bed once she'd put the loft back in order? "I can ask you anything on my list and you'll answer?"

Elbows on the chair arms, he propped his fingertips

together under his chin, shrugged again with just one shoulder. "Unless it's something I don't want you to know."

"Aha!" She bounded to the edge of the sofa, pointing a finger. Four of the bras at her shoulder slithered down into her lap. "I knew there was a catch."

A brow went up. "There's always a catch, Macy. But go ahead. Try me."

There *was* always a catch, wasn't there? Macy thought, folding her renegade laundry. And the catch in finding out what she wanted to know was that Leo would be asking the same in return.

But she'd be damned if she wouldn't ferret out at least the one item she remembered seeing on her list. "Okay. Tell me this. Where is the most bizarre place you've ever had sex?"

Leo blinked slowly, thoughtfully, looked at Macy over his index-finger steeple. Then he removed his hands from his face. "Geographically bizarre? Like Bangkok?"

"Bangkok? Hmm. No, actually I mean strategically bizarre. On the back of a horse, in an airplane bathroom. That sort of thing." She stacked the lingerie on the arm of the sofa and turned an expectant look on him.

Leo turned an expectant look on her stack of lingerie. "In a box seat. At the theater. Wearing a tux."

The theater? A tux? And his date in formal wear, too? How could they— Unless— Macy had about ten-thousand logistical questions, but then Leo said, "My turn."

With a sudden flutter of nerves, she pushed an unruly mass of hair from the right side of her face, repeated the gesture on the left. "Ask away."

"Exhibitionist tendencies. It's a question on my list."

Macy looked his way slowly, sensing a strange, compelling touch, as if his finger had tipped up her chin and turned her head toward him. "And you were wondering what, exactly?"

His jaw tensed. The tic of a pulse throbbed at his temple. He glanced again at the arm of the sofa and at her lingerie.

"Oh, that." She laughed lightly, ignoring the twisting, tightening tickle spinning like a roulette wheel beneath her rib cage. "I usually don't make a habit of exposing my underthings, no."

"But would you?"

"Strut my stuff?" Did she have it in her to be so bold? Her lips curved upward. And here she'd thought Leo so conventional and conservative. "I might."

"Now?"

"Now?" She glanced toward the bras. "You want me to…"

He gestured with his chin. "The one on top. Put it on."

The novelty print? She had black lace, silver lamé, zebra stripes, silk and satin. And he wanted Tinkerbell and Peter Pan?

One corner of his mouth almost lifted. "Just put it on."

She was absolutely out there to be considering this. Such a strange turn for her scavenger hunt to take. But wasn't this what she'd wanted? To see where her games might go? Besides, putting it on didn't mean she had to take anything off.

Keeping that tidbit to herself, she stood, hung the bra around her waist and fastened the single rear hook. The cups and straps dangled over her belly. She slipped her arms out of her sleeves and down inside her T-shirt, working the straps up over her shoulders beneath the narrow pink top.

She exposed a whole lot of belly in the process, but managed to get the bra into place without too many awkward movements. All that was left now was to wiggle one arm, then the other, back through the T-shirt's armholes and, ta-da!

He didn't move a muscle. Not so much as an eyelash. No tic in his jaw or fingers clenched on the chair arms, nor was there any other dead giveaway of a man holding his fierce lust in check. Then again, what was there for him to lust over?

Wait a minute. What in the world was she saying? She had plenty to lust over. Yet she was thinking like...like a man instead of like a woman who knew size didn't matter.

Milk came in everything from gallon jugs to coffee cream thimbles. It was still milk. Just like the dimensions of the banana found in a man's pocket mattered less than the way he peeled his fruit.

The blinders on Leo's eyes had to go.

She took a step closer, and closer still, until her knees bumped into his. Bracketing his legs with hers, she scooted aboard the chair. Her knees sank into the cushions on either side of his hips. Her lap sank into his.

The move put Peter Pan and Tinkerbell level with Leo's eyes, though the perky little characters were safely covered by her shirt. "Anything else?"

"Well, now that you mention it," Leo began, his voice less Prince Charming and more husky frog, though he met her gaze directly, his intent as evident in his expression as it was beginning to be in his lap. "You can take off your shirt."

She knew she ought to probably put more effort into

resistance. But she was putty, soft and malleable, made for easy play. And for hours now, she'd wanted to feel the touch of his hands. "You first. Take off your tie."

He hesitated a nanosecond. Then he loosened the knot, slipped the strip of colored silk free from his collar. She reached for the tie at the same time she took hold of his free hand, and before he could prepare an argument, she started binding his wrists together.

He studied her ongoing handiwork. "Bondage? This would be the dirty little secret you've never shared with your best friend? The one I need to find and mark off my list?"

She pressed her lips together because she so wanted to blurt out that he'd just lost his edge, breaking the rules of the game like that, telling her point-blank one of the items he'd be working to discover.

Instead, she concentrated on making another loop, another knot, totally ruining a designer accessory that had to have cost a small fortune.

"Are you done?" he finally asked when there was only an inch or two of tie end left hanging.

Pleased with the results of her efforts, and even more so with the progression of the game, Macy dropped his bound hands into his lap. "Just making sure you're not tempted to get all hands-on here."

That she would kill to feel his hands on all parts of her body wasn't the point. The point at this point was… She had absolutely no idea of anything except that she wanted to get naked with Leo Redding.

"Macy?"

At his softly spoken question, she met his gaze. "Yes, Leo?"

"I've changed my mind. I'd rather you leave your shirt on."

He'd rather, would he? He'd seen enough of what wasn't there to see, was that it? No, that wasn't it. Because just as she'd started to reach defiantly for the hem of her shirt, she realized that was exactly what he wanted her to do.

"You're a sneaky one, aren't you? Using reverse psychology on a psychology major won't earn you any points, mister."

"I don't need help earning my points. I'll talk you out of anything I want to know."

"Is that so?" Ooh, he was so close to crossing the line to her bad side. "Then what's with the shirt on, shirt off business if you're not trying to sneak past my defenses and get a head start on your list?"

"There's a lot to be said for a man's imagination."

"I thought men were from Mars. That you preferred relying on all those eyes you have instead of flexing your imagination."

Leo lifted his glasses, lowered them back into place. "I am using my eyes."

"Oh yeah?"

"Yeah. Not that I'll stop you if you're determined to lose your shirt."

Now she was battling confusion as well as hormones. Did he want her? Or was she imagining the activity of his third Martian eye?

"I think I'll leave it on." She gave her answer with utmost ambiguity.

"Good. Because that'll make doing this a whole lot more fun." Leo looped his bound hands behind her neck. He held her still and his eyes flared sharply. The corner of his mouth lifted with the secret he was thinking.

And then he leaned forward and gave Tinkerbell a tongue-lashing.

Oh and *my* were the only two words Macy could remember. The rest of the noise in her throat was either a moan or a groan. Leo's mouth covered her breast until her T-shirt and bra were as wet as he'd find her panties.

He pulled on her nipple with his lips, scraped the tip with his teeth, then moved to Peter Pan, leaving damp circles of cotton and nylon and skin. He traced the line of her tattoo with the flat of his tongue, circling the tip over the Celtic knot that dipped between her breasts.

Macy's own fingers gouged into her thighs because she was afraid she'd reach for the buttons of his shirt, or the hem of her own, or his head to better guide him, or his other head to see exactly what he had to offer.

Why was she wearing anything at all? Why weren't they both naked and in bed?

Okay. This madness had to stop. She pressed a hand to Leo's chest and pushed him away from the grand work he was doing. His eyes were brighter than she'd ever seen them. His mouth was damp, and red from the contact with the fabric of her shirt.

She opened her mouth to speak, but he grinned. The impish, devilish, cocky grin of a boy caught with his hand in the cookie jar. Or his mouth in the make-believe cleavage of a woman he didn't know. Hmm.

"Leo? What are we doing?"

"Breast-feeding?"

At that, she cuffed the back of his head. "An Eric Haydon comment if I ever heard one. Hey, what are your hands doing untied?"

"Doing this." One hand held her nape. "And this." The other hand he splayed flat across her collarbone, his palm resting on her cleavage, which was still damp from his mouth.

Macy knew he was taking the measure of her heartbeat, her arousal in reaction to his touch. Men enjoyed that, knowing they held a woman's orgasm in the palm of their hand. "Are you thinking of snapping my neck? Tossing my limp rag-doll body down the elevator shaft?"

One hand slid up toward her throat. "Why would you think I'd do that?"

"Easiest way to eliminate the competition."

He didn't say anything for a minute, then murmured, "Rag doll?"

She narrowed her eyes. "Don't be getting any ideas."

"I don't know. I like the idea of having my own personal plaything."

She tilted her head to one side. "The idea does have merits. I could use a boy toy of my own."

One brow went up, came down. "Boy toy? I guess I could live with that."

"I'm sure you could, but don't think you'll be so lucky. We've fraternized enough for one night."

"I thought fraternization was the secret to your scavenger hunt. Best way to learn all about one another." Leo laced his fingers behind his neck and leaned back, knees spread wide as he considered the wet spots he'd left on her shirt.

"I never said I was going to make this easy for you." She backed off his lap and onto her feet. "We're going to be at each other's throats before the end of the month, you know."

He studied her over the rims of his glasses. "Throats? I can't say that would be the first thing I'd go after."

"Don't tell me you're actually considering sleeping with the enemy."

For a moment he remained silent. Unmoving. Then the slow blink of his eyes, plus the rapid tapping of a single index finger along the outer edge of the chair arm, suggested conflicting thoughts must be running through his mind.

Finally, he pushed to his feet and reached for his cell phone. A self-directed shake of his head offered little insight into what decision he'd reached.

His voice, as he ordered a cab, was calm and collected, unlike the look on his face, which had Macy wondering what part of her comment, the sleeping or the enemy, had switched the thermostat from sauna to freeze.

He snapped the phone closed and returned it to the case at his waist. Then he moved toward her. She refused to back away. Instead, she lifted her chin and the stakes of this game.

"A tactical retreat? So soon? Why, Leo, you surprise me."

"Sleeping with the enemy is against my code of ethics." He ran the tip of one finger the length of her tattoo.

A shiver reached her bare toes. "You're a lawyer. I didn't think you had a code of ethics."

"If I didn't, I wouldn't be leaving."

So he did want to sleep with her. "So you do want to sleep with me."

The words hung in the air as he wrapped one hand around her waist and used the pressure of the other on her backside, pulling her up and into his erection.

Oh, he was gloriously huge, gloriously hard, and

Macy could barely find her voice to say, "Is that a subpoena in your pocket or are you just happy to see me?"

The tic at Leo's temple twitched with the grinding of his jaw. "Is everything a joke to you? Or only the things the rest of us tend to take seriously?"

"Laugh and the world laughs with you," Macy said, her breath coming fast, in heated bursts.

"I'm not laughing." He let her go. "I'm leaving."

"What? You're not interested in finding out the truth about the dirty little secret I've never even shared with my best friend?"

"The scavenger hunt can wait. I've learned enough of the truth for one evening."

And then he left, walking to the elevator, a scene that was becoming all too familiar and predictable. The lift came and went, taking Leo bodily away, leaving behind the picture of his backside on the balcony, of his hands spread wide on the arms of the chair.

Of his mouth making wet and wild with her chest. Of his cocky attitude and his cocky grin and his cocky, er, okay, his cock pressed like a probe to her belly.

Too bad she couldn't toss the memory of the night after him down the shaft.

5

Lauren lay on her stomach on the soft navy sheets covering Anton's mattress, her fingers laced, her forehead resting in the cup of her hands, her body bare but for the comforter draped over her lower legs.

She alternately winced and groaned, depending on which group of muscles Anton worked with his fingers, which he dug into with the heels of his palms. He'd been manipulating her body long enough that her tension should have eased.

But how was she supposed to relax when his fingers were walking the length of her spine, reaching her tailbone and exploring lower, dipping between her legs to make her ready, only to pull away as she lifted her hips?

She whimpered when he returned to her shoulders to begin the process again. With soft brushes of lips to skin, he eased her back from completion, working the stress from tendons and muscles as stiff and unyielding as the part of his body pressed firmly to the crevice of her bottom.

A quiet laugh escaped as she worked her legs farther apart. She may not have intended for her mind to wander, but she couldn't help entertaining the fleeting thought that maybe, by the end of the month, Macy would be lying this way beneath Leo Redding, his erection sliding over her bottom as he moved.

Oh, but Lauren liked the way Anton slid over her

bottom as he moved. Forward as he pressed down between her shoulder blades, back as he kneaded his way to the base of her spine. Eyes closed, she allowed a smile to touch her lips. Her limbs became jelly, then melted like butter, and she no longer knew the difference between the sheet and her skin.

"Tell me what you're thinking."

She couldn't think clearly enough to speak. His fingers grazed her sides, teased her breasts. Her nipples puckered into the sheet; his erection probed between her legs. Deeply aroused, Lauren inhaled the aroma of the citrus and vanilla massage oil enhanced by the mating of skin.

Coils of tension unwound, only to tighten anew at the feel of Anton's heavy sex stroking to the rhythm and the motion of his hands. She wanted him inside her, and reached back with one hand to measure the soft weight of his testicles, to run her thumb over the wet tip of his glans.

He moved away as she did, and even her soft plea didn't bring him back. Lauren closed her eyes briefly, steeling herself before she rolled onto her back and propped herself up on her elbows. She wanted to ask why he'd stopped, what she'd done.

Why did she always jump to the conclusion that it was something she'd done?

But one glance at Anton and she couldn't think of anything but the way his skin looked in the room's candlelight, how the soft fuzz on his chin caught the glow from the flames, as did the blond curls in disarray on the top of his head, the bare dusting of hair that covered his torso.

He'd sat back on his heels, his hands on his thighs, his sex strong, hard, jutting upward. She wanted him.

Desperately. She'd always thought men possessed the more powerful sex drive, but with Anton, she could never get enough.

Tonight, however, before he'd take her, before he'd allow either one of them the climax to which they'd been building, there was something else he wanted. She knew that about him after all the time they'd been together. Knew, too, the power she held over him with the satisfaction he found in her body.

Strangely enough, right now, she didn't care what he wanted. She wanted to be the one in control, to experiment with that power, to discover exactly the depth of that hold. She wanted to stir in Anton an emotional response, to see if he felt any of the unease she was feeling after reading Macy's list.

That list...that list had jarred Lauren deeply.

Out of the dozen items she should know about the man in her life, she couldn't name but two. She knew him sexually, but intimately? The question prodded her conscience to answer. She refused, and she didn't like what that refusal said about her commitment, what it said about her as a lover, as a friend.

She moved up and around on all fours, and she didn't miss the flare in Anton's eyes as she crawled behind him, draped her arms over his shoulders and pressed her breasts to his back.

She moved her hands over his collarbone, rubbed light circles over his chest with her thumbs. ''I was thinking about your hands.''

She nipped at his earlobe, slid her palms with tormenting leisure down his torso. ''Thinking how much I enjoy your touch.''

She reached down, teased his erection with fluttering

fingers. "Thinking how lucky I am to have you in my life."

Anton's shoulders remained rigid under her ministrations. He didn't believe her. She was going to have to confess the error of her ways. "And I was wondering how long it would be before Macy ended up in bed with Leo."

Anton turned his head, his chin brushing her cheek. "Macy and Leo? Are you serious?"

She slowed for a moment, then picked up her stroking rhythm again, her fingers moving up to tug lightly at the hair covering his chest. "It was just a random thought, so no, not really. Why? You don't think they could get something going?"

"No. I don't."

Lauren's hands stilled. Her fingers slid up and off his shoulders. She sat back and crossed her legs, wondering if he didn't know she would come to the defense of her friend. "I think you're jumping the gun. From the way things looked earlier tonight, they seemed to be hitting it off without a snag."

Anton turned to face her, pulling her crossed legs forward and into his lap. "Don't take this as a slam against Macy, Lauren, but you've seen the women Leo dates. Macy's not in his social league. She's not his type physically. And she doesn't exactly come equipped with the résumé he's used to."

"I don't really care what the man's used to." She couldn't help but be protective of Macy. Lauren didn't take her best friend's best-friend rules lightly. "Leo's way too narrow-minded. I mean, does he really think he'll find what he's looking for bedding only designer labels in his designer label bedding? Give me a break. I think Macy and her scavenger hunt might be just what he needs to change his way of thinking.''

Anton studied Lauren's face intently. ''Do you think it will change my way of thinking?''

This was what she'd been waiting for. This feeling of losing her footing at the first beckoning finger of dread. ''What do you mean?''

''If you think the scavenger hunt could change Leo's mind about Macy, what's to stop it from changing mine about you?'' He reached up to toy with a long strand of her hair. His eyes finally softened. ''Or yours about me, for that matter?''

So her fears weren't entirely unfounded. Anton shared her concerns…as if that were any sort of consolation. She smiled sweetly, refusing to let him see how the evening's events had left her unsettled.

''C'mon, baby. You and I both know that Leo has no idea who Macy really is. His opinions aren't based on anything substantial.'' Lauren ran fingertips up and down Anton's outer thighs, moving her teasing touch into the pit of his knee before working her slow way back toward his groin.

''You, on the other hand, know me. You know me very—'' her fingertips grazed the base of his softened penis, delved below the heavy sac beneath ''—very well.''

''Are you sure?'' He held her hands and halted her arousing progress. ''I'm serious, Lauren. This game of Macy's that you think capable of changing lives… Have you looked at your list?''

She nodded and, working her captured hands free, shared an idea that had been forming. ''You know, we could cheat. I'll fill you in on anything you don't know about me, you claim the prize, and we're off for a week of fun.''

This time he took hold of her wrists and pulled one hand close, grazing her wrist with a nibbling, calming kiss. ''Instead of cheating, we could actually give it a shot. Aren't you the least bit curious?''

''What's to be curious about?'' Besides ten out of her twelve items. ''I know you wear sexy little bikini briefs, when you bother to wear anything at all.''

''Underwear. Right. What else is on your list? How many things don't you know?''

She didn't want to answer, to admit that her infatuation had sprinkled fairy dust in her eyes. She was giddy with the way she'd fallen so amazingly hard for this man, and blind to what she didn't want to see.

Like the fact that the schedules she and Anton kept had them stealing quick lunches or spending what time they had together in bed, where talk ran the gamut from endearments to smut.

Turning the tables was the easiest response. ''What about you? How many things do you or don't you know about me?''

She waited while he stared into her eyes, and she watched the flames of dozens of candles flicker in his, playing tricks with their color until she couldn't remember if they were really that close to navy or that lighter shade of ocean blue.

Such a little thing she couldn't remember, and the resulting worry tightened the muscles of her stomach even more.

''Let's see,'' he finally said, and smiled, a slow revelation of beautifully deep dimples. ''I should know your addictions. Nothing narcotic or alcoholic. Not even chocolate.''

He went on, even after she stuck out her tongue. "I'd have to say television. Specifically, every endlessly rerun episode of *Frasier* and *Friends*."

Lauren reached out and punched his shoulder. "Don't be making fun of my fun. I could be addicted to porn, you know, spending all my money on smut books and wanker flicks."

He gave a quick shake of his head. "Did you just say wanker? I can't believe you said wanker."

"Excuse me?" This time Lauren's punch was a shove, sending Anton flat to his back. She crawled up over him, glared down into his face. "I know my share of dirty words, big boy."

He cupped her breasts in his hands. "So I've noticed."

"Is that a complaint?" she asked, and lowered her weight onto his naked body, chest to chest, thighs to thighs, feet and knees tangled and soft sex ground against hard.

He shuddered and held her still. "No healthy, red-blooded man is going to complain when his woman talks dirty in bed."

"So you do like the way I use my mouth." She opened her lips over the hollow of his throat, teased his skin with tiny flicks of her tongue.

Anton groaned. His sex pulsed, growing thick and strong. "Yes, I like your mouth. I also like that you have a mind to go with it."

Lauren lifted her head, propped her chin on Anton's collarbone and forced a sultry pout. "Does that mean you want me for my brain and not my body?"

"It means I want the combination." He bunched a pillow beneath his head and studied her down the length of his nose. "You wouldn't be here if you didn't have intelligence and an incredible wit. If you didn't give good conversation.''

He reached for a lock of her hair and tested its texture with his fingers. ''And I wouldn't be here if you didn't rock my world in bed.''

A tack-sharp sting spread from the base of Lauren's spine to burn like an aggravated ulcer. He wanted intelligence and wit. He wanted conversation. And he'd just put both on a pedestal above sex. Her stomach muscles clenched to hold in the pangs of anxiety. But she made certain not to reveal any of the turmoil she was feeling.

''Is one more important to you than the other, then?''

''Are we talking long-term or short-term?'' Anton's initial scowl softened from thoughtfully tense to tender. ''Or is this about the scavenger hunt?''

''I thought we were talking about you and me.''

That hand that had been slipping in and out of her hair joined the other wrapped around her shoulders and holding her close. ''Then I guess you have your answer.''

She didn't have anything of the kind. But analyzing the dynamics of their relationship would have to wait. Their bodies were not to be denied. It was the one constant in her swirling awareness, this extraordinary physical attraction they shared.

Moving the way her body, instinct and Anton had taught her pleasured him most, Lauren took control of the mating. His strangled gasp signaled his surrender. His hands worked their way down her spine to her backside, which he squeezed before moving to the tops of her thighs.

Using strong fingers, he spread her legs, giving himself room between. His erection was full, and once settled, she closed her legs around his length, holding him still.

Then finally, when she was ready, when imminent ecstasy had erased fear of the unknown, she let him go and shifted her lower body, slowly settling herself over the tip of his sex until he was fully sheathed. Totally captured. Completely hers.

Rotating slowly, she lifted and lowered with alternating strokes. Faster, harder, slicker, hotter. She tossed her mane of hair and sat up, splaying her hands across his shoulders and using that base of muscle as leverage, setting a rhythm that had him urging her with his hands on her hips to slow the pace, to gentle the mood. But slow and gentle would have to wait.

She wanted rough and mindless.

From her kneeling position atop his prone form, she used her toes to pry apart his legs, and worked her feet down between his thighs. He groaned, but gave in and spread wider, groaned again when she reached back and caressed him, exploring his skin, slick with the fluids they'd stirred, and the skin beneath, now tight and drawn close to his body.

She knew by his sharp intake of breath she'd more than hit her mark. And seconds later he proved it, flipping her onto her back, keeping their bodies fully engaged as he leaned his weight into his elbows on either side of her head.

"You're an amazing woman, Lauren Hollister." He brushed his lips over her eyelids, her cheekbones, the line of her jaw and her chin, whispering against her mouth, "You have no idea how sexy it is for a woman to respond the way you respond."

"Of course I respond." Men could be so simple-minded, she thought, and shivered from the feel of his body made one with hers. "Why wouldn't I respond? I love you."

And she did. She knew she did.

Yet this time, when she came, the intensity she'd always found with Anton wasn't there. Still, she hugged him fiercely, held him tight, tracing soothing patterns across his muscular back and receiving in return a sleepily mumbled, "Mmm."

Mmm? That was it? She forced her frown to relax. What had she expected? A declaration of love? Why would now be any different than before?

Anton rarely spoke of his feelings at all, a trait he shared with many men. He'd actually confided more tonight about what he thought important, what he wanted from their relationship, than she could remember him ever sharing before.

It was foolish for her to need more in order to settle the unease she'd been feeling for a while now. Words were just words. She'd never hungered for them in the past, so what was the difference tonight?

This time, foolish girl, his silence doesn't make you question his honesty and commitment, an inner voice jeered.

It makes you question your own.

IT WAS THREE DAYS later before Macy, curled up on the sofa waiting for Lauren to finish her shower, had access to quality girl talk.

Lauren hadn't been home since leaving the loft with Anton after Saturday's game night. She kept enough of her things at his place to stay for weeks at a time if she wanted. Her rule of thumb was never to stay more than two or three days.

Years of roommate experience, not to mention the

faux roommate contract she'd been forced by Macy to cross her heart, hope to die and sign, had persuaded Lauren that prolonged peace, quiet and solitude would send Macy over the edge.

Macy knew this, and when she counted her blessings, Lauren's name topped the list. Not many people, not even everyone Macy considered a friend, would have the patience with her quirkiness that Lauren never failed to show.

Macy had to be the only living person she herself knew who considered private time the equivalent of solitary confinement. She hated being alone. Hated the sound of silence. Hated the depressing sense of isolation, the unnatural withdrawal from the outside world.

Okay, she'd heard enough psychobabble to know her reaction was textbook classic. That of a party girl, searching "out there" instead of "within" for peace. The quintessential live-for-the-moment extrovert. But one who well understood an introvert's moments of loneliness and despair, the unparalleled depression, the accompanying tears.

Which is why she no longer cried.

Well, there was the occasional bout of PMS. And her sappy addiction to romantic videos that coincided with the blues brought on by those days. She'd sobbed her heart out when Hugh Grant came back for Emma Thompson at the end of *Sense And Sensibility*. When Kevin Costner's Robin Hood told Maid Marian, "I would die for you."

And how could she forget Niles finally telling Daphne he loved her? If not for Lauren, Macy would never have gotten so wrapped up in watching *Frasier*. The sitcom's nightly reruns had become a Hollister and Webb evening tradition—one Macy had gotten too used to.

The way things were going between Lauren and Anton, Macy knew her best friend's loft-living roommate days were numbered. Macy couldn't panic. Wouldn't panic. Not just yet. Not until the very last minute…when she'd probably do something stupid like take in boarders.

But now that it was Tuesday evening and Lauren had managed to find her way home, catch up on her laundry and fix herself a bean sprout to eat, Macy was ready to get back to their normal routine…starting immediately, with the two weeknight back-to-back reruns of *Frasier*.

Right on cue, Lauren breezed in smelling of citrus shampoo, plopped down on the sofa and scrubbed her wet hair with a towel. She tucked her feet between her cushion and the one on which Macy sat, then frowned at the television. "I've seen this one."

Casting a sideways glance at her roommate, Macy scooted onto the next cushion and off of Lauren's feet. "What are you talking about? You've seen all of them."

"I know. They quit being as funny when you already know every punch line."

"You always laugh at every punch line no matter how many times you've seen the episode." Macy gentled the tone of her reminder. Lauren often returned moody from Anton's, wanting to stay, knowing she had to go. "Do you want me to turn it off?"

Twisting her hair into a topknot and her mouth into a foul-looking grimace, Lauren shook her head and reached for the bag of pretzel sticks she'd set on the floor with a can of diet soda. "I need the noise. Keeps me from having to think."

Having to think? Interesting development from the woman who prided herself on always thinking of everything. "If you've seen this episode, then I have a feeling you'll be thinking instead of watching, whether the television is on or not.''

Lauren didn't reply, just shoved a dozen or so sticks into her mouth and smiled with pretzel teeth.

Undeterred by her roommate's antics, Macy said, ''That teeth thing works better with an orange wedge, you know.''

Lauren chewed, then swallowed. ''Fine. Slice me an orange. And while you're at it, bring me a banana, an apple and a vat of dipping chocolate.''

Macy muted the television, leaving Niles with his mouth wide-open. ''Quit obsessing and speak to me.''

''Can't talk,'' Lauren mumbled. ''Food in mouth.''

''That didn't stop you fifteen seconds ago.'' Macy leaned forward to grab her roommate's can of diet soda from the floor, handed it over and waited until Lauren had washed the pretzels away before asking, ''Now, what's going on?''

Lauren sank deeper into the sofa cushions and curled up into a long-legged ball of cropped khakis. ''I don't like your stupid scavenger hunt.''

Yes and hallelujah! sang the devil on Macy's shoulder. ''Why not? I figured you and Anton spent the last few days packing for the trip.''

''What trip?''

As if Lauren's sarcasm could throw Macy's bloodhound nose off track. ''Hello? Sydney's trip? The scavenger hunt prize?''

''Why would you think we'd be packing for that?''

''The game should be a piece of cake for you two.''

''Yeah. You'd think so,'' Lauren said, punctuating her comment with a snort.

Oh, but it was hard to keep a straight face, a level tone, the appearance of being an innocent bystander.

"You mean you and Anton don't know everything about each other?"

"No we do not." Lauren slid a narrow-eyed, sideways glance at Macy. "And I have a feeling you knew that."

"What're you talking about?"

"Don't give me that crap, Macy Webb." Lauren demanded Macy's undivided attention. "I dare you to deny that this scavenger hunt wasn't some grand master plan to set me up."

Uh-oh. Not quite the reaction Macy had anticipated. "Set you up how?"

"The list. You knew I wouldn't know all those things about Anton."

"Now you're being paranoid. I mean, yeah. I made up the lists. But it's not like I had any control over who would know what about their teammate. Or if the lists would cause problems for anyone," she added, though she probably shouldn't have gone quite that far. Too much curiosity was rumored to be deadly.

Lauren crossed defensive arms over her retro peasant blouse of embroidered white cotton. The long red draw cords hung over her wrists. "Uh-huh. Right. Sure you didn't."

"You don't believe me?"

"What I believe is that you couldn't wait, that you *can't* wait—" Lauren pointed an accusing finger "—to find out how much trouble you've caused for me with Anton."

"That's a load of crap." Macy hooked her finger around Lauren's and twisted until she cried uncle. "The scavenger hunt is work. It's for my gIRL gAMES column. It's not about you and Anton. Or Eric and Chloe. Or Sydney and Ray. You know that."

Sitting back to sulk, Lauren rubbed at her reddened

skin. "Yes. I know that. I'm just trying to avoid facing up to the fact that I didn't make much of a dent in my list."

"Duh. You've only had the list for, what? Three days? I never intended it to be *that* easy. And you're way ahead of me. I haven't had a chance to learn a thing about Leo." Except that he had the love 'em and leave 'em game down pat...not that Macy planned to share those particularly humiliating details.

"If you can't think of it as fun, then think of it as a job. My job. Which effects your job. Do I need to do the gIRL-gEAR song and dance here?" Macy threatened to get up and shake her booty.

Yanking her back to the sofa by one of the dozen zippers on her cargo pants, Lauren trumped Macy's trump card. "This scavenger hunt goes above and beyond my gIRL-gEAR duty."

Lauren left her no choice. Macy pulled out the big guns. "What about your best friend duty?"

"I don't remember anything in the rule book about you being allowed to turn my life upside down." Lauren reached for the pretzels again.

"It's not upside down." At Lauren's look of incredulity, Macy extended a trembling hand. "Okay. Maybe a little shaky."

"A little?" Lauren shrieked, tossing pretzel sticks at Macy's head. "The only thing I knew for sure was Anton's type of underwear."

Funny, but Macy hadn't wondered until now what Leo wore beneath his corporate uniform of crisp whites and pressed grays. "Well? What does he wear?"

"Ha! Like I'd tell you after the hell you put me through."

And she'd only just begun. Macy started picking bits

and pieces of pretzel from both the cushions and her lap, and building a small log cabin on the back of the sofa. "It wasn't really as bad as all that, was it?"

She was met with another telling sideways glance. Another volley of pretzels.

"Okay. I believe you. It was really that bad." Now, of course, she was dying to know the details.

"Yes it was." Lauren chewed and thought. "Are you sure you don't remember what was on the list you gave me?"

"There were ten lists. No, twelve, since Kinsey and Doug didn't show." Lying by evasion. How harmful could it be? "I don't remember all the items on every single one."

And that remark was the absolute truth. Of course, Macy might remember more of the grueling torture she'd assigned her best friend if she wasn't having so much trouble dealing with her own list.

She shook off thoughts of Leo Redding. "So, give me an example."

"Okay." Lauren turned her body and her attention toward Macy. "What characteristic found in a woman, whether physical, emotional or intellectual, plays the biggest part in his decision to commit to a long-term relationship?"

"Hmm. Wow. That is a toughie. I'd forgotten about that one." And bears didn't poop in the woods. "Do you know the answer?"

"No."

"Did you at least guess?"

"It didn't do any good."

"Why not?"

"Because Anton doesn't know the answer."

"Whoa! What? You're kidding." Macy'd wanted

Lauren and Anton to connect on a deeper spiritual level. But to score a touchdown at kickoff? "You're kidding, right?"

"Nope."

"You mean, he couldn't decide on one? Or he'd never analyzed your charms individually?"

"He just doesn't know." When Macy remained silent, Lauren emphasized, "As in, he doesn't know. Because he's never consciously decided to pursue a long-term relationship."

"Until now."

"No. Ever."

Macy wasn't sure exactly what to say. She'd expected her questions to cause both Lauren and Anton to think about their relationship. But she hadn't entertained the idea that what the two had together wasn't a relationship at all.

That had to be Anton's male denial. Because Macy knew exactly how Lauren felt about her man.

Didn't she? "So, what are you going to do?"

This time Lauren picked up the remote control and flipped off the television. She scooted forward on the sofa, sitting cross-legged, her knees only inches from Macy's feet. "I wanted to talk to you about that."

Macy felt the first stirrings of uneasiness as Lauren nervously studied her nails.

"I don't know Anton as well as I should, after being with him for a year. We never have any quality time, what with both of us working like we do."

"That's not so unusual. It happens that way for a lot of couples." Enough attacking for one night. "But you're right. It's tough when you can't find the time."

"It is. I mean, how are we supposed to make a go of

this if we can't even get to know each other? I mean, really know each other, the way a couple should.''

"Maybe this scavenger hunt will be a good thing for the two of you.'' And hadn't that been Macy's plan all along? "You can dig a little deeper and win a fab vacation in the process.''

"Well, that's only going to happen if we have the time to work on the hunt. Which is why I've decided—'' Lauren took a deep breath "—I'm going to move in with Anton.''

"What?'' Really, Macy *had* been meaning to get her hearing checked. There was no way Lauren would leave her living all alone. "I don't think I heard you right.''

Lauren nodded. "You heard me right. Anton asked me a few months ago to move in with him. I put him off then. I wasn't sure I was ready. That *we* were ready.''

"And now, because of the scavenger hunt, you've changed your mind.'' What was the saying? *Be careful what you wish for.* Oh, this was not at all what Macy had wished for. "Whose idea was it this time? For y'all to move in together?''

"It was mutual.'' When Macy responded with a skeptical look, Lauren added, "Okay. I broached the subject. But Anton agreed. We have to do something. Otherwise how can I trust what we have to be real?''

"But doesn't moving in together seem to be drastic? What if you're there a week and decide you want out?'' And who was Macy going to get to take Lauren's place?

Oh, good panicked grief.

Lauren bolted to her feet and paced the length of the sofa. "Oh, thanks for having so much faith in our relationship.''

"It's not that—''

"Maybe not. But try to give me a little credit. If anything feels wrong, I'll move back out. Even if I have to find a new roommate.''

A new roommate. Where was Macy going to find a new roommate? ''I don't think I'll replace you in a week.''

''I know you better than anyone, Macy. And I'll bet my entire share of gIRL-gEAR stock that in the last thirty seconds you've already made a list of potential replacements.''

''It's a blank list, if that makes you feel any better,'' Macy admitted, anxiety testing the limits of her antiperspirant.

''Yes. It does. I like knowing I'm irreplaceable.'' Lauren tugged Macy's legs down flat and sat in her lap, wrapping an arm around her shoulder.

Macy leaned her head into the crook of Lauren's neck and sighed. ''Don't ever let Anton forget it.''

''Are you kidding? He's a guy. I'll be reminding him constantly.''

''Good.'' Macy whispered the word, closed her tear-filled eyes and swallowed. Oh, she was going to miss her best friend.

''I know a lot of this for him is physical. Who am I kidding?'' Lauren chuckled. ''I lot of this for *me* is physical.''

''You are such a slut.''

''And damn proud of it.''

''As well you should be.''

''Do you really think so?'' The wistful question begged for reassurance, not psychoanalysis.

''Of course I do.'' Macy sat up and looked Lauren squarely in the face. ''It's not like men should have a monopoly on enjoying sex.''

''I know. But I wonder sometimes if that's all our

relationship is about.'' Lauren sighed. ''I mean, I know it's not, but it seems like we're always in bed when we finally find time to be together.''

''Well, this way, you'll have time for other things, too. Now—'' Macy patted Lauren's knee, needing freedom, needing air, needing to get to the toilet before she puked on the floor ''—get your booty out of my lap before you break my legs.''

Since you've already broken my heart.

6

WELL, SO FAR THIS scavenger hunt idea of hers sucked.

It was Monday, and since springing the game on her crew a week ago Saturday night, Macy had lost her roommate, spent the last two days alone in a loft that now resembled a crypt, and been felt up by a man she hadn't seen since.

And she'd had the nerve to call Lauren a slut.

Living alone was obviously getting to her, not to mention this was no way to win her own scavenger hunt, being totally out of touch with her partner.

Today was the first time she'd grocery shopped for one. A half gallon of milk. Whole milk. No more watered-down skim for this girl. Sour cream. Real butter. Cream cheese. Oreos.

Without Lauren along to reshelve half the things Macy picked out, she was going to reach the checkout counter with a heart attack in a shopping cart. She might fuss at Lauren for her birdlike diet, but at least when Lauren was around Macy ate a healthy balance of nutritious foods.

With Lauren around Macy also managed to work instead of staring out the loft's sliding glass doors while sitting at her desk. She hadn't even written up half the notes she needed for tomorrow's departmental meeting.

Which went to prove that she was going to have to do something about this roommate dilemma. When she couldn't string together one coherent sentence on a subject she'd worked out in advance, well, something was going to have to give.

The fact that she thrived on chaos was not exactly a secret or a surprise. Growing up the youngest of six meant she'd never had the luxury of quiet time. She'd been the runt of an oversize litter, scrabbling for what attention she could get in a family where attention was inevitably spread thin.

Not everyone would've enjoyed the noise or learned through the years to work in the uproar as Macy had, but pandemonium had always been so much a part of her life that both madness and mayhem were as comfortable as a pair of worn sneakers.

She pushed her cart, crackling with bags of blue corn chips and organic potato chips and curly cheesy puffs, out of the snack food aisle and into the produce section, where the choices of fresh food seemed to stretch for red-and-green acres.

She gave a pathetic little sniff. Lauren loved this market more than any other for this very reason.

Okay. Macy could deal with this. Buying green beans for one was not the end of the world. Choosing three apples, two bananas instead of a half dozen of each meant less to carry home, less to go bad, and guaranteed Macy the pick of the crop.

Iceberg lettuce, none of Lauren's fancy, frilly red and yellow types. A bag of mini carrots, one small Roma tomato and that would do it. Simple salad makings instead of the gourmet fare Lauren always chose.

Buying all this roughage on her own... Lauren would be so proud, Macy wistfully mused, missing her best friend's critical eye as she tested the waxy skin and weight of the cucumbers.

"It's not really true. What they say."

Macy glanced up into the face of Leo Redding. She blinked, blinked again, but he didn't vanish into thin air like a good little figment of her imagination. "What's not true?"

Leo directed his gaze to the produce in her hand. "Size doesn't matter."

Bad enough that he'd caught her fondling cucumbers. Now he'd managed to make her blush. Searching for a comeback, she took her time, added the cuke to her cart, then poked an index finger at the honeydew melon in his carry-all. "I guess we both have our fantasies."

She glanced up to see how close to the mark her barb had landed. And then she wished she'd kept her eyes front and center and focused on the miles of fruits and veggies. How, in the span of a week and two days, had she managed to forget how devastatingly gorgeous he was?

His eyes were a soft lettuce-green, his dark beard just beginning to be visible along the solid line of his jaw. He stood a good head and a half taller than her, giving Macy the perfect perspective to visually measure the breadth of his chest and shoulders, both impressively masculine and tempting to her hands. Those hands remembered the resilient give of muscles. Remembered, too, the feel of that hint of whisker grazing her cheek, scraping her mouth, tickling the tips of her fingers.

She sighed. There really ought to be a law about who was allowed to shop in public, and given a moment, she'd think of one. Here she was, about to drool all over herself *and* all over the produce. Surely that violated all manner of health codes and store policy.

Of course, and thank goodness, Leo seemed totally unaware of her lust-ridden dementia. He'd reached into the breast pocket of his crisp white oxford shirt only to pull out, instead of his grocery list, the list from the scavenger hunt.

He actually had it folded in his pocket and was carrying it with him. He was mocking her. She couldn't believe he would keep the thing on his person for any other reason. Macy shook her head. "What are you doing with that?"

He adjusted his glasses, shook open the sheet, frowned and peered closely. "Checking to see if there's anything on here about favorite foods...or a food fetish."

She put her cart into motion, waiting to see if Leo followed. He did and she felt a little thrill. No, a chill. That was it. The refrigerated cases were around the corner.

"I can tell you right now any fetish I have is going to be of the chocolate-covered-cherry variety. Maybe even peanut butter. Or popcorn."

"Popcorn?" he asked from behind.

"Forget it. Hey. Wait a minute." She jerked her cart to a complete stop. Leo sidestepped and avoided the collision. Macy glared in his direction. "Are you stalking me?"

Leo blinked. "Stalking?"

"It's Monday afternoon." She glanced at her Winnie-the-Pooh watch. "Three-fifteen. Shouldn't you be at work doing something legal? Instead of engaging in whatever questionable activity brings you to this part of town?"

An aristocratic brow arched upward. "Grocery shopping? A questionable activity?"

"Exactly. Especially since you are doing so miles from your home turf."

"Sorry to burst the bubble of your conspiracy theory,

but this store isn't miles from my home turf. At least not any longer.''

Perfect. Just dandy. Of course he was living nearby. She gripped the cart's handlebar, twisting one hand forward, one hand back, nearly cracking the red plastic cover. ''You've already moved?''

''Yes and no. I bought one of the Neville and Storey condos downtown. Closing won't be for another week, so I'm camping out in an extended-stay suite. I didn't want to add another month to my lease when we're only talking a matter of days.''

She glanced over her shoulder before pushing the cart forward again, and mumbled to herself, ''Stalking. That's what it is.''

''What was that?''

''Nothing.'' Change the subject. Forget how close he was, er, he'd be once he moved. Forget that he was driving her crazy at the same time he was driving her…crazy. ''Can I ask you a question?''

Leo picked up a bunch of fresh spinach, a tub of butter lettuce. ''Shoot.''

''What *is* the most strategically bizarre place you've had sex?''

Leo chuckled. ''Since the last time I answered that question?''

''Oh, I give up.'' Macy started pushing her cart toward the front of the market. Leo, of course, still followed. He continued to follow, and even stopped when she stopped at the olive bar to load up at $6.99 a pound.

''You're actually going to pay that price?''

''Why not? I'm worth it.'' She went for the Greek style and the jalapeño stuffed. ''Besides, I'm drowning my tears in salt. Lauren had olive issues. She refused to allow them into the house. But I can eat anything I want to now that she's gone.''

"Gone? Where'd she go?''

"She moved in with Anton over the weekend.''

"You're kidding.''

"Nope.'' Macy popped an olive into her mouth.

"So.'' Leo ladled $6.99 a pound olives into a small plastic tub of his own. "You're living in that great big loft alone. And I'm living by myself in a glorified hotel.''

"Yes, I am. And don't think I don't know what you're thinking because I do. The answer is no.'' She popped another olive because, even though she'd made a weak effort to head him off at the pass, a sense of where he was about to take this conversation had her heart racing, her toes tingling, her dread of having the loft to herself ready to invite him to stay.

"Why not? It's the perfect solution.''

"Solution to what? I don't see any problem here needing solving.'' She circled her shopping cart around the olive bar, turning to the barrels of fresh-roasted Sumatra Mandheling coffee beans.

"Rent money? I could make up Lauren's half. Go a few dollars extra.''

Money she didn't need. Money she was fine with. It was the prospect of silence and solitude making her crazy. Crazy enough to realize that Leo Redding—why, of all people, Leo Redding?—had just provided a short-term answer to the question of what she was going to do about her living arrangements.

She shoveled a pound of the coffee beans into a paper bag. "Money's not a problem. But you know that. You know how much gIRL-gEAR is worth.''

Leo gave an acknowledging shrug and pointed her

toward the barrel of Hawaiian Kona. "That's still a lot of space for one person to manage."

"I'll manage," she answered, frowning when she realized she was actually scooping up the beans he wanted. Expensive tastes, this one had. But then she knew that about the man, didn't she?

"I'll bring my espresso machine."

"There's a Starbucks on the corner." She tossed the Kona into his basket, wheeled her cart around and made for the bakery before she actually handed him her extra house key.

This was absolutely insane. Leo Redding? Living in the loft? There was no way she could share her space with this man. He was the chalkboard beneath her fingernails, the hot leather car seat beneath her short shorts. So why was the prospect of having him under her roof, even temporarily, such an incredible turn-on? The idea should've turned her off completely.

Her nerves fired a round of thrilling jolts. She reached for a three-pack of apple-bran muffins, a loaf of oatmeal-cinnamon bread. She wondered if Leo liked oatmeal-cinnamon bread. She looked up to catch him watching her. "I suppose you have a bread machine, too."

"Too much trouble."

"And pulling your own espresso isn't?"

"Priorities," he said, and shrugged with one shoulder, his white shirt drawing tight over his muscles as he moved.

"Mine are in order, thank you." She pondered the garlic-topped onion rolls. Bad breath. The perfect repellant to ward off sexy, broad-shouldered men. She added a bag to her cart.

Leo reached for a bag of his own. "Your scavenger hunt isn't a priority?"

Screw the scavenger hunt. Who needed a cruise, anyway? If she needed anything it was a reversal of the lobotomy she'd undergone between the olive bar and the onion rolls, because she was actually close to saying yes.

She had to get out of this store before she lost any more of her mind. "I didn't think you wanted anything to do with the scavenger hunt."

"What I said was that it could wait."

He had said that. He'd also said he'd learned enough of the truth for one evening. A comment Macy still hadn't quite decided how to take. "And now? You're done waiting?"

"Timing seems right." Leo started toward the front of the store.

Macy hurriedly followed. "What timing? Right for what?"

"For playing with you again."

Oh, but her heart lurched at that. "Very funny."

"The scavenger hunt, Macy." He cast a glance back over his shoulder. "Isn't that what we've been talking about?"

"You hardly need to move in with me because of the scavenger hunt." She couldn't think of any reason for him to move in with her. Not a single one.

Rent money wasn't a legitimate issue. Leo wanting more space than the hotel allowed was bogus. He could deal with cramped quarters for an additional few days.

And she could not, would not have him moving in because she was desperate to avoid living alone. She didn't want it to be Leo Redding who kept her company, who made the noise she needed in order to think.

She didn't want Leo Redding for anything. She didn't want him moving in at all. She didn't want him, most of all, to know she'd become a consummate liar.

"I wouldn't be moving in because of the scavenger hunt," he said, and made his way to the end of the shortest checkout line.

Macy chose the line to the left. Not too close, not too far away. "Why then? I can't think of any logical reason."

He pulled off his glasses, tucked them in his pocket and looked at her then. He held her attention for the longest time, his steady gaze compelling, his entire presence commanding.

Macy couldn't do this. She couldn't do this! She couldn't give in, not after holding out this long. All she had to do now was pay for her groceries and get out of the store. Another five to seven minutes and her mind would once again be hers.

Who was she kidding?

Nine days ago she'd crawled up into this man's lap and demanded his smile. He'd given her that much, given her more, and in exchange had captured her interest. He'd kissed her full on the mouth, left behind his texture, his taste, the temptation of his wicked wit, making sure she would never forget him.

And then Leo ruined her plans for escape anyway by giving her a reason she couldn't refute.

Simply, he said, "Because you can't think of a reason to say no. And because I dare you to say yes."

Oh he did, did he? One eye narrowed, she asked, "When did you say the condo would be ready?"

"Two weeks. A month at the outside."

Two weeks she could handle. A month might be tougher. Maybe she could light a fire under Anton to get the condo finished ASAP. Or get Lauren to do the lighting, since she was responsible for leaving Macy in this roommate lurch.

On the other hand, she was stupid for even considering this madness. Especially when Leo didn't even have the humility to beg with a poor-pitiful-me puppy-dog look, but instead met her gaze directly with a triumphant expression.

She lifted her chin and met his challenge. "If we do this, don't even think I'm going to let my guard down for a minute. I will not pay for your groceries. I will not do your laundry, clean your toilet or wash the dishes you use. And you won't be gaining any scavenger hunt advantage because of our proximity."

"Face it, Macy. I'm going to win this scavenger hunt of yours whether we're living together or not." And then, as if he had every right, he left his line, moved into hers and added his entire collection of purchases, melons and all, to her cart.

"Correction." She would make this one thing perfectly clear because, the way her pulse was racing, her heart thudding a heavy beat from the hollow of her throat to her toes, she needed the reminder herself. "We'll be living under the same roof. That's not the same as living together."

He shrugged. "Semantics."

"As long as we're on the same page here, then—" she couldn't believe she was saying this, knowing full well he'd use those semantics to his advantage "—give me your money." She held out her hand. "I'll check out. You go pack up your stuff and meet me back at the loft."

LEO WASN'T SURE he'd ever hit such a stroke of good fortune in his life. Capitalizing on it had proved to be tougher than he ever would've thought—at least before last week. He was learning fast that every inch gained with Macy, whether measured in physical or mental terms, was hard won.

But oh, was every inch sweet!

Not many people went toe-to-toe with Leo Redding and enjoyed, as he did, the feints and jabs, the thrill of the fight, the battle to go one better than his opponent. Certainly no woman had ever sparred so adeptly, so directly, as Macy had.

He'd yet to work out how this thing with her was going to go down. He kept insisting the attraction was all about the game, about a woman who had a competitive streak and cutthroat spirit he'd never found in another player.

But the piercings, the tattoo, the unconventional hair style, the wardrobe right out of a high-school classroom...it was all a bit much to deal with. She was a strange composite: everything he wanted in a woman and everything he avoided at the same time.

He wondered what her issue was about growing up, how long she'd continue to flaunt convention with the unorthodox way she dealt with the world around her. He could see her a year or two from now, taking off on a quest to ''find'' herself. His Bohemian, avant-garde mother all over again.

So, what in the hell was the appeal? Was he seriously looking beyond the exterior trappings and her obvious Peter Pan syndrome? Looking deeper, and seeing his own ambitious nature in a package meant to complete?

How Jerry Maguire was that?

Leo chuckled to himself, swung his garment bag over his shoulder and reached into the back seat of his Lexus for the duffel and overnight case that contained most of the belongings he'd need until he could move the rest of his things from storage into his new place.

His new place. It had been quite awhile since he'd been this excited about a change. Not that he'd necessarily been suffocating. He just hadn't been in a mental place where he'd felt jazzed about much of anything.

Moving into the city was a personal victory of sorts. He'd established himself, had worked hard enough to afford the better things in life without a second thought as to how finances would effect his future. It was an incredibly intoxicating freedom, and he knew he'd made his father proud.

But his caseload of late was routine. The social functions he'd attended recently had failed to hold his attention. As had the women whose company he'd been keeping. A shake-up was definitely in order. And maybe Macy Webb was about to give him what he wanted.

The gate on the loft elevator closed and he began his ascent. For once, he wasn't going to analyze. This time with Macy was something of a vacation. He was going to enjoy her scavenger hunt the same way he would enjoy sailing the deep gulf waters this summer.

And then, when he was baking in the sun and the solitude, he'd give more thought as to why this woman appealed to him at such a visceral, soul-searching level. And what exactly he was going to do about it.

The elevator ground to a stop; the gate groaned and creaked open. Leo half expected to find Macy in a warrior woman stance, wearing golden Valkyrie armor with longbow and six-foot spear at the ready.

Instead, the loft was quiet, the track lighting brightening the hardwood floor immediately in front of the elevator, but casting the rest of the main room into shadows. He walked inside, dropped his three bags onto the yellow-and-red plaid armchair.

He knew from Anton's description of the loft's layout

that Lauren's rooms were to the right, behind the entertainment center. Macy's rooms were the other direction, isolated from the rest of the loft by the design of the kitchen. He heard a quick blast of water and the whir of the garbage disposal off to his left. He headed that way.

Macy was still dressed as she had been earlier, at the market. On her feet she wore black sneakers with the thickest wedge sole he'd ever seen on an athletic shoe. Obviously sports had nothing to do with the design.

She wore no socks, and her denim pants reached an inch or two below her knees. They were a bright red, and her top was a form-fitting cropped number in black cotton covered with red polka dots.

He took it back; she didn't dress like a teen, but more like a kindergartener. She would've looked like a kindergartener, too, except for the obvious fact that today she wore one of her push-up bras. Strangely, his heart and his mood both lightened. He'd bet on the plain white bra. It fit her ingenuous look.

She finished scooping the pulp from the honeydew she'd filched from his groceries, and took an attack cleaver to the watermelon half she'd bought. Leo enjoyed a private smile as another piece of the puzzle clicked into place. The wild child was nothing if not dramatic.

He stayed on the breakfast nook side of the open serving counter, away from the sink and the cutting board and the bits of flying fruit. "So, we both pay for our own groceries, but all food is fair game?"

She wielded the cleaver like a professional chef. "What's yours is mine and what's mine is also mine."

He felt the corner of his mouth crook upward. "I thought that was how this was going to work."

"I had faith that, being the smart lawyerly type, you'd figure it out."

"Do we need to talk about it?"

"About what?" She hacked the melon into pieces. "The fact that I've obviously lost my mind?"

She mumbled the question, so he wasn't sure if she really wanted an answer. That he was going to give her one wasn't even in question. "Sure. We can talk about your mental health. Or about how you want to handle expenses while I'm here."

"There won't be any expenses. I've changed my mind. You can't stay."

"Too late. Possession is nine-tenths of the law." When she looked at him askance, cleaver in hand, he added, "You've taken possession of my melon. I've taken possession of Lauren's bedroom. It's too late for either of us to back out."

"Humph. Melon possession. What kind of law is that?"

"Leo's law."

She stopped and considered his answer, then demanded, "What's the difference between a lawyer and a catfish?"

"One's a bottom dwelling scum sucker. The other's a fish."

Thwap! Bright red melon juice splattered the sink's splash guard. "I'll find one you haven't heard one of these days."

"I doubt it. I've been around awhile."

"You've been around? Or you get around?"

"Is there really much of a difference?"

"Depends on who's asking, I suppose."

"You're asking. What exactly do you want to know? I'll give you this one for the scavenger hunt."

She whacked the point of the cleaver into the plastic cutting board. "What do I want to know?" she finally asked, and he realized he'd been staring too long at the hand she'd had wrapped firmly around the cleaver's handle. He glanced up into her face and nodded.

"Family, genus, species and name of your first pet."

Back to the scavenger hunt. "Canine. Dog. Irish setter. Bandit."

"A boy's pet." Her surprise was evident.

And surprisingly annoying. "I was a boy."

"Are you sure? You look like you've been grown-up for a very long time."

Leo glanced down at his white oxford shirt, his navy slacks and his belt and shoes of faux black alligator. He shrugged. "I've looked like this for about ten years now."

"That's not what I mean. You look…you act like you were born wearing Hugo Boss instead of a birthday suit."

Now there was an image to make him smile. If he were given to smiling. Which he wasn't. Usually.

Uh-oh.

Sobering, he propped a hip against the counter while she carefully cubed the honeydew and scooped balls from the meat of the watermelon. Fruit salad for dinner, he presumed. No need to help, since she seemed to have it under control.

He settled more comfortably, the better to watch her brow furrow in concentration, her dainty white teeth worry that plump lower lip. She radiated energy and purpose, and a childlike deliberation he found enchanting.

He blinked. Uh-oh.

Leo Redding enchanted? If that wasn't clue number one that he was in some kind of trouble here, he didn't know if he'd recognize clue number two. But he did. The word *childlike* only compounded the mess.

Macy spooned the melon pieces into a big ceramic bowl, went to the fridge for red grapes and grapefruit. "How long did you have Bandit?"

Yep. Trouble. Nosey-woman trouble. "Not long enough."

She looked up over the top of the refrigerator door. "What happened to him?"

"Long story."

The door slammed. "You in a rush to get somewhere?"

Only out of this suddenly too intimate conversation, this too cozy domestic scene. He straightened and made a show of stretching. "I wouldn't mind a hot shower before dinner. Do I have time?"

A tiny fist went to her tiny hip. "Counselor, are you evading my question? May I remind you that you're under oath to tell the whole truth?"

Now she was using his profession to her advantage. *What next*, he thought, and reached across the counter, filched a chunk of melon and lobbed it into his mouth. "My mother took off to find herself when I was thirteen. Took Bandit along for the ride. He loved taking road trips, sitting in what he considered *his* seat, with the window wide-open."

Leo had loved road trips, too, but she'd chosen to invite his dog instead. Old news. Old pain. Long since dead, buried and forgotten.

Macy's gaze sharpened, a steel shovel of focus. Damned if it didn't seem to pierce straight through to the coffin lid. Those eyes...those intelligent, perceptive, Jack Daniel's gold eyes were dangerous.

She was a piece of work, this one. Complicated as

hell. Whatever time he spent here, two weeks, a month, was going to be wild.

"Leo?"

"Hmm?"

She plucked grapes from the bunch and dropped them into a colander for washing. "You need a dog. Once you get settled in your new place you definitely need a dog."

More of her pop psychology. "I don't have time for a dog."

"If you had a dog, you'd make the time." She finished with the grapes, reached for a plump ruby red. "You really do need to make the time."

That was certainly backing into a solution. "You don't say."

"I do say, even if no one else will. Learning how to relax is your biggest challenge. I don't think you're genetically uptight. You've just forgotten to nourish your inner boy child." She seemed awfully pleased with herself.

"Really."

"Absolutely. I knew there had to be a reason you're always such a stick-in-the-mud," she said, scoring the grapefruit rind and peeling back the skin in even quarters.

"I'm a stick-in-the-mud because my mother took my dog?"

Not because his mother had taken away anything resembling a childhood, leaving him to be raised by a father who never admitted to failure, never allowed his son to fail.

No. Macy had narrowed down his psyche to the loss of one dog. So much for dangerous.

She shrugged. "It's not all about losing Bandit. I

mean, you lost your mom! At thirteen, that's as good as saying goodbye to your childhood. And what about your father's reaction? I'd guess he expected you to be perfect, considering how much you hate to fail.''

Leo stared, then finally managed to answer, ''Thank you, Dr. Webb.''

Macy screwed up her face. ''I know. It's one of the hazards of the degree. And it's already cost me one roommate.''

''Lauren moved out because you told her she needed a dog?''

''Hmm.'' She sectioned the grapefruit, cut each wedge into four pieces. ''Maybe I should have tried a dog instead of the scavenger hunt.''

''You know, Macy,'' Leo began, circling the end of the counter into the kitchen proper. ''Your mind works in mysterious ways that I'm not even sure I want to understand.''

''You mean, you find me an, oh, I don't know.'' She faced him head-on. ''A challenge?''

He remembered the morning he'd thrown the insult into her face. He'd been wrong when he'd thought she wasn't an enigma. That still didn't make her his type, even if he could appreciate the puzzle of her mind.

He nodded a silent touché. ''Out of the ordinary, at least.''

''You won't admit to finding me a challenge. Only that I'm strange.'' She added the rest of the fruit to the bowl and washed her hands of the sticky juice and of the conversation. ''Much more of this sweet talk and you'll be wearing your melons.''

I'd rather be wearing yours. Leo blinked, surprised by the renegade thought. And then he smiled. Again. He couldn't help it, though he tried his damnedest before giving it up.

Wild wouldn't even begin to describe these next few weeks. He lightly cleared his throat. "So. Back to the house rules?"

She nodded. "If I make dinner for one, I'll make it for two. As long as you're home. If you're not, you're on your own. If I'm not in the mood to cook, you're on your own. Basically, when it comes to food—"

"I'm on my own. Got it. And consider the reverse to be true, as well. If I cook for myself, I'll cook for you."

"Okay." She held up one warning finger. "But don't touch my laundry."

"Don't do your laundry or don't touch your laundry?" he asked, this time going for the grapefruit, giving her a second to ponder his question as he chewed. "Because last time I was here you had different rules about touching your laundry. I just want to get things straight."

"Grr." She tossed the cleaver and the cutting board into the sink, grabbed a bag of potato chips and a package of Oreos and stomped from the room.

Grinning to himself, Leo served up a bowl of fruit salad, pulled a rib-eye from the freezer and set the microwave to thaw. He found fresh garlic and butter and an indoor grill.

Maybe intimate and domestic wasn't so terrible. Maybe he'd worried over nothing. So, she was perceptive. So, she was too damned attractive for his peace of mind.

So far Macy's house rules suited him just fine.

7

ANTON NEVILLE LEANED against the railing that ran along the second floor landing of the home he'd made in an abandoned warehouse. To the average observer, the place gave no hint to the aesthetics hidden in the framework, the oddly slanted roof sections, the placement of windows.

Anton's gift was being able to see with more than the naked eye. The way Beethoven looked at a piano's ivories, the way Michelangelo looked at a block of marble. This was how Anton's mind worked. He looked at buildings long since left to decline and visualized the possibilities.

Which was why, now, looking down at Lauren, who sat working at the computer station he'd added to their home office, a sense of dissatisfaction chewed at the contentment he'd lived with since she'd moved in.

She had amazing potential, a potential that guaranteed more career possibilities than he knew she'd imagined. gIRL-gEAR was a fantastic launch to her multimedia career, but she was still thinking inside a smaller graphic design box than her position gave her boundaries to explore.

Lauren insisted the artwork she created for the company's Web site fit the image Sydney and the others agreed best conveyed gIRL-gEAR's upbeat and energetic attitude.

But Anton couldn't help thinking that Lauren was stifling her creativity, stunting her artistic growth in a way she wouldn't be if she were to expand her graphic portfolio.

"Are you going to stand up there and stare at me for the rest of your life? Not that I'm complaining, mind you."

"I don't know. Sounded like a complaint to me." Anton made his way to the central staircase, descended leisurely. He kept his hand on the polished aluminum railing, his eyes on Lauren.

"Then I guess I need to make my meaning a bit clearer, don't I?" She swiveled in her chair and crooked a finger his direction.

Anton gave in to the smile that tugged at the edge of his mouth. Since the day he'd stepped from his car and found Lauren waiting to tour the loft in which she and Macy had lived, he'd fought what felt like an unhealthy obsession.

He had her under his roof now. The obsession should have eased. The fact that it hadn't said a lot about the way he'd let her get under his skin. He had plans for the long term and he wanted to include Lauren.

What he didn't want to do was forget about his future because he'd gone and fallen in love.

Once he reached her chair, he braced both hands on the padded arms, leaning down to nuzzle her hairline from temple to ear. Lauren moaned and Anton pulled back, but only far enough to snuggle his nose to hers. "Still complaining?"

She nodded, and this time he moved to look into her eyes. "What's wrong now?"

She slipped the noose of her arms around his neck. With her lips brushing his in light butterfly kisses, she whispered, "You're not naked and I'm wearing too many clothes."

"A single-minded wench, aren't you?"

"Now who's complaining?"

Giving in would be so easy. Too easy. He finished the kiss she'd begun, then ducked away from her hold. "That would be me. But only because I'm meeting Leo in twenty minutes. Not enough time for a wench of your nature."

"Oh, now suddenly you're the expert on my nature."

"I do know your nature, Lauren." His voice was soft and coaxing, convincing. This was one thing he didn't think she understood. "Better than I think you know yourself."

"I'm some sort of mindless bimbo. Is that it?" She'd tucked her heels up on her chair, pulled her knees to her chest. A childlike defense. Fetal. Protecting herself from his prying eyes. As if he needed to see her to know her.

He'd taken too long to answer, and she'd started to fidget, rolling her thumb over the trackball of her mouse, sending the cursor in a jerky flight across the screen. He knew her well enough to lay odds on her imminent flight.

Five, four, three, two, one. She was out of her chair.

"I can always move back in with Macy. I'm sure she's climbing the walls by now, being on her own."

"You think I wouldn't be climbing the walls if you left?" He'd taken hold of her shoulders to prevent further flight. Now he drew his palms in a caress down her arms to her wrists. "I want you here, Lauren. With me."

Her chin went up a notch. Her eyes glistened.

He refused to be swayed by her tears. "You're beautiful, creative, intelligent. But that's only the tip of the iceberg. I want to learn everything there is to learn about you. I want you to know me in the same way."

She looked away, found her composure, then met his waiting gaze. "Isn't that why I'm here? Because we wanted time together? Time we didn't have living apart?"

Anton closed his eyes briefly. He wanted to say things to Lauren he knew she wouldn't want to hear. It had always been his way to push. Both himself and those around him. His put-up-or-shut-up method produced results.

But this was Lauren, he reminded himself. And toned down the words he wanted to say. "I want you here. But you have to want to be here and to believe in us for this to work. You have to be as honest with yourself as you are with me."

"Why would you think I'm not honest with myself?"

"I don't know that you're not. I hope you are." He paused, took a breath. "What I don't want, Lauren, is for you to...settle. For me. For anything. Not if you can do better."

Lauren waited through several long seconds, then pulled free of his hold. She gave a disgusted shake of her head. "This is about gIRL-gEAR, isn't it? You still think I'm wasting my time there."

"I never said you were wasting your time. Or your talent," he added, before she cut him off.

"Maybe not in so many words." Lauren began to pace. Her sandals slapped lightly over the espresso-colored Italian marble of the room's flooring. "Why would I want to leave gIRL-gEAR?"

"I didn't say you should leave gIRL-gEAR."

"I love what I do. I'm good at what I do. I love the people I work with. It's a dream job. I'm making tons of money." She stopped, pressed fingertips to both temples. "I can't even believe this has come up. Again."

He leaned back against her desk and crossed his arms. "I don't want you to leave gIRL-gEAR. I only want you to recognize that you can do anything you want."

"I *am* doing what I want. I know you're not crazy about me working in an industry dependent on fads and styles. But you know what? You're doing the exact same thing. Turning your talents to supply the demand for the—" she rolled her eyes, made air quotations with her fingers "—oh-so-fashionable lofts and warehouses. So don't give me crap about not knowing myself."

She returned to her desk then, closed out the file she'd been working on.

"Macy's new logo?" he asked after the screen went blank.

"Yes, as a matter of fact. And I'm very happy with the design, thank you."

Anton had to admit it was time to back off. All he wanted was for Lauren to live up to her potential. But he'd yet to figure out how to make his point without ruffling her feathers. Her defensiveness had a source he still hadn't discovered.

And that was why she was here, wasn't it?

"Look," she said, finally. "If we're going to do this housewarming, I've got to get busy. And I could use some help."

"I'm all yours," he said. His truest statement of the day.

"I HAVE AN IDEA." Cradling her first coffee of the morning, Macy barely gave Leo time to set foot in the kitchen before she pounced. "Coffee's hot. Get a cup and I'll tell you all about it."

He lifted one brow in answer. A small fan of laugh lines spread toward his temple, but nothing resembling a wrinkle or a droopy, under-eye bag marred a face well-suited for an eight-by-ten glossy. The man could at least have the decency to look half-asleep first thing in the morning. But no. He'd been here three days now and he still had no decency whatsoever, looking as if he'd stepped from the pages of a sleepwear fashion shoot.

He wore black, pin-striped pajama bottoms and a matching calf-length robe. The bottoms served to emphasize the length of his legs, the robe the breadth of his shoulders. His only faux pas was the pajama top he'd skipped, wearing, instead, a form-fitting white T-shirt. Macy approved of the gaffe.

Each of his movements—reaching up into the cupboard for a coffee mug, lifting the brimming carafe to pour, bringing the white stoneware to his mouth to blow across the steaming surface and sip—teased her with glimpses of his lean waist, his muscled chest, the bulge of a shoulder rising just above his collarbone.

Discreet glimpses, of course. Modest glimpses. Totally innocent, acceptable glimpses. No bare skin or—

"Macy?"

"Hmm?"

"You have an idea?"

"Idea? Oh, yeah." She shook off her lust and set her mug on the countertop, scouring the pantry shelves for the box of Cocoa Krispies she'd hidden from Lauren. "Let's play a game."

He lifted his stoneware mug. "It's seven o'clock in the morning, I haven't even finished my first cup of coffee and you want to play a game. Not to mention that I need a shower. Or that I haven't had breakfast."

She wiggled both brows, shaking the box of Cocoa Krispies.

Rolling his eyes, Leo started to leave the kitchen. "I have to be in court at ten. Chocolate isn't going to cut it."

Macy reached out and, grabbing the belt of his robe, gave a quick yank. "I'll make you a deal. An omelette. Cheese. Ham. All the protein your brain can handle."

He slowed, since she wasn't giving him a choice, and, sipping from his mug, considered her offer. "What's the game?"

Macy grinned. Men were so easy. "Twenty questions. Sort of."

Leo breathed deeply. "Your *sort of's* worry me."

"C'mon," she pleaded, telling herself she really wanted that sailing vacation. "For the scavenger hunt. How hard can it be?"

"Can't." He drained his coffee and made to leave the kitchen. "I've got to get in the shower or I'll be late."

He hardly needed three hours to get to court. She knew that. After the past few days of his off-and-on company, she'd learned things about him she never thought she'd know.

He wasn't as uptight as she'd accused him of being. He had a sense of humor, a real sense of humor, not just the sarcastic wit he wielded so well. No doubt he hid other redeeming qualities. The one thing he didn't hide was his impatience with her playful nature, or with her tendency to open mouth, insert foot.

She winced and tried again. "C'mon, Leo. How long can it take?"

"Considering the way your tricky little mind works? Fifteen minutes, give or take a week." He set his empty mug on the counter and headed for the back of the loft.

Grr. She took it back. Men weren't so easy, after all.
"Hey. What do you mean, my tricky little mind?"

She followed, enjoying the light slap of his bare feet
on the hardwood floor. Hmm. What was Mr. Designer
Pajamas doing with bare feet, anyway? What happened
to his coordinating designer house shoes? "Leo. Answer
me."

"I'm taking a shower, Macy."

She stopped when he stopped in the hallway, waiting
while he grabbed a towel and a washcloth from the loft's
single linen closet. "I can't believe you're saying no to
an omelette."

"I'm not saying no to an omelette." He closed the
closet door and looked down into her face. "I'm saying
no to a game of twenty questions that will end up being
twenty-two thousand after you get through."

"Ha."

He continued toward the bath and she continued to
stalk, er, to follow. He turned into Lauren's rooms,
looked over his shoulder only when he reached the bathroom door. "Macy. I'm going to take a shower."

She crossed her arms and stood her ground. "No one
here is stopping you."

He took her up on the dare with only one arch look
before he walked into the room tiled in red and black.
Macy didn't let him get too far ahead. It was her gauntlet
he was walking away with, after all.

She moved into the doorway and swore she caught a
hint of a smile on the mouth of the beast. That did it.
He couldn't pay her to leave. She'd stand here until night
fell if she had to. She would not be the first to back
down.

Apparently Leo was of the same mind-set. He'd
draped his towel on the rack, his washcloth on the

shower head. His glasses he set on the shelf above the pedestal sink. And then he turned and shrugged off his robe.

His eyes never left Macy's as he reached behind the door for the clothes hook, and she wasn't about to be the first to look away. His T-shirt came first, off and over his head. The devil on her shoulder went pitchfork crazy, but Macy refused to move her gaze from Leo's face.

Temptation had never been so hard to resist. With her eyes only marginally popping out of her head, she took total advantage of her peripheral vision and sucked in the picture of Leo's hard body.

His pecs were well defined, his abs sported a six-pack. The body of a man who worked out for stress relief instead of competition. His chest was free of all but a feathering of dark hair, soft hair, hair she wanted to feel against her bare skin.

She wanted to melt into a girl puddle at his feet, but managed to do nothing more than wet her lips, clear her throat and say, "I could easily stand out here and ask my questions while you shower."

"You could just as easily fix that omelette instead." He hooked both thumbs in the elastic waistband of his pajamas.

"No questions, no omelette."

"No omelette, no pajamas."

He wouldn't. No way. She snorted her disbelief. "Oh, this I gotta see."

"If you insist." And he showed her. Though she didn't see a thing because at the first sign of male belly and the stripe of hair spreading out over Leo's lower abs and lower other things, Macy shut her eyes tight.

She ignored both his laugh and the prurient urge to

peek, listening for the snap of the shower stall's door latch catching, finally. Listening, too, for the first blast of water from the shower head.

When the spray at last hit the tiled stall wall and the drain took its first gurgling drink, she peeled open one eyelid, still expecting to come face to crotch—er, face to face—with a naked Leo Redding. But she found herself alone.

Disappointed, Macy debated her next move. Whipping up an omelette bribe? Standing her ground and demanding answers? Taking off her clothes and sliding her bare soapy skin over Leo's, getting a closer look at that spread of belly hair, an eye-level look at the wash of soap and water slicking that hair to his skin, an up-close-and-personal look at everything bold and male between his legs?

She took a deep breath to dispel the image of the last option, which held so much appeal. What was it about a wet naked man? A wet, soapy naked man? So much clean skin in which to bury her nose and breathe, in which to dart the tip of her tongue and taste.

Inhaling the steamy, soapy-skin-scented air was no less arousing, she decided as, eyes closed, she inhaled all she could of Leo.

"Macy? Are you cooking yet?"

If he only knew, she mused, surfacing from her wet dream to find her fingers fiddling with the tiny white buttons running from V-neck to waist on her pajama top of hot-pink flannel covered with hot-orange flames.

"I was thinking of bringing a couple of eggs in here and poaching them in this steam." She waved her hand in front of her face to clear the air that was fogging her view of the shower stall's door.

Leo blew out a gusty huff. "If that's your idea of

cooking, I think I'll take my chances with the courthouse cafeteria."

Macy frowned. "I know perfectly well how to cook."

"I haven't seen much evidence so far."

"You've had my fajitas. My fruit salad."

"Fast food."

"Fast food? I don't think so. And what's wrong with fast food, anyway?"

"Nothing." He paused, moving beneath the water, shooting droplets over the top of the door that hit Macy in the face. "If you're into instant gratification."

She lifted her face for more. "And you're not?"

The shower stall opened a crack; Leo's dark wet head appeared in the opening. His grin was white and wicked and extra appealing for its rarity. His eyes flashed beneath spiky clumps of wet lashes.

"If you tell me you are, I'm going to be more than a little disappointed in you, Macy Webb," he said, then disappeared behind the closed door.

Well, she couldn't have that, now, could she? "I suppose you're right. But you can't tell me that a quick... bite now and then doesn't have its advantages."

All movement in the shower stilled, as if Leo's mind was traveling the path of Macy's last remark. Following her mental meanderings into a territory made more dangerous by the fact that he was wearing no clothes and she could be out of hers at the snap of his fingers.

She ran the palm of her hand over the mirror to check her reflection, just in case he started snapping. "I mean, sure. It's nice to linger over a meal. But, really. Who has the time?"

"You don't think it's worth it to make the time?"

"I suppose I'm more the spontaneous type." Putting her body in motion always helped her think, so she paced the small room. "I don't tend to plan many of my...meals in advance."

"And here I thought you were a connoisseur of fun."

She stopped and frowned. "Obviously we disagree on what makes a good time. My appetite is hardly being short-changed just because I carpe diem."

"Does your mouth water?"

Macy's heart skipped a beat. "Excuse me?"

"In anticipation. While looking forward. At the prospect of what's to come."

"Sure. Why not? The same way it waters when I'm not even aware of being hungry until I come across what I want."

It took him a minute to respond, and his voice verged on husky when he asked, "How do you feel about appetizers?"

Foreplay? Was that what he'd said? "Uh, appetizers?"

He opened the door, poked his sopping head out and repeated, "Appetizers."

And then he was gone, leaving her scrambling for an answer and reaching for his towel to dry her arms. "I wish you'd quit doing that. You're making everything out here wet."

Again Leo's movements stilled. Macy replaced the towel and moved closer, into the direct path of Leo's steam. She leaned one shoulder against the warm black-and-red tile that abutted the shower stall's door.

"This is a bathroom," Leo said. "The word itself implying water and the probability things will be getting wet."

"Sure. In the bath. Or, in this case, the shower. Where the water belongs."

"Then maybe we should be having this conversation in here."

Macy's heart kicked a hard beat against the knot of breath caught in her throat. The stall door's silver handle drew her gaze. Her fingers flexed; her nails scraped her palms.

Was he serious? Or only tossing out the challenge as a tease? Did he expect her to make the first move? To pull open the door and boldly step inside?

"Macy?"

His voice had dropped to a level made even more suggestive by the fact that it was her name he had spoken while he was naked and they shared the same steam.

"What's the matter? Afraid of how wet you might get in here?"

She closed her eyes at his dare, took a deep breath and promised a quick murder-suicide if she screwed this up. Her hand was halfway to the stall's metal handle when the magnetic latch clicked and the door eased open.

It was then she got her first unintentional look at Leo's body. A quick flash of skin and dark body hair only, before she jerked her gaze away and to his face.

The devil's face. The face of an arrogant beast, wearing a grin that wasn't a smile but an expression of ego and conceit. The brief look she'd caught was enough to confirm he had good reason.

Besides, at the moment, she was willing to forgive him just about anything. Water streamed down his face, dripping from spiky lashes, matting his hair to his head with a boyish charm.

The complete picture destroyed her resolve and she stepped into the shower, pajamas and all. He went straight for her buttons, the pressure of his knuckles pin-

ning her to the warm tile as he opened her top, top to
bottom.

He took hold of the lapels and parted the edges, baring
her skin as he lowered his head. His mouth covered hers.
His chest pressed against the skin he'd bared and he was
wet and he was warm and he was delicious, rubbing, as
he was, dragging the edges of her parted top over her
nipples.

The friction of the thin layer of flannel, now wet and
no barrier between his eyes and her skin, between his
skin and her skin, between his wide concave palms and
her skin, or his tongue, which had moved from her
mouth to flick at the tips of her breasts, his lips, which
drew both nipple and pajama top into his mouth, where
the material scratched and his tongue soothed...

Oh, good orgasmic grief. She couldn't even finish her
original thought.

But she didn't care. Splayed the way she was against
the wall, her head thrown back, her hands flat on the
tiles beside her hips, her legs barely managing to keep
her upright, because now Leo had lowered himself to his
knees and had raised the hem of her top, giving himself
permission to drink the water from the skin of her belly.

His hands nearly circled her rib cage completely and
his tongue pressed to her navel, then lower, as his palms
slid down her sides. His fingers curled around the elastic
waistband of her pajama bottoms and slid them down.
She wasn't sure if she'd had on panties, but now she
was bare to her knees. And her brain still refused to
work.

And really, she should have cared, but she couldn't,
not when Leo's fingers had moved between her legs and
spread open her sex so he could find her clit with his
tongue. Which he did. Oh, he did.

She moaned, her hands holding his head, because she was afraid she would fall, the way she was standing, moving up on her toes, and down, opening her knees when Leo slid the length of a finger through her folds and found the entrance he'd been seeking.

His finger was thick, the second was thicker, his tongue was a butterfly flitting, tickling, tiny soft touches that weren't enough. She reached down with two fingers, pulled back her own skin to expose the tight center of nerves in ardent need of a harder, faster pressing stroke to match the motion of his fingers as he turned her inside out.

"Oh, Leo," she moaned. "You're making me come." And she did, in sharp spasms that tightened her around his fingers. He stayed where he was until she finished, and even then she had to hook her fingers over his shoulder and pull him to his feet.

He kissed her immediately and she tasted herself, tasted the water, tasted him. She placed her hands flat on his chest, slid her palms down his abdomen, reaching into the thatch of hair and below, taking the weight of his balls in one hand, the thick shaft of his penis in the other.

He was tall and she was short. But who cared about physics and logistics and geometry when he was full and throbbing and ready and she couldn't wait for that first filling thrust? She lifted a leg. He lifted his mouth.

"Macy, I need a condom."

She grimaced. "Where? I'll get it."

"No. I will. In my things."

"Wait." She stopped him from reaching for the stall door. "This is Lauren's bathroom. Look in the medicine cabinet."

He paused for only a second, and she could only

imagine him wondering if he'd find condoms in the bathroom off her rooms. But he didn't ask, so she didn't answer. She only waited, nerves raw and on end, as he stepped from the shower, leaving the water to beat her into a mindless mess.

He stepped back into the shower already sheathed. And he wasted no time, his hand sliding over her hips, his fingers digging into the backs of her thighs as he lifted her off her feet. He pinned her to the wall with the strength of one arm. His other hand made sure she was ready.

She wanted to laugh and tell him not to waste his time, but his fingers played her so nicely that she let him have his way. And then he buried his face in the crook of her neck, buried his cock in her warmth.

She pulled in a whimpering breath and groaned.

He shuddered to a stop. "Did I hurt you?"

"Not yet. I'll let you know when you get it right."

He shoved himself deeper. She gouged encouraging fingers into his taut backside and he moved just so, his hips rotating, grinding, using the motion to press the swollen base of his shaft high and hard to her center.

She gasped.

And he asked, "Am I hurting you yet?"

"Oh, yeah," she managed to answer, feeling the stretch of her body as she adjusted to accommodate the invasion of the beast.

Animal lust. That's all this was. A raw primal mating. Bodies doing what bodies for eons had done.

Steam swirled in wet ribbons. Water spilled in a fall of erogenous heat. Soapsuds slipped from Leo's neck and shoulders and seeped between the press of chest to chest.

Macy moved and rubbed, swept up in the sensation

of skin on skin, of skin in skin, of hands and fingers exploring, of mouths mimicking the fiery passion of spearing thrusts and reluctant retreat.

She couldn't get enough of Leo, couldn't feel parts she wanted to feel without releasing parts she wanted to hold for as long as he was willing. She wanted to feel Leo come. To take in his shudder and know his vulnerability.

But then he slowed his movements and stopped, hitching her legs higher around his waist and holding her impaled and suspended. His legs were shaking, his muscles beneath her drawn and taut.

She hated the thought of having to move. "If I'm too heavy, you can let me down."

"Such a generous offer."

She adjusted an arm, flexed a hip, caught him deep inside and groaned. "Don't worry. I'll make sure you...finish."

"Oh. I intend to finish." He rolled his hips one way, then the other. "But I should warn you."

"Warn me?" He moved again, both hands holding her backside as he slid nearly all the way out. She shuddered. "Warn me about what?"

He eased his way back in. "I never come first."

She rolled her eyes, in part because of his arrogant claim, primarily because of the pleasure rendering her incapable of conscious thought. Barely cognizant as he bit and nipped at her collarbone, she rushed to admit, "You won't be coming first this time, either."

His mouth found hers again. "I want you to come. Again. Trust me. I'll get mine."

Who was she to argue with his logic? She lost herself in the act, the mating of tongues and of intimate flesh.

Her breathing once again grew shallow; her blood rushed with the powerful beat of her heart.

Then she came, the release drawing forth a loud cry. Her neck arched, her head bumped the tiled wall. And what she felt next—the tension in Leo's body, the loss of the control he'd kept close and tight...the sensation blew her away.

He buried his face in her neck and let go.

Macy closed her eyes and held on for the ride.

WHAT IN THE WORLD had she just done?

Macy stood in the shower stall, empty now but for her soggy pajamas and her even soggier mind. After an awkward few minutes of sharing soap and shampoo while neither one spoke, Leo had left her to sort out her thoughts and her clothes.

But all she could think about was how she longed to feel him again deep inside her body.

She wanted to better experience the fit of their tangled limbs and the friction of skin on skin. What she didn't want was to open the door and find him gone, but she braced herself for the probability.

She cut off the water, pushed open the stall door and grabbed a towel for her hair. Bending at the waist, she twisted the towel into a turban and straightened, stepping out of the shower...

...and in range of Leo's reach. She was wet and naked and he hadn't even bothered with a towel while he'd been waiting, and modesty was obviously no issue because he was once more boldly erect.

Oh, but he was beautifully made. And she shivered, both from the chill and from the fever in his eyes. A fever of desire and expectation and the desperation to continue what they'd begun.

His impatience burned with a heat Macy knew well. He took her by the wrist, pulled her from the bathroom directly to bed. Nothing about his actions was hesitant. Neither did he ask. What he did was pull off the towel and replace it with his hands, holding her head for his mouth.

His kiss was the kiss of a starving man deprived. His tongue mated with hers, giving her the pleasure she wanted to take. With her hands caught between their bodies, she measured the beat of his heart with her palm. His breathing came hard and heavy, and warmed her skin, still cool from the shower and the water in her hair.

His mouth on hers, Leo reached for her hand and drew her fingers down his body to wrap around his erection. He kept his hand over hers, used the fluid he released to ease the stroke as he thrust in and out of her hold.

Macy wanted to lift her leg, make him ease the ache between her thighs. So she moved her hand, moved her mouth and shoved him down to the edge of the bed. All he did was raise a brow and sit right where she wanted him, his weight braced on his elbows as he spread his legs and leaned back.

She couldn't help but lick her lips. He was a delicious feast and hers to devour. She knelt between his legs, her chill forgotten once she encountered the intimate heat of his body. With her hands spreading his thighs wide-open, she moved in and nuzzled the sac beneath his full penis.

Leo shuddered. She lifted her eyes, locked her gaze with his and took him in her mouth. His nostrils flared. He pulsed against her tongue. Macy smiled, moving her lips in a stroke to imitate the earlier motion of her hand.

She watched his face, judged her success by the fire in his eyes, his grimace, the rapid rise and fall of his chest. With the palm of one hand pressed flat to his belly above his shaft, her thumb beneath the solid base, she wrapped her other hand around his length, leaving her lips free to work the swollen head.

She sucked hard, drawing her tongue up the underside and her upper lip over the top. She repeated the process, stroking, sucking, using the moisture of her mouth and his release of clear fluid, until Leo tossed his head back and roared.

He scooted back out of her reach. She followed him up onto the bed, crawling over his body, shuddering as his erection strained against her belly. She lifted her hips to take him. She was so very ready to take him.

But he hooked his leg over her hips and flipped her onto her back. He silenced her ''Oomph'' with another demanding kiss.

Macy tried to work her legs free, but he'd caught her fast. She shivered and submitted, unbearably aroused by her inability to move. Leo lifted his hips, but only enough to slip one hand down her belly and into the crevice at the apex of her thighs.

She whimpered at his touch, at the contact with her clit. But she was captured and couldn't move to show him how to use his thumb to pull back that hood of skin and how to take a fingertip and lightly brush the edges of that knot of nerves and how to open her wide with the rest of his hand.

And if he didn't stop what he was doing she was going to come all over the place when she wanted to come to the stroke of his tongue while his fingers played intimately with her sex.

She pulled her mouth from beneath his to tell him that it was her turn, that she was not going to take this bossy business lying down. Though she was, and she was loving it. But she didn't get out a word because Leo used the break from her mouth to order, "Turn over."

She had no spine, so she flipped as he'd ordered. And when he tucked a pillow beneath her belly, hiking her backside up into the air, she didn't even think to say no.

He knelt behind her, and Macy anchored her fingers over the side of the mattress, aroused and certain Leo had caught the scent. With her heartbeat rattling her whole chest, from her ribs to her throat, Macy waited.

Leo settled his weight, pressed his thighs to hers and leaned forward. She held her breath. He placed a hand in the small of her back...placed the dual vibrating heads of Lauren's back massager right below.

The sensation sent Macy's eyes rolling up into her head. She audibly groaned into the sheet as the rumble of the massager shook her bones. Oh, she couldn't believe this was happening. Sex had never been this way before.

Leo moved his hand to the base of her neck, her nape a starting point for his erotic massage. He drew the massager slowly down her spine. Macy melted into the mattress, her cheek, her shoulders, her breasts humming, her belly pressed into the pillow and humming, too.

But it was her backside, raised and waiting, that took the full brunt of the electrically charged shudder, Leo now sweeping the massage heads over her derriere and down one thigh, to the pit of her knee, the sole of her foot, her toes.

He reversed direction on the other leg, and once he reached the crease where thigh met buttock, he lowered the speed to a tempered buzz, settled the head on her bottom and left it there.

Macy tensed, waited, totally disconnected from everything but the heat of Leo's body behind her and the unbearable edge of excitement cutting off her ability to breathe.

Leo shifted, his erection probing between her legs, where a finger spread her wetness. She was beyond aroused. She ached, she burned, she hurt with the pleasure of his touch.

And then Leo inserted a finger and her world came to an end. It was too much to take, the vibrations skittering over her network of nerves and now the invasion, the finger he used to explore, pressing downward, pulling up and into her center.

She couldn't stand the wait, the anticipation, her body shifting and swelling and wanting. And then he moved his finger to her clit, moved the massager down so that his touch was an extension. And just when she wasn't sure she'd live to find her release, he slid his sheathed cock into her body.

The sound she unleashed was wild and untamed. Her body burned with Leo's every thrust. She felt the vibrations on her backside, in his finger and his cock. It was all too much and she let go, crying out as she came, shuddering over and over again until she knew nothing but the way he filled her.

Leo tossed the appliance aside, grabbed Macy by both hips and drove into her, his rhythm fast and furious, and then he peaked, shuddering, growling from a place so deep Macy felt the hum where he joined her body.

Once finished, he didn't move or withdraw, almost as if the connection they'd shared was far too painful to break. But that was her imagination talking. Or a case of wishful thinking.

This was all about sex. It had to be. There was no other sane way to look at what they'd done. They hadn't talked about a relationship. They hadn't even talked about attraction. They'd just screwed each other's brains out.

Physically, Macy was replete. But her soul remained disappointingly unfulfilled.

8

LEO WASN'T REALLY a party guy. He attended *functions*. Business dinners. Fund-raisers. Receptions. Soirees. Rarely did he make an appearance without an agenda. Never did he volunteer his involvement without the guarantee of a return.

And then came Macy's monthly game night. Which proved the folly of active participation. Look what that lapse had gotten him. Moving from a perfectly suitable extended-stay suite into the midst of madness.

He'd never been late to court in his life. But yesterday morning he'd barely managed to drop his butt in his seat before the bailiff called, "All rise."

He'd spent as much of the past two days at the office as he could find work to fill. With his current caseload, if he'd wanted, he could've spent the night. Sleeping on the sofa in his office wouldn't be anything new. And there was the law firm's efficiency apartment to consider.

But last night, he'd returned home, wanting simply to hear Macy breathe. He didn't want to talk. He didn't want to listen. He'd only briefly thought about wanting to get her naked. But then he'd seen her sleeping, and acting on the thought hadn't even been a consideration.

The door to her rooms had stood open. In the four days he'd lived there, he hadn't once ventured to her private corner of the loft. Personal space and privacy had been part of their agreement. She'd been the first to break the bargain when she'd interrupted his shower.

If he'd found her in bed wearing lace and black silk, sleeping on satin sheets, or if her blankets had been kicked to the bottom of the bed and she'd been lying there wearing nothing but her wild-child tattoo, he'd have been more inclined to strip out of his clothes.

As it was, he could only stand and stare.

The room was aglow in nightlights. One plugged into every outlet. Others burning low in the trio of lamps marking off three corners of her room. Each lamp spun on a solid base, its shade casting liquid shadows of sea life from the floor up the walls to the ceiling.

The ceiling was what struck the blow to knock him off balance. The blue-and-green-toned mural stretched corner to corner, with every undersea creature imaginable looking down on Macy as she slept. This was a child's room, not one where a man would make love to a woman.

Yet the woman curled in the center of the queen-size bed could flash him a look with her whiskey-wise eyes and he'd have a hard-on to hammer nails. Either she was a witch or he was sick. And since he didn't like either option, he'd turned and left the room.

He'd fared no better at his end of the loft. He'd been too wound up for sleep, and standing in the shower underneath the warm spray, all he could think about was taking her up against the wall.

He didn't know if he'd ever had sex explode the way it had with Macy. He'd had it in the heat and the spur of the moment, unexpected, hot and fast. But never had it been that blast of fire and passion.

Her body, when bared, had been as slim as he'd expected, but feminine and belonging to a woman, not a child. As much as he enjoyed indulging his fetish for the rich and the lush, Macy had offered him more. Her hunger and her honesty had no parallel in his experience. And that had the whole of his gut tied up in knots.

So now, twenty-four hours later, he found himself at Lauren and Anton's housewarming, no closer to figuring out where he and Macy stood or where they were going...if anywhere.

Standing at the second-floor railing in the home Anton had made of a warehouse, Leo looked down to where Macy huddled with Lauren in the main room's office corner to review her new logo concept and design.

She'd arrived only a few minutes ago, while he'd been upstairs on the second-floor tour. Lauren had pulled Macy aside immediately, giving Leo a few minutes to reconcile last night's girl in hot-pink pajamas with the woman showing off sexy shoulders in a top that was nothing but two handkerchiefs held up by a band of velvet encircling her neck.

The fabric was glistening and black, with a rose of muted reds and pinks centered over her chest. The skirt was red and knee-length, with a flippy sort of hem, and even her shoes matched: the barest of sandals with narrow straps of black and pink and red.

It was a damn sexy outfit.

And she was a damn sexy woman.

And he hoped like hell to get moved into his condo before she had him on her balcony howling at the moon.

HIP PERCHED ON THE CORNER of Lauren's desk, Macy studied her new logo. Both the black, lace-fringed web and the Gen-X girl spider Lauren had designed were to die for.

The spider's legs were overly long and jointed, and

all eight feet sported funky high-tops in a combination of gIRL-gEAR's lime-green-and-orange color scheme. A broad-brimmed painter's cap in hot pink and bright yellow sat at an angle behind eyes twice the size of the spider's head.

It was absolutely perfect. Macy laid her cheek on Lauren's shoulder. "Oh, Lauren. This is so incredibly cool."

"I'm not sure it's all that." Lauren clicked the computer file closed, shut down the graphics program and tucked loose strands of hair behind her ear instead of into the ponytail caught low on her nape. "But I'm glad you like it."

Uh-oh. This wasn't the Lauren Macy knew. Down in the dumps *and* wearing a plain Jane barrette that was *not* a gADGET gIRL accessory? Macy drew her best friend around the end of the desk and into the corner where French doors opened onto a courtyard.

She nudged the door part of the way closed, shutting out the chatter of the party that was, by now, well under way. "Are you okay? You're wearing an awfully big party-pooper face. And it's your party you're pooping on."

"I'm fine. Just tired." Lauren worked hard for the smile she finally produced, lifting her face to the cool night air. "Work was a bitch this week."

"Because of my logo?"

"No," she said, and shook her head. "A problem with copyrighted images being lifted from our Web site. Sydney took care of it."

"Then why do *you* look so stressed?" Macy's hands went to her hips. "And why didn't you call me to help with the party?"

"Anton helped." Moving back inside, Lauren shuffled through a stack of envelopes she lifted from the desk. "At least he helped when we weren't fighting."

Dare Macy ask if the scavenger hunt was to blame? "Don't tell me you're fighting over the toilet seat being left up. Or squeezing the toothpaste from the wrong end of the tube."

Lauren's smile came more naturally this time. "*That* I think I could handle. It's nothing, really. I fell in love with a control freak and I'll learn to live with it. If not, I'll get counseling."

Macy grabbed at the envelopes—an obvious distraction—and slapped them back on the desk. "You say that way too much like you meant it."

"Which part? The learning to live with it or the counseling?"

"Both. Either. You know if you get all stupid on me, I'm going to have to kick your ass."

At that, Lauren did laugh. "Wouldn't that be breaking all your best-friend rules?"

"My prerogative as the rule maker," Macy said, following Lauren's suddenly distracted gaze to the second-floor landing where, next to Anton Neville, stood Leo Redding.

Both women sighed, the release of appreciative breath a more eloquent expression than words. Anton and Leo were close to the same height, the former no more than an inch taller. In build they were near mirror images as well, with Leo only slightly broader and Anton the perfect definition of surfer lean.

Lauren leaned over to whisper into Macy's ear. "You realize, don't you, that from my artistic perspective, that's an amazing exhibition. Well worth the price of admission."

"And here I was trying to put what I'm witnessing into words. Editorial being my specialty and all."

But now that she'd taken in the whole picture, Macy only had eyes for Leo. He had on dark khaki slacks, leather deck shoes and a black linen shirt worn loose.

His casual look was more put together than her own paltry professional wardrobe. Imagining them as a couple required a huge stretch. They sure didn't fit together like peas and carrots, like peanut butter and jelly, like...Tinkerbell and Peter Pan. Macy shivered. If anything, they fit together like a round hole and a square peg. Except Leo's peg wasn't square. Leo's peg wasn't even a peg. More like a...

Sensing Lauren's probing stare, Macy pulled her gaze from the landing and turned it on her best friend. "What?"

Lauren's eyes cut from Macy to the second floor and back again. "If I didn't know you better, I'd swear I wasn't the only one mooning like a lovesick puppy here."

"I'm surprised you'd admit to mooning or being lovesick."

"You're avoiding my question."

"Did you ask a question?"

"What's going on between you and Leo?"

"Not much." Macy shrugged. Lauren would dig out the truth whether Macy went for subtle or explosive. She decided to drop the bomb. "We played Spin the Webb and he kissed me. We're paired up for the scavenger hunt. He moved into the loft."

"What?" Lauren shrieked and a dozen heads turned. She took hold of Macy's arm and propelled her across the main room and into the kitchen, where she immediately pounced. "And just when were you planning to share this wealth of good news?"

"I never said it was good news."

"You didn't have to say anything. I can put two and two together."

"What two and two?"

Arms crossed, Lauren looked Macy up and down. And up and down. "What you may not have said in so many words, you have screamed with that outfit. Macy Webb? Wearing the latest in gROWL gIRL party wear? Give me a break."

Macy knew she should've stuck to her usual party wear of clogs and capris. Or stuck to her pajamas. "What? All I'm trying to do here is give my wardrobe a little oomph."

"Hello? This is me, Lauren."

"I know who you are."

"Then let's be honest. It's not your wardrobe you're looking to oomph, is it? Not that I wouldn't be the first in line to take you shopping if that were really the case."

"Oh? And that line would be how long?" As if she needed to hear Lauren's insults on top of Lauren's prying.

One hand had moved to Lauren's hip. She used the second to gesture the length of Macy's body. "C'mon, Macy. You may have a thing for gROWL gIRL's lingerie, but that's about it. You wear pajamas like most people wear blue jeans. Or business suits. Or even formal wear."

"They were Oriental silk and they were the dressiest thing I had and I only did it one time." Macy stopped her rant to push her hair back from her face. Nothing she said in self-defense would throw Lauren off track.

As predicted, her friend chugged right along. "Pajamas are made for sleeping. Which is why most people only wear them after dark. When they go to bed.''

''Yes, but most people have to leave the house to go to work. I have the luxury of working from home.''

''What about Leo?''

''He does the biggest part of his work at the office.''

''That's not what I meant.''

''Then say what you mean.''

Lauren's eyes threatened to pop from frustration. ''Do you wear pajamas when he's around? Or is what you wear more revealing?''

''Like what?''

''Like your bare skin?''

Macy's earlobes steamed. ''What kind of question is that?''

Lauren glared. ''Are you sleeping with him?''

''Sleeping with Leo Redding? You're kidding, right?'' Showering, yes. Sleeping, no.

''Okay then. Not sleeping. Are you having sex with him?''

So much for evasive semantics. ''No. I'm standing here in the kitchen talking to you.''

''Have you *had* sex with him?''

Macy took too long to come up with an answer. Her body still tingled from what she'd done with Leo thirty-six hours ago. Thirty-six hours. Had it really been that long?

It seemed like only minutes since they'd tumbled wet and naked into bed, not bothering with the towel Leo had pulled from the linen closet, but letting skin and satin sheets make quick work of the water. Neither had said a word, but had let hands and mouths run wild.

That second time in bed—that wild unreality of sweet hot sex and reckless abandon—had been as fast and fu-

rious as the one in the shower, and Macy couldn't help
wonder if it had been a long time for Leo, or if she'd
whet his appetite that fiercely.

"I knew it. You *are* sleeping with him." Lauren's
stage whisper had enough volume to be heard over the
salsa music setting the festive party tone in the main
room.

Macy shushed her best friend. "I am not having sex
with him. I had sex with him. It was a loss-of-
consciousness sort of encounter. We didn't plan it and I
sure don't intend to let it happen again."

"Why not?"

"What do you mean, why not?" A question Macy
was still trying to answer for herself.

"Don't tell me he wasn't any good. You can look at
the way the man walks and tell he knows how to move
in bed."

"We weren't exactly in bed." And the amazingly intimate way Leo moved would remain her secret. "At
least that first time in the shower."

"Oh, and so now the story changes." Palms held flat
like the scales of Justice, Lauren weighed Macy's answer. "From not sleeping with him to keeping count of
the number of times."

"Two times, Lauren. Two." Macy held up two fingers. "That's all. One right after the other."

Lauren's expression conveyed her respect for Leo's
stamina. "Nice. When?"

"Not that it's any of your business. But…" Macy
searched Lauren's face, finding not a hint of disapproval,
but only a best friend's interest.

And, okay, a best friend's prurient nosiness.

"But?" Lauren prompted with both the question and
the encouraging flutter of fingers.

"But...oh, Lauren." Macy buried her face in her hands. "I've never had anything like this happen to me before."

With a long sigh and a shake of her head, Lauren reached into the refrigerator for two fuzzy navel wine coolers. She opened both bottles and handed one to Macy. "Anton's mixing margaritas and whatever else out in the other room. But this can't wait. So, spill already. I'm dying here."

Macy sipped, sipped again, then quit pretending she hadn't been needing a drink since ten o'clock yesterday morning to calm the nerves that still sparked and burned every time she remembered the feel of Leo buried in her body.

She set her half-empty bottle on the counter behind her, braced the heels of both palms on the countertop edge. "Things like this don't happen to me, Lauren. When it comes to guys, you know? This is like a pure beefcake fantasy. Like taking a shower with Ben Affleck or Mark Wahlberg or Heath Ledger."

Lauren finished a sip of her own drink. "Leo Redding's just a man, Macy. He's no better or different than anyone else. Except maybe in his own mind."

A week ago, Macy would have agreed. Especially that Leo held himself in high regard. But until she'd had him underfoot and done her best to return the favor, she'd only seen the starch in his collar and the "Esquire" at the end of his name.

He was no more just a man than she was just a woman. "No. He is different. And, in a lot of ways that matter to me, he is better. And you can get your mind out of the gutter, because I'm not talking about being better in bed."

"So?" Lauren's comeback held less confusion than

curiosity. "Yes, he's gorgeous and sexy, but so is Anton. So is Eric. So is Ray. There are a dozen gorgeous, sexy men out there."

Macy wasn't even sure she could explain. Or if any explanation would make sense. "Okay. For one thing, he gets my jokes. He doesn't laugh, but he gets them. And he comes right back with his own."

"Okay, gorgeous, sexy and funny."

"Actually, he's not that funny. At least he's more funny sarcastic than funny 'ha-ha.' It's an intelligent humor. A bit dry, a bit wry…"

"That's still not doing it for me, Mace. You've gone how long between men? I want to know why Leo?"

"Why Anton?"

"Now *that* was love at first sight. Which I don't think is the case with you and the lawyer."

"Love? Leo? Screw you for even saying, even thinking, that word."

"Then tell me what it is you're thinking because, I've got to be honest, Mace." Lauren shook her head. "I've thought about the two of you. A lot. Especially after the last game night and the way you two were all over each other during that kiss."

"I don't know. I don't know anything. Not what I'm thinking or what I'm doing or what I'm feeling. Nothing." Her shoulders drooped as the exhaustion she'd held at bay took over. "All I know is that he makes me ache. My body and my brain."

"You said he gets your jokes but doesn't laugh."

Macy nodded.

"Okay, then. Does he make *you* laugh?"

"What?"

"Does Leo Redding make you laugh?"

She had to stop and think. She pulled out a chair from

the breakfast nook table and sat, stunned less by the admission she was about to make and more by the implication. "No. He doesn't. And I haven't even noticed enough to care."

"Don't get me wrong here. I can't think of anybody Leo Redding could use in his life more than you. But for him not to make you laugh when your number one goal in life is to have fun..." Lauren let the thought trail away.

"That's just the thing that's so confusing, Lauren. I am having fun."

"Leo Redding has to rank at the bottom of any fun-guy chart ever put together. Every time you've dumped a guy, it's been because he bored you silly."

"Leo definitely doesn't bore me silly. Unless you mean bore, as in...oh, I don't know." Macy couldn't help herself. "Drill?"

Lauren rolled her eyes. "I meant bore as in dud. Not bore as in..."

"Thud?" Macy suggested in all innocence.

"Thud, huh?" Lauren sipped her wine cooler, studied Macy over the end of the bottle. "Is that like a sound? Or an action?"

"Or maybe the sound of the action? Like in a really bad porn movie." Macy went into an orgasmic display of moans and heavy breathing.

Lauren choked on her drink and poured the remainder down the drain. "Eww. Way too much information. Look. I have an idea."

"I can hardly wait," Macy muttered.

"Since he doesn't make you laugh, but you are having fun, in an admittedly warped and twisted sort of way—" Lauren stuck out her tongue in answer to Macy doing the same "—why don't you go out there and demonstrate what it means to party? See if he's capable of showing you a good time in public.

"Because, no matter how much fun you say you're having now, Macy Webb, you're not going to keep having fun in any relationship—sexual, platonic, whatever—where there are issues about you taking this kid-at-heart thing to the extreme. I know that. You know that. And Leo Redding, especially, needs to know that."

Macy shook her head, because that was what frightened her most. Facing him again. Hearing that they'd made a mistake. She didn't have stars in her eyes. She didn't think she and Leo were headed for Eric's dreaded matrimonial bliss. But she didn't want to hear that they'd made a mistake.

"That would mean I'd have to talk to him. Acknowledge his presence. Maybe even look him in the eye."

"Oh, you don't want to talk to him, but you'll shower with him. That makes no sense whatsoever." Lauren grabbed Macy by the elbow, pulled her up out of her chair.

"Now. It's time to face the music. Let's see if you two can have as much fun with your clothes on as you seem to be having with your clothes off."

BY THE TIME LAUREN and Macy joined the group—a group that seemed to Leo to be the same bunch to have witnessed him fall prey to Macy's Spin the Webb—the public housewarming was over and the private party was on.

A flick of a switch dimmed the overhead lighting, leaving the room awash in Mardi Gras flashes of yellow, green and royal blue, the light thrown by paper lanterns cleverly suspended from beams crisscrossing the room's high ceiling.

The music was loud, a blend of sexy Latin pop and funky Brazilian bossa nova that added its own electronic spice to the fiery drinks and appetizers. The evening's main courses offered a flavorful Asian flair to the multicultural experience.

Anton mixed margaritas by the gallon to wash down the fire of the jalapeño hors d'oeuvres. Whether stuffed with cheese and crab meat, or breaded and fried, the peppers packed an eye-watering, throat-scorching punch. Leo stopped after three.

He stopped, as well, after three margaritas. The drinks gave him a nice buzz without making him stupid. At least not stupid enough to find a secluded corner and drag Macy away from the party and into the dark.

He wanted to lift her skirt, to see what she'd chosen to wear beneath. He wanted to measure the heat of her skin. To gauge her reaction to the boldness of his touch, because he still wasn't certain that what had happened between them had burned with the heat he remembered.

Tonight they'd wound up seated at the far end of the long dinner table. She sat across from him, but had managed to avoid eye contact through most of the meal. The main conversation was to her right, to his left, which gave her plenty of reason to keep her gaze averted.

Not that she needed more reason to ignore him than what they'd done thirty-six hours ago in the shower. And then again on his bed. Because after the fact—after the act—they hadn't spoken except to mumble niceties and dress in their respective rooms for their respective days.

He hadn't seen her since except to watch her while she slept, until he couldn't take any more of her undersea world of Jacques Cousteau. Avoiding her hadn't been intentional. But neither had time and space put what had happened into any sort of logical perspective.

He wasn't the love 'em and leave 'em type. True, he was more into conquest than into commitment, but the women he dated knew that going in. His relationship policy, whether short-term or long, had always been to make sure he and his partner were on the same page.

He and Macy hadn't even opened the covers of the book.

They'd just fucked.

"Whoa, Chloe, baby! Pour that hot stuff this way!"

Eric Haydon's rowdy shout brought Leo out of his musings. He glanced toward the big room's fireplace, crafted from the belly of an old woodstove, to see Chloe and Lauren dancing in front of it. A dance that set the bump and grind tone for the rest of the party.

The inviting crook of Lauren's finger was all the encouragement Anton needed. He slipped out from behind the bar and in between the two women, who writhed and popped to the hot salsa music, arms overhead, hips grinding, heads thrown back, hair whipping as they moved.

Chloe blew a kiss Eric's way. He bailed out of his chair to join the other three, spinning Chloe away from the ménage à trois and into their own private party. Ray took over bartending duties, pouring straight tequila shots, while Jess made like a sideshow knife-thrower and quartered the last of the limes. He tossed a requested wedge to Melanie.

She caught it, squeezed the juice into her Corona longneck. Then she and Sydney upped the revelry, whooping and hollering, banging beer bottles and mugs on the table, egging on the four dirty dancers and the dynamic duo tending the bar.

Macy, Leo watched surreptitiously. She had yet to say much of anything, but he didn't doubt for a minute that she was having a good time. Her entire upper body rock 'n rolled to the beat of the music and the rhythm of the dance. Her smile was infectious and he caught the disease.

Caught himself starting to relax.

This was so unlike him, this casual partying, this giving it up for fun. This total inability to stay focused on the game. Macy made it too easy to forget that he was here for the win and the win only. He had to remember that his involvement with this group was of a limited duration. One month. The length of Macy's gIRL gAMES scavenger hunt and no longer.

The same should they continue their affair. He could afford a short-term diversion. He'd enjoy her company, take pleasure in her body as long as the arrangement suited both their needs. His were suited perfectly. Hers hadn't yet been established. He'd see that they were tonight.

The more he thought about it, the more he liked that plan. Yeah. He liked it a lot. An affair he could definitely handle. That Macy was as willing as she was, as talented as she was...a man would be out of his mind to say no. But he'd be a fool to consider any sort of long-term investment in a woman, any woman, whose approach to life was more sophomoric than strategic.

Macy's sudden and animated cry of, "Go Lauren!" brought Leo's head back up in time to catch Anton working to pull a wedge of lime from between Lauren's lips with his teeth. Lauren refused to let go, earning her cheers from the women, earning Anton a ribbing from the men.

He hooked an arm around her waist and pulled her tight to his body, using his tongue where his teeth had failed and prying loose the lime. By this time Lauren wasn't putting up much of a fight; was, in fact, doing what she could to ditch the wedge, making Anton's win all the sweeter. Leo had yet to meet a man who didn't savor a woman's surrender.

And then there was Eric, never willing to be outdone. He grabbed a shot glass from Jess in one hand and Chloe by the wrist with the other. "C'mon, woman. Let's show these yahoos how a real tequila kiss is done."

Chloe speared her own wedge of lime from the bowl on the bar and gave Eric the full evil-eye treatment. "I'm only letting you get away with that woman remark because my payback is going to bring you to your knees."

"Give it your best shot, baby." His grin was wide as he leaned into Chloe's space. But he didn't lean too far, considering Chloe still held the lime on the end of Jess's paring knife.

The four supporting females called encouragement to Chloe, Melanie taking an empty longneck bottle in each hand and pounding a punctuating beat. "Payback! Payback! Payback!"

"Eric Haydon, you are in such deep shit. You are not going to know what hit you." This from Lauren, who stood encircled in Anton's arms, snuggling back into his chest now that they'd traded in their public exhibition for the intimate embrace.

Even normally serene Sydney leaned an elbow on Ray Coffey's shoulder and blew an ear-splitting rah-rah whistle. Having hung up his bartending apron and returned to the woman who'd held his attention most of the evening, Ray tugged his earlobe and shook off the deafening aftereffects.

Watching as Eric circled Chloe like Sylvester the Cat preparing to pounce and devour a tiny, defenseless

Tweety, Macy was the last to give a shout, clapping as she added her chant to Melanie's. "Chlo-e! Chlo-e! Chlo-e!"

As if Chloe needed any more encouragement. She'd already lowered both spaghetti straps of a black velvet top, a top held in place by nothing but full feminine curves and a whole lotta luck. And now she fluffed her powder puff hair and cocked a hip in a show of Mae West attitude.

Leo sat back in his chair, crossed his arms and extended his legs. His foot bumped Macy's. He left it in place. He wasn't surprised when she did the same. But then she pressed her bare sole to his bare ankle. On purpose. And Leo felt the evening's first true stirrings of intrigue.

Anton jacked up the volume until tambourines and maracas rattled the windows and walls. Chloe trailed the lime across the tip of her tongue and her lips, rubbed it over Eric's mouth, then squeezed the wedge against her chest, trickling droplets of juice into her cleavage.

Staring at the wet and tempting trail, Eric remained unmoving and at a loss for words. A rare thing, even Leo had to admit, but it didn't last for long. Seconds later, Eric let loose a wild animal howl, baying toward the ceiling and the full moon beyond.

Leo's pulse ripped like an unexpected shot through his veins. He felt the urge to echo the primal sound. Because, as Chloe sprinkled salt over the damp trail of skin, as Eric smacked his lips and rubbed his hands together, as Leo wrapped his hand around—he swore—his last margarita of the night, Macy's toes begin a slow crawl up his leg.

He tensed, then forced himself to relax, not wanting to make a move that would dissuade her exploration, wanting to see what she had on her mind, if he'd read her right. Later tonight they'd be taking the time with one another's bodies they'd not been able to take in the shower or in his bed.

He wanted to spend time, learning her hot spots, feeding her hunger. Making her wait until she turned on him and devoured. But he'd had too much to drink, he mused, then realized he hadn't had enough. Between thoughts of getting her naked and the way her toes were tickling the pit of his knee... He drew in a sharp breath and held it, forced his attention out of his pants and back to the show.

Chloe presented her salted skin to Eric, pulling the neckline of her top even lower and holding the lime wedge, pulp out, between even white teeth. Eric made as if to give thanks, hands piously together and eyes closed, until Chloe hooked her fingers in his belt loops and yanked him forward. He wrapped his free arm around her waist, finishing the move she'd started by pulling her lower body hard into his.

He settled the flat of his tongue in the salty hollow of her throat, mumbled and hummed his appreciation of her taste into her skin. Chloe arched her neck, giving him better access and an encouraging invitation to continue.

Macy's invitation followed. She shifted in her chair, leaning back far enough to rub her curved arch over the muscles of Leo's inner thigh. His hand tightened around his drink and he spread his legs wider. She repeated the caress, first one side, then the other. Her toes flexed into the fabric of his trousers and a snarl rumbled through his chest.

Eric's tongue grew bolder, licking away the trail of salt, flicking across Chloe's upper chest and earning him a playful ear-boxing and a reprimand to get back to work. He laughed into her skin and corrected his downhill course, approaching the valley between her voluptuous hills.

Macy needed no course correction whatsoever. The toes of her second foot had worked their way beneath the cuff of Leo's khakis. Her skin was cool and smooth. His was heated and hair-roughened. The simple anatomical contrast between the sexes raised the heat of the blood pooling in his groin.

It was a sad state of affairs when he let a sprite of a wild child turn him on with her toes. Yet he couldn't remember another woman's conventional seduction getting him so hard, so fast. This was what he so enjoyed about Macy. She was bold and adventurous, not the least bit shy when it came to going after what she wanted. Or insisting things be done her way.

So far he'd given her what she wanted. He'd let her have her way. She'd gotten a roommate, a teammate and his attention. Now he intended to get his. This private under-the-table lap dance was not a bad place to start. And by the time Eric had managed to dip his tongue deep into Chloe's cleavage, Macy's soles strategically rested in the V of Leo's crotch.

Eric licked away the last of the salted trail of juice, lifted his head from Chloe's chest and grinned like the devil. Then he tossed back the shot of tequila, shuddered, settled his mouth on Chloe's and sucked the juice from the waiting lime.

But he didn't stop there, when the lime was spent and the Jose Cuervo burn had eased. His tongue scooped away the pulp and rind and swirled freely into Chloe's mouth. And when Chloe reached out and grabbed his ass, the crowd roared.

Eric and Chloe had the room's attention as they

moved from the kiss into a hands-on set of dirty dancing. Lauren and Anton joined them.

And Jess was just reaching for Melanie when Leo felt a shift in Macy's gaze, from the dancers to his face.

9

It had been thirty-six hours since he'd had her.

And the last thing Leo expected was to look up and see Macy drawing a bite of fried rice from between two chopsticks, her tongue curling around the food, teasing the tips of the wooden skewers the way she'd teased the head of his dick.

He hadn't expected to see her lightly nip at the flesh of a pork rib, leaving the bone whistle clean, licking the sticky sauce from her lips and the tips of her fingers. He hadn't expected to see her pinch the tail of a grilled jumbo shrimp, closing her lips around the thick meat, sucking the seasoned juice from the shell.

The ball of her foot stroked the burgeoning bulge behind his fly. Her chin lifted; her eyelids fluttered and closed. She opened wide and swallowed the whole thing deep down in the back of her throat.

Leo came close to upending the table in a ferocious exhibition of his inner Gladiator. Fortunately, Macy was the only one to notice the way he shoved the edge of his dinner plate hard against hers when he reached across the table, wrapped his hand around her wrist and pulled her to her feet.

She didn't resist or object, but made the long reach for her drink to wash the food from her mouth before she followed where he led. In this case, the far edge of the impromptu dance floor. As far away from the rest of the group as Leo could get without leaving the room.

With Ray and Sydney deep in conversation at the table, and the rest of the couples caught up in the music or in each other, the timing of Leo's abduction could not have been planned any better. No one noticed the commotion, his desperation or the erection straining the fly of his pants.

He put his back to the room and pulled Macy tight to the front of his body. She nestled into him like a pearl into the shell of an oyster, right where it belonged. The admission struck him hard with its corny truth.

What the hell had he gotten himself into?

She looked up at his face and caught him considering his flight options. Her innocent expression was more of a lie than Leo could stand. There was nothing innocent about Macy Webb. She was the original black widow spider, spinning the sticky threads of her deadly man-snare.

"Were you wanting to dance? Or did you just want to get your hands on me?" She could hardly keep a straight face as she wrapped her arms around his waist, hooking her thumbs into the belt loops at his sides.

Even wearing shoes, she wasn't tall enough to reach around his neck, and here she stood in nothing but bare feet. Comfort over etiquette. Just like the kid she insisted on being. Instead of the woman she was, the woman now working to mow down his beliefs about what he needed from the opposite sex.

What he needed was to get his head on straight.

His forearms rested on her shoulders; his hands met in the center of her back and pressed her close. "What I want right now is probably better left unsaid."

"Why? You think I'm not adult enough to handle it?"

She looked up again, eyes wide once more. Innocent again.

He wasn't going to fall for her act. Not this time. "Is that what you want me to think?"

She gave a small shrug. "I don't really care what you think."

He maneuvered them away from the crowd and closer to the front foyer, tiled in a rich Italian marble of an equally rich espresso color. "You'll never make a very convincing witness with that lousy Swiss cheese testimony."

Macy sighed in capitulation, resting her cheek on his chest. Good. He was finally getting her attention. But then she snuggled up to him and asked, "What's the difference between a lawyer and a vampire?"

Leo could only roll his eyes. "A vampire only sucks blood at night."

"Hmm. What's the difference between a lawyer and a leech?"

"A leech quits sucking your blood after you die."

She tsked. "You would know all the suck jokes."

He spun them around, backed them almost the entire length of the foyer. And then he stood in place and did no more than shuffle his feet and sway from side to side. "You're hopeless. Do you have one single serious bone in your body?"

"Nothing compared to what you've got going on." She looked up into his face. Their bodies slowed until their feet remained unmoving, their knees sandwiched together, their hips aligned in a way that had nothing to do with the dance. "I mean, I knew you had a Jones for playing games...."

Leo felt heat pool and spread, felt a compelling need to ease the building pressure. He dropped a hand to

Macy's backside, held her close and pushed forward into her belly. "This is not about playing any game."

Her eyes drifted shut, drifted open. Her smile was nothing if not tickled pink. "And here I was beginning to think you were the one who was hopeless. You are allowed to have fun just for fun, you know."

When he wasn't quick enough to refute her allegation, she slowly frowned, slowly added, "Or didn't you know?"

He knew she was thinking about the time they'd spent in bed. The time in the shower that had started on a dare she'd been more than willing to accept. Even now he was rising to the private provocation she'd boldly issued both above and beneath the dinner table.

She was right. Enjoying her body, her wit and her mind had nothing to do with competition, with making his mark, with getting ahead. It was fun and games with no agenda, no ulterior motive.

So, what was he doing here?

His life was a study in focus, success and striving to excel. He surrounded himself with the people, bought his way into the games designed to make it happen. He never lost sight of the goal.

So, what was he doing here?

The possibility that he was here for more, that he wanted more and wanted it from Macy, landed with a gut-deep punch. A punch he should've been able to dodge. He'd forgotten his own fundamental rules of play.

So, what in the hell was he doing here?

"You never did tell me what it is you want," she said, her voice too soft and sweet, too concerned female, too not-Macy for his liking.

"Never mind," he muttered gruffly, because he

wasn't quite sure what he wanted any longer and was afraid he wasn't going to like it when he finally figured it out.

"Fine. Whatever." She shrugged off his comment and his attitude, drawing herself up stiffly in his arms. "It's not like I'm going to lose any sleep worrying about it."

Leo gritted his teeth, forced a deep breath and blew out his self-directed ire. He might not like what Macy had done to his mind, but he was solely to blame for this inexplicable lapse in concentration. And he owed her an apology for acting like a son of a bitch.

He realized all this as he stroked a fingertip along her jaw, repeated the caress on the opposite side. Her eyelids grew heavy, her mouth dreamy. The tip of her tongue peeked from between her lips as Leo lifted her chin and asked, "Do you lose sleep over anything?"

"Only when I have a good reason." She looked up then, met his gaze. And what had been a look of the sweetest surrender became an invitation best suited for a corner in the dark. "Do you have one to give me?"

He shook his head.

"No?" Her eyes widened, then narrowed to a scowl.

He shook his head again. A piece of work, this one, like hot and cold running water, needing nothing more than the turn of a handle to alter her mood. "That wasn't a no."

"What was it then?" She tried to slip her arms from around his back.

He caught her fingers, so cool and tiny in his hands, and held them at his waist. He wanted to dispel her skepticism—even if the effort cost him more points than he gained. "That was me. Enjoying you."

And at that, her expression blossomed into a look of

pure bliss. Her soft sigh warmed his skin straight through the fabric of his shirt.

"See?" She nuzzled his chest with her cheek, burrowed her nose into the loose folds of black linen. "I knew you were capable of having a good time."

He held her where and how she wanted to be held while listening to the strains of the music drifting into the dimly lit foyer from the main room beyond. Mood music. Hot and throbbing and utterly untamed. And Macy's mouth making wet and wild with that bared section of his skin.

A deeply drawn groan, primal and raw, rolled from his gut to his throat. He pulled her farther into the shadows. "So getting me all worked up? This is what you consider a good time?"

"I consider it a start." Glancing up, she wiggled both brows, her tongue slicking over her lower lip. "It's not like all that fancy footwork was just for you, you know."

When he didn't, couldn't, immediately respond, she quit with the nuzzling and burrowing and hit him lightly in the shoulder. "C'mon, Leo. We showered together yesterday morning. It's not like I came on to you in there out of the blue."

He wasn't going to argue. If anything had been out of the blue it had been Macy stepping into his shower. He was still recovering. Not from the sex, but that she'd taken him up on the dare.

This wasn't the time or the place, but he wanted to know why. Why now, but even more so, why then? Had sex been one more tactical move in her game plan? Or had she shed her clothes and her inhibitions because the sex had been with him?

"Why?"

"Why what?" she asked as he returned her hands to

his waist and put their bodies back into slow motion. "Why did I come on to you?"

"Yes. And…"

"Why did I come all over you?"

He crooked up both corners of his mouth, the smile a private appreciation of her candor, when another woman would've gone for coy. He didn't think he'd ever enjoyed a seduction—or a seductress—more.

"That one is easy. And obvious," she said, answering her own question without giving him a chance to start thinking with the head on his shoulders. "I'm easy. And I'm obvious."

What she was was clever, quick-witted and quite confident that he wouldn't think her either easy or obvious. "I wouldn't say that."

"What *would* you say?"

" 'Take off your clothes,' for starters," he said, keeping one hand centered on her back, working the other between their bodies and up under the fabric to her belly.

"Leo?"

"Hmm?" Her skin was tender and soft, her curves the perfect fit for a man's hands.

"What are you doing?" she asked, and shivered.

He was learning her shape, the way she wanted to be touched, what he could do to heighten her pleasure. "Getting even for the fancy footwork."

"The only skin to skin contact I made was my toe to your shin." The party lights reached only as far as the edges of her eyes, tinting her irises the intoxicating gold of aged brandy.

Irises and aged brandy. Leo knew he had to be drunk. "Feel free to grab my ass anytime."

And at that, Macy reached behind him…and turned the brass knob on a door he hadn't noticed.

A bathroom. A tiny guest bathroom. With nothing but a toilet, a basin and a lock on the door.

Click!

He held Macy by the waist and lifted her onto the edge of the countertop of espresso-and-indigo-colored porcelain. Her hands went straight to his backside.

"Greedy wench," he managed to mutter before his mouth descended, covering hers, one hand around her back, the other finding its way between her legs and under her skirt. A simple thong, nothing more, easily breached, and he did, his fingers finding her ready, finding her wet and wild.

She backed away from his touch, pulled her mouth from his and looked down, mining the wallet she'd dug from his slacks pocket. "Not greedy. And not stupid."

She waved the condom she'd found, then went to work freeing him from his boxers. He ripped open the foil packet, caught her watching, her lips parted, her tongue pressed to her two front teeth.

When he offered, she accepted, taking the protective sheath and checking the direction of the roll. At the first touch of her hands he swallowed hard, thrust forward, and she covered him completely.

He wanted to wait, wanted Macy to go slow, but this wasn't about taking his time. This was about here and now and tamping down the flames of this particular fire. Macy had braced her heels in the small of his back; her palms straddled the basin for support.

Her eyes were closed, her head thrown back, and Leo was done with taking his time. One hand held the damp thong to the side; one hand held his cock and guided. He was in and she was tight and nothing mattered but the look on her face. A look that said he'd done good.

It was the reflection of his own face in the mirror that told a different truth.

THREE DAYS LATER, Lauren finally put the finishing touches on Macy's new logo. Her eyes aching from hours spent staring at her monitor, her back aching from sitting too long, Lauren now stood at the backyard pool railing, leaning against the custom-made iron grille that separated the covered patio from the pool, where Anton was swimming his scheduled laps.

She shivered lightly. The night air was cool, the moon high and full. The heated pool would be warm. Her cover-up hung unbuttoned over her suit. Both remained dry. She'd had every intention of joining him in the water when she'd stepped outside ten minutes ago.

But then she'd stopped to watch him swim.

The pool's underwater lights cast his sleek form in shadow—a dark phantom slicing through the water in perfect, long-armed strokes. He never missed a beat. He never faltered or sputtered or tired. His disciplined control never wavered.

He swam by rote: a certain stroke, a set number of laps. She admired his commitment to his athleticism, his health and his routine. He managed to fit exercise into his daily agenda no matter what else he had going on.

Lauren sighed. She was kidding herself to think she'd ever live up to his expectations. She wasn't even sure that his expectations, for himself but especially for her, fit in with the plans she'd made for her life.

And none of this would she have known if not for the scavenger hunt and her impetuous move into his house.

She smiled to herself, a rueful private expression of her current unsettled mood. To kiss Macy or to kill Macy. That was the question. One thing was certain.

Lauren had a decision to make. Unless what she had was a decision in need of unmaking.

What would Anton say if she admitted this move in together had been too much too soon? That there was still a lot they needed to explore about their feelings for one another, their feelings about their relationship; what each wanted to give, what each expected to take?

She'd wanted to be open and honest, candid about her needs and desires. She'd wanted to be free to let go, to hold nothing of herself back. She hadn't expected Anton to feel he had every right to remake her into what he thought she should be.

As if he knew her well enough to know what he was changing. At twenty-five years old, she didn't even know herself—except to be certain the inevitable changes she made in her life would be *her* changes. Not Anton's. Not any man's.

He made another turn at the near end of the pool. She watched the way he moved. The strength that allowed him to pull his body tirelessly through the water. The same strength he used to hold himself in check long after he'd seen to her intimate pleasure.

Mind over matter, he said. A battle of inner and outer wills.

Why didn't he ever just let go?

Maybe Macy had the right idea. Maybe Peter Pan was not such a bad role model. Right now Lauren wasn't sure adulthood was the way to go. Her move toward deepening her relationship with Anton had backfired in a big way.

She doubted he would agree. According to Anton, their issues were minor. All couples experienced series of ups and downs. Adjustments were to be expected. Anything less would be suspect, cause for worry.

"Easy for you to say," she murmured to his shadowed form. It wasn't his life, his choices under scrutiny. She really had thought the honeymoon would last longer than three weeks. Instead of using the time to grow comfortable with one another, Anton had started in with his man plans, analyzing, fixing...driving Lauren crazy.

He shot out of the water now, his exit an energetic leap from the shallow end onto the pool's concrete apron. He shook the water from his skin, then slicked both palms back over his head, dragging loose shanks of long blond hair behind his ears, where Lauren knew it would dry in wild ringlets.

"I thought you were going to swim with me," he said, catching sight of her and making his way to the patio.

She handed him the towel draped over the railing. "I like the view from back here."

And now that he was closer she wondered if she had the strength of will to share her feelings. Her doubts and reservations. Her resentments.

He was so much of a man. Physically, but emotionally and intellectually as well. He was straightforward and self-assured, and his body was broad and lean and built to inspire both her passions and her confidence. Lauren sighed.

Anton scrubbed the towel over his face, draped it around his neck. His hands gripped the patio railing. He leaned forward and smiled. "I see what you mean. About the view."

His gaze roamed boldly over her body, intentionally clad in the scantiest suit she owned. She wanted him to want her. Sex seemed their strongest bond of late. She wanted to hold on to what she could of their relationship, even when it felt like she was grasping at snapping straws.

She shrugged out of her cover-up. "Are you finished with your laps?"

"With the right amount of inspiration—" his expression said he was halfway there "—I could manage a few more."

"Then give me a ten-second head start."

"You're on."

Lauren caught but a fleeting glimpse of the wicked flash of Anton's grin. She tossed her cover-up into his face and over his head, hoping to gain more than the ten seconds. Even counting on Anton's quick reflexes, she badly misjudged, and he was on her heels before she reached the edge of the pool.

"Ten seconds!" she screamed, then made a clean dive into the water. She was on her return lap when he caught her. Or, more accurately, when she reached the point midpool where he'd stopped, waiting, stalking.

She stayed out of his reach, but just barely, dunked her head and smoothed back her hair, sputtering as she surfaced.

"Are you okay?"

She shivered. "You cheated and I'm freezing."

"Cheated? How? I gave you your ten seconds." He didn't comment on the fact that her teeth were chattering.

His weren't, so she decided to grin and bear it. "Ten seconds by whose watch? Anyway, you were supposed to swim with me. Not chase me down."

"I am swimming with you." He treaded water, drew closer, using only the long strokes of his legs to make his move. "But you wanted a head start. That usually means chasing you down. Then you chasing me down..."

Lauren shook her head, set off in a slow backstroke

for the edge of the pool, where she planted her feet on the textured bottom. "I've had all the chasing down I care to these past three weeks."

Anton joined her in the shallow water. The surface lapped around his rib cage. He held Lauren's gaze, but made no move to touch her. Or to warm her. "Are you talking about the scavenger hunt?"

"What else?" She evaded his question when what she really wanted to do was admit the truth and tell him that she had based the most important move of her life on a stupid game.

She deserved to lose the prize. Deserved to lose any of Anton's respect she hadn't lost already with her defensiveness and refusal to consider that his input into her life choices was made out of his concern for her happiness as much as with her potential in mind.

She'd accused him of butting in where he had no business butting. She'd tried to bury the very real problem of miscommunication under the cover of night, beneath his sheets and his body. This time, sex wasn't the panacea she'd always found it to be.

Anton toyed with a lock of her wet hair. "A few days ago you were all gung ho to cheat and win Sydney's vacation. What gives?"

With a shiver, Lauren ducked her shoulders beneath the warm water and lifted her face to the sky. "Who needs a vacation, anyway? We have the perfect getaway right here."

Anton wasn't convinced by her flippant comeback. "A getaway from our getaway sounds like a good thing to me."

"Then let's go. We don't need to *win* a trip. Let's *take* a trip. We can rent our own sailboat." The more she thought about it, the more she liked the idea. And the faster she talked.

"Or we don't have to go sailing at all, though I know how you are about the water. We can go to New York. Or San Francisco. Ooh. Why don't we go to Canada? To Banff. Skiing sounds like—"

"Lauren, hold on a minute." Anton moved close to her side. Their legs brushed lightly. He used one arm on the lip of the pool edge for balance. His free hand came to rest on her belly beneath the cover of water and night. "What's going on here?"

"Nothing really." *Deep breath, Lauren. Keep it together.* "I just started thinking about taking a real vacation. You and me. Together. We've never done that, you know."

"There are a lot of things we've never done together. We'll get around to most of them. Just takes time."

"I know. It's just..."

She leaned her head back, kicked her legs out in front of her, dislodged Anton's possessive hand when she moved. She didn't know how to say what she had on her mind. Or if she wanted to keep silent and work out her own problems in her own time.

Obviously Anton shared none of her hang-ups. Obviously he had his life and his act together, his head on straight. "It's just what? What's going on, Lauren? You're running from something."

Her legs stilled, her eyes closed. "What makes you think I'm running away from anything?"

"You mean besides the fact that you're working up to an underwater hundred-yard dash?"

"That's ridiculous. I'm trying to warm up." And seemed to be getting colder by the minute.

"Lauren." Anton moved in front of her, used the

nearness of his big, heated body to lessen her chill. "I'm a guy. You're going to have to spell this out."

She wished finding the warmth she was missing was so simple, so physical. She had to do this. As blissful as the thought of feigning naiveté was, she couldn't be the child Macy got away with being.

One hand retained a firm hold on the edge of the pool. The other stroked the stubble on Anton's cheek and came to rest in the center of his chest. She met his gaze. "Do you ever wonder if we're rushing things?"

An eyebrow went up. "You mean do I believe in love at first sight?"

She shook her head and wistfully smiled. "No. That one is my fantasy. You're much too practical."

"Practical?" He seemed to consider the idea, then shook his head. "Not always. But I do give my best shot to being realistic."

"What have you done lately that was impractical?" *And please don't say letting me move in here with you.*

"Agreeing to Macy's harebrained scavenger hunt."

That wasn't what she'd expected. He hadn't given any indication of being burned out or drained by the emotional process. But then, him being a guy, the process wouldn't be about emotions, now would it? Lauren mused. Anton made no secret that thought and logic far outranked feelings.

She, of course, disagreed and showed him so, running soothing toes up the back of his calf and thigh. "Why is the scavenger hunt impractical? I thought you liked discovering all my deep dark secrets."

Anton toyed with one strap on her suit top. "I want to find out all your deep dark secrets on my own time. Not on Macy's schedule. And not using Macy's list."

"You don't like what you're discovering?"

"I love what I'm discovering." He wedged his knee between her legs and moved intimidatingly closer. "At least I'm loving most of it."

What wasn't he sure about? And then it hit her. "The yearbook."

His hand stilled on her shoulder. "Would you have told me?"

That she'd been voted the girl most of her male classmates wanted to sleep with? "At the time it was perversely flattering. What girl doesn't want to be considered sexy? Now I realize it was more about being considered easy."

"Were you?"

"Easy?" Her high-school days had not seen any of her finer moments. She hadn't even shared the complete truth with Macy. But in the name of an honest relationship, Lauren couldn't lie to Anton. Instead she disguised the facts. "I was a party girl. Not a slut."

"A tease."

She considered her response in light of her, so far, successful sin of omission and let one hand drift to the drawstring of Anton's suit. "A selective tease."

Only the cutest boys. The most popular boys. The boys who could increase her own hot-stuff reputation. She'd never been shy about using what she had to get what she wanted.

Surely she'd outgrown such an immature way of pursuing success.

"How old were you when you lost your virginity?"

Lauren looked up sharply. "Is that on your list of questions?"

He shook his head. "I'm just curious."

"Why? Is it going to make a difference in our relationship? In how you see me?"

"No. But I think it might make a difference in how you see yourself. And it might have something to do with the way you are about sex now." He moved away, moved to stand at her side, his elbows on the pool edge for support and positioned to give her space.

She didn't want space; she wanted space. She faced him so at least she'd know where she stood. "What's wrong with the way I am about sex? Am I oversexed? Do I give it too much importance?"

Anton bit his tongue except to say, "You're putting words in my mouth, Lauren."

"You make it easy to do when you don't say anything." Exasperating man, adding frustration to her heartache and her stress. "I went to a counselor once. He was like that. Saying nothing. Sitting back and waiting for me to talk myself into a corner."

A frown furrowed Anton's brow. "When did you see a counselor?"

Lauren huffed. "More of my dirty laundry, right? Phobias, fixations and fears? Is that another question on your list?"

"C'mon, Lauren. This is not about the scavenger hunt." He looked away, looked back, his eyes dangerously bright and a near transparent blue beneath the light of the moon. "This is about you and me. You're the one who asked if I thought we were rushing things."

Leaning her head onto the arm she'd propped on the pool edge, she softly answered, "Because I think we have."

"You're making that call after, what? Three weeks?"

"How many times have we argued in the last year? How many times in the last three weeks?" Funny how easy it was now to talk, now that she'd stopped avoiding the uncomfortably sensitive subject.

"An adjustment period. It's not unexpected."

She pressed her palm to her chest. "I didn't expect it. I thought a year together would count for something. That we'd gotten beyond being...petty."

"You think I'm being petty?"

Maybe he wasn't. Maybe she was the one overreacting. She just didn't know anymore. And she'd never be able to figure it out while she was living here. "I don't know if it's you. It's quite possibly all me."

"I see." Anton backed away and boosted himself up onto the side of the pool, dangled his legs over the edge. "So, what are you saying?"

The last thing she wanted to do was hurt him. But she wasn't sure if that was best avoided by staying or by leaving. At least leaving until she had a better idea of why so many of her feelings were at odds.

"I think...for now...I should move back in with Macy. At least until we—you and I...until you and I have... No." She had to do this right, because she'd done it so wrong the first time. "Until we *take* the time to get to know each other. The important things. Hopes and dreams. Fears, even. Not ridiculous yearbook captions or underwear preferences."

He didn't say a word, didn't even look in her direction. He only stared at the surface of the water lightly ruffled by the cool evening air. Then he took a deep breath and shook his head, a shudder, really, as if ridding himself of a disturbing pest.

Lauren waited for his answer, but he slid back into the water, a sleek otter at home, in his element and safe from harm. He took off for the far end of the pool in a brisk execution of his earlier leisurely stroke.

Still she waited, climbing the submerged stairs at the end of the pool. She found her cover-up where Anton

had draped it over the back of a lounger. She shrugged
it on out of habit, certainly not out of need. At least not
any need she could feel. Since she couldn't feel. Anything.

She waited until she had nothing left to wait for, then
returned to the house to pack.

10

"LADIES. We've talked the scavenger hunt to death. Can we please get back to gIRL-gEAR business?"

Sydney Ford had to raise her voice to be heard above the chatter of the corporation's partners. Five of the six, Sydney included, with Lauren having yet to make an appearance, sprawled across the living area of Macy's loft in a gathering that suggested pajama party and not strategy session.

This was Macy in her element. The noise of interaction. The frenzy of flying ideas. The creative inspiration of five like-minded brains. She couldn't imagine having to keep any sort of regular schedule in any sort of regular office, wearing any sort of regular clothes.

Lauren had been right about Macy's predilection for pajamas. Tonight, however, she'd considered the professional nature of the get-together, made the concession and dressed in a camouflage tank top and army-green fatigues. She'd been doing that a lot since Leo had moved in. Getting dressed.

And making concessions.

Doing what she could to give him space when the whole point of having him in the loft was to keep him underfoot. Stocking up at the whole foods market on the coffee he liked, when her original roommate guidelines demanded every man for himself. Swabbing a mop over his bathroom floor, since she was mopping her own anyway, and his was only another ten minutes of work, or would've been if she hadn't stopped to smell his soap, his aftershave, his bathrobe hanging on the hook behind the door.

She'd yet to sit down in her bedroom on the stool facing her vanity mirror and have a true heart-to-heart about the reasons for following rules. How rules were designed to keep one out of trouble, especially the trouble caused by sexy attorney types who lured unsuspecting females into shower stalls and guest bathrooms.

Or maybe she needed Lauren to do the talking since, sometime during the past couple of weeks, Macy had forgotten every rule she'd ever set down about exploring guest bathrooms and shower stalls with sexy attorneys. Not to mention that she'd discovered the small thrill that came with doing Leo Redding's grocery shopping. And the satisfaction she'd found in giving him the peace and quiet he needed.

It was like she'd been channeling Carol Brady.

"C'mon, Sydney." Kinsey Gray's plea offered a welcome interruption to Macy's musings over living a domestic sitcom as harebrained as *The Brady Bunch.* "I missed out on the whole scavenger hunt. I'm doing my best to stock up on vicarious thrills here."

"Besides, dear CEO," Chloe added, settling back onto the dais she'd made of bolsters and pillows, and making sure she had Sydney's attention before saying more. "You haven't revealed a single, solitary, noteworthy thing about Ray."

Both Macy and Melanie hurried to add their seconds to Chloe's comment, Melanie admonishing, "You can't hold out, Sydney. The rest of us have shared at least one good gory guy detail."

And Macy stating, "Think of it as work, Syd. It's all

about the column, and with our current readership numbers, that means the bottom line.''

Sydney looked around the room into four expectant faces, and when her eyes rolled up, her eyelids closed and she shook her head in weary defeat, Macy and Melanie shared a triumphant high-five.

From the floor in front of Macy's chair, Melanie moved to the sofa and snuggled down into the cushions opposite Sydney's end. Macy stayed where she was, having a bird's-eye view.

Kinsey was the one who couldn't sit still, pacing the strip of floor between the sofa and the entertainment center until Chloe tumbled her down into the pillow pile.

''One thing,'' Sydney said, when the shenanigans were over and she finally had the attention she'd been trying for ten minutes to get. ''But then it's back to work.''

She tucked her loose curls behind her ear. ''He doesn't talk about it, but he did tell me it's not a big secret, so I'm not breaking his confidence here.

''Anyway, Ray has a scar on his chest. It's about six inches long and cuts up and over his heart,'' she said, and demonstrated. ''He got into a fight in some Caribbean bar.''

''Wow.'' Macy wasn't sure what else to say in response, but had no trouble asking the obvious. ''What was he doing stirring up trouble in the Caribbean?''

This time Sydney pinned each partner with a look designed to up the curiosity ante. ''Searching for his younger brother, who's been missing for three years.''

A hush settled over the room and Macy had no doubt the other women were seeing stoic Ray in the same brand-new light. What was the saying? Under that calm exterior beats the heart of a... What? It would come to her in a minute. But even more notable than Ray's new larger-than-life dimensions…how had Sydney discovered his hidden scar?

Macy was about to ask the pressing question, but Melanie started giggling. Hiccups at first, then hysterical laughter that she tried desperately to stifle, digging herself in deeper with the effort.

"What is wrong with you?" Macy finally asked when it looked as if Melanie would never recover.

"I'm sorry. I'm sorry." Melanie fanned both hands in front of her face. "It's just that…here I thought the scar on Jess's breastbone was impressive."

"What's up with all the guys and their scars? I feel so cheated." Chloe frowned and pouted her way deeper into the pillows. "I wonder if Eric's been holding out on me."

Macy thought of the scar she'd never asked about but had first noticed when she'd showered with Leo. "Leo's got a nice big one."

After a moment of supreme silence, one after another the women shrieked, whooped and cackled. Macy rolled her eyes. Oh, good foot-in-mouth grief, she thought as the laughter continued.

"And just how big is it?" The obvious question finally came from Sydney—proper, genteel Sydney, of all people.

"I was talking about his scar. But you can forget it. Just forget it. I'm not saying another word." Judging by the burning heat, Macy's face had to be bright cherry red. "You want anything else, you'll have to wait for Melanie to give up Jess's secret."

"Yeah, Mel. What happened to Jess?" Kinsey prodded, giving Macy a quick wink.

"He'll kill me for this, but…it seems he got talked

into posing as Michelangelo's *David* for a drawing class at the Art Institute. The instructor, the wife of one of his co-workers, I think it was, asked if he'd mind shaving his chest.''

Melanie fought to keep a straight face, but burst out with a side-splitting laugh, shouting, ''So he did. And he cut himself shaving. We're talking four stitches, cut himself shaving.''

At least five full minutes passed before a single gIRL-gEAR partner could draw a breath without dissolving into a fit. Not that any of them wished harm to Jess, Macy knew. But the picture of the incredibly introverted Mr. Buff and Gorgeous requiring stitches? After shaving?

How had anyone talked him into stripping down in front of an art class, anyway? And how had he kept the incident quiet for so long? Trust Melanie—

''Ladies! Now that we've all had our fun at Jess's expense, let's finish up this meeting.'' With Sydney's request and a round of deep cleansing breaths behind them, the women settled down and got back to their notes.

''I know it's hard to get jazzed about winter and holiday fashions in February, but such is the makeup of our business. Now.'' Pen in hand, Sydney checked her notes. ''Looks like we're up to gIZMO gIRL.''

Melanie tucked two pillows in her lap and resituated her notebook computer. She adjusted the bright red headband holding back her shiny brunette hair, worked her glasses around until she was happy with their fit on her nose.

''Uh, anytime, Mel.''

Melanie stuck out her tongue at Macy, then turned to the group. ''Am I the only one here who feels like I'm never living in real time? That I exist in a strange sort of gIRL-gEAR vacuum? You know, that I'm sick of Christmas by the time Christmas gets here because I've been in Christmas mode for the past six months?''

"By the time Christmas gets here you should be in bikini mode," Sydney pointed out.

"I will never be in bikini mode, are you kidding? All that waxing?" Melanie shuddered.

And then, out of nowhere, Kinsey interjected, "I did it. Had a Brazilian wax done."

Sydney buried her face in her hands and moaned.

Melanie cried, "Yuck!"

Macy yelped and whimpered like a dog in pain.

Chloe, calm as always, simply said, "I'm sorry, but I don't have the urge to show off my ass in a thong badly enough to let someone pour wax down my crack."

"No one pours wax down your crack. It's more like...swabbed on." Kinsey screwed up her nose and made a paintbrush-to-canvas swabbing motion that mutated into an over-the-top, all-hands-on-deck action, and sent her into another fit of laughter.

"Swabbed down your crack, then." By now Chloe had resorted to her compact mirror to check the truth-in-advertising of her waterproof mascara. "And onto other places from which I don't even want to think about hair being ripped away. I prefer to shave, thank you."

More groans erupted. More whoops. More hollers. Another five minutes of hilarity before Melanie tapped the eraser of her pencil to the earpiece of her glasses. "I can't believe what we have to go through as women. Can you imagine what it must be like to be a man? To get up every day, run a razor over your face, shower, throw on a suit and go?"

"No hot rollers."

"No tweezers."

"No eyelash curler and no hot wax."

Macy waited for the others to finish, then shrugged. "Half the time I don't mess with more than mascara."

That earned her all the pillows Chloe and Kinsey could throw. Macy ducked until the bombardment fizzled, finally looking up to find four glares aimed her way. "What did I say?"

Melanie stage-whispered from behind the back of one hand, "I think it had something to do with the mascara."

"Exactly. Not all of us are lucky enough to have hair that naturally looks like we spent hours with a stylist." This from Sydney, who wore her dark-blond hair in elegantly sleek chignons to match her elegantly sleek temperament.

"And not all of us have skin that wouldn't know the meaning of a zit or a T-zone." The comment came from Chloe who, in her position as head of gRAFFITI gIRL's skin-care line, was the resident expert on zits and T-zones.

Macy crawled out from under the pillows to sit on the arm of the red-and-yellow plaid chair. "Maybe not, but then the rest of you have one big thing I don't." She held up two fingers. "Make that two things."

"I know, I know," Kinsey yelled and, in unison with Melanie and Chloe, cried out, "Boobs!"

Sydney gave up, sank down to the sofa and knocked her forehead repeatedly against the portfolio now folded across her knees.

Chloe admired her new manicure in a light spring green. "And most of us don't have to resort to decorative scribbling to draw attention to our assets."

Macy gasped at the indignity of it all. "My tattoo is not about drawing attention. It's about self-expression."

''Yeah. Expressing that you need attention.''

''I do not need attention. If I did, you can bet this tattoo would be down the side of my neck and not hidden under my shirt where there's nothing to see.'' Macy jumped to her feet and pulled down the straps of her tank top so that everyone would know she was not seeking attention.

And there at the head of the hallway that lead to his temporary quarters in Lauren's old rooms stood Leo Redding.

He wore a scowl like Macy had never seen him wear, and not much else. Nothing on the top half of his body, nothing on his legs or feet. And his long-legged briefs in dynamite red left little to anyone's imagination.

''There may not be much to see,'' Leo growled. ''But there's a hell of a lot to hear.''

Macy pulled her straps back over her shoulders, feeling reprimanded and strangely self-conscious, then telling herself to get over it. This was her house. He was only a visitor. His opinion didn't matter. She didn't give a flip what he thought. *Do, too! Do not! Do, too! Do not!*

''Why Leo, sugar.'' Chloe reclined on the few remaining pillows, looking like a queen waiting to be served. ''I would never have guessed that red is your color, but is it ever.''

Macy circled around the back of her chair and approached her scavenger hunt partner, because that's all he was. That's all he was! Her temporary roommate and scavenger hunt partner. And if Chloe didn't close her mouth...

Macy hadn't known herself capable of possessing such a jealous streak until it shot its pointed, dartlike end straight into her heart. She took him by the upper arm, her fingers coming nowhere close to making a dent in his bicep.

"Trust me," she whispered, and guided him back down the hallway and out of the sight of prying eyes. Once in Lauren's room, Macy let him go, reluctantly, unsure whether to stay and make the group's apologies as well as her own, or to walk away and leave him.

She didn't want to leave him.

She didn't want to walk away.

He made the choice an easy one because he made it for her. He pulled on a pair of gray jersey shorts and a plain white T-shirt, shoved his feet, sans socks, into running shoes. "Trust you? To do what? Tell your girlfriends everything you've learned about me? See if I'm good for a laugh?"

"Leo, it's not like that at all."

"Oh?" He recklessly stuffed notepads and folders and two thick law books into his satchel. "You think I should relay that info to Ray and Jess?"

Macy crossed her arms over her chest. "If you were eavesdropping, which obviously you were, then you know I didn't say a word about you."

He hefted the satchel and made for the door.

"Leo, please stop."

When he paused, she spoke to his rigid back. "So we shared our scavenger hunt finds. What's the big deal? You can't tell me guys don't gossip over a cold beer. Besides, Jess and Ray are like family. We love them. We'd never share their secrets with outsiders."

"What about my secrets?" He slowly turned, his glare touchingly vulnerable. "I'm not a part of the family. Will some stranger be talking about my 'big one' over a cold beer next week?"

He'd heard her gaffe in explaining about his scar.

Which meant he'd heard enough to know she'd been talking about his scar, damn it. Now what? Macy tried for a casual shrug. "You told me once that size doesn't matter."

"Well, I was wrong, wasn't I?"

"Wrong?"

"Dead wrong. It seems we both were. Because we've just proved that three-thousand square feet isn't enough living room for two people, now, haven't we?" With a mocking nod, he swung around and headed for the elevator.

By the time she found her voice, the motor's hum announced his swift descent.

Funny how her own stomach dropped to her toes.

COMING TO THE OFFICE had sounded like a good idea an hour ago, Leo thought, staring at a point between the far edge of his desk and the closed door across the room. Slumped back in his chair, one ankle squared over the opposite knee, he mindlessly rolled the barrel of his pen up and down the legal pad propped on his thigh. He wasn't getting a damn thing accomplished.

It was all *her* fault.

At the loft, his concentration had been cracked by the pecking of ten thousand hens. Feathers ruffled, he'd barged into the coop, prepared to demand silence—only to be met with the same. Immediate and total. Not a cackle. Not a peep. At least not until the flock started in on his underwear...

His frustration level already hovered at an all-time high. The eye-popping stares, the clucks and the twitters, had splintered his thin shell of patience. Unable to face another frustration on top of his inability to keep his mind on work and his hands off Macy, he'd taken flight.

And now here he was, as disturbed by the lull as he had been by the storm.

It was all *her* fault.

He picked up the pen, sketched the head, the beak and the eye of a chicken, added a comb and feathers, penciled in the wings, the breast and a Celtic tattoo. Funny how five women had the capability of sounding like fifty. Or maybe what was funny was the way he'd strained to hear Macy's voice above the others.

Of course, the funniest thing was that none of this was funny at all. Macy Webb had turned his world upside down. And for the first time in his life, he was at a loss as to how to fix what never should've been able to break.

His concentration. His focus. His single-minded drive for success.

How had this moppet of a woman, this wild child, this little girl all grown up, made such a mess of his life? No. How had she managed to get *him* to make such a mess of his life? Playing silly kid games that weren't even a means to an end. Partying with no purpose but to have fun. Living in a madhouse run on no schedule but that dictated by Macy's whims.

It was all *her* fault.

Why had he ever thought he'd get any work done living—even temporarily—at her place, in an atmosphere that crossed a carnival with a cartoon? Look at him now. Paperwork shoved into his satchel without a care for organization. Gray jersey sweat shorts over his red cotton knit boxers. A plain white undershirt. Hightop Nikes, untied, no socks.

There wasn't a member of his firm who wouldn't think him off his rocker if they caught him in the office looking like the dragged-in leftovers of a thousand cats. He couldn't name a single woman he'd dated who wouldn't pay cash to get a good look at how far he'd fallen from the standards he'd held so high.

Using bold capital letters, he scratched the word *LOSER* across the top of the legal pad, then returned to the chicken and filled in the feathered details, outlined a pair of clogs over the three-toed feet, drew a pair of knee-length pants over the legs.

If only his father could see him now. The son who'd never disappointed, who'd never failed, who'd followed the footsteps so precisely measured and positioned along the path to success. The son who'd gone on to lose his mind over a woman as unsuitable as the mother who'd rebelled against the life his father had demanded she live.

Rebel. The word described Macy from the piercings in her ears right down to the flannel pajamas she insisted qualified as business casual. Leo snorted. Flannel pajamas weren't even bedroom casual...except he couldn't see Macy wearing anything else when she crawled into his bed.

She was like no woman he'd ever known, and he didn't know what to do with her. Women didn't wear Walt Disney underwear. Women didn't eat pancakes with their fingers, licking away sticky syrup while laughing at his over-the-breakfast-table stories. Women didn't sleep with an entire plush zoo of endangered species, in the glow of a dozen night-lights, beneath iridescent starfish pasted to a ceiling painted to look like the ocean floor.

Leo groaned. He wished he'd never stepped foot in her bedroom. She'd tempted him to swim in her dangerous waters, coaxed him to dive headfirst into the unknown. He'd done both, only to sink to the bottom like a stone. And now he was drowning in confusion.

He'd screwed up in a big way, wasted a lot of time playing her childish games. He was no better off now, no further ahead today than he'd been three weeks ago, he realized, studying the rooster he'd drawn wearing a studded choke collar, restraints around both ankles and a long leather leash.

In fact, he'd obviously taken a big step in reverse, judging by the caliber of notes on his notepad. Another hour had passed and what did he have to show for his time but a funky chicken and her henpecked cock?

"Leo?"

He looked up sharply to see Macy standing in his doorway, rubbing the toe of one chunky black boot over the calf of the opposite leg. He hadn't even heard the door open. Hell, he hadn't even heard her knock.

"Is this a bad time?" she asked.

His gut knotted. He shook his head, tossed the pad onto his desk, lobbed the pen on top and watched it slide to a stop between the two birds. He turned his attention to Macy, turned the pad facedown while answering, "I've done all the damage I can for tonight."

She smiled shyly, pushed back the hair from the right side of her face, repeated the gesture on the left. "I wouldn't have come except that I wanted to apologize. For the noise and all. We sorta got...out of control." She scrunched up her nose. "I'm sorry."

They'd more than *sorta* gotten on his nerves, but he shrugged it off and relaxed against the high leather back of his chair. He was much more interested in the here and now. "How'd you get in? How'd you know where I'd gone?"

Her fingers fluttered near her waist. She twisted her hands together. Her body language told the apprehensive truth her steady voice concealed. "You're fairly predictable, Leo. If you're not at the gym, you're at the office. That is, when you're not at home.''

Home. The knot tightened, drew into a ball of twisted, tangled nerves.

''Besides,'' she quickly added, before he could remind her and himself that he was nothing but a temporary guest, ''I followed you.''

He kept his hands on the chair's armrests. His fingers gouged deep dimples into the rich brown cordovan leather. With a concentrated effort, he managed to keep from asking why when his body was already stirring with the need to know.

''That's the thing about these old renovated buildings.'' She took one tentative step into the office. ''The builders like to use what they can of the original fixtures.'' She took a second, bolder step. ''The door downstairs didn't latch all the way, so I invited myself in. I was hoping you wouldn't mind.'' She took her third step, the bravest yet, bringing her far enough inside to close the door behind her. ''Do you?''

''Do I what?'' He didn't even remember what she'd been saying. He only knew she was here and that he was supposed to breathe.

''Do you mind that, technically, I committed a breaking-and-entering sort of crime?'' She shrugged both shoulders, tilted her head to one side. ''You being an upholder of the law and all.''

He waved off her worry. ''I should've made sure the door was latched.''

''It's latched now.''

''Good.'' It was all he could say as she leaned her light weight back against his heavy office door.

Her small shoulders and slim hips weren't even as wide as one of the decorative panels. She was a child.

She was a woman. She was everything he wanted and all that he'd learned in life to avoid.

"Anyway, I came here to apologize for the noise."

"You did that."

"Oh, right. I did, didn't I?"

Her anxiousness intrigued him. He'd never known Macy to be anything but full steam ahead when it came to letting him know what she wanted. "It's your place, Macy. You can be as loud as you want."

"Well, you're living there, too. I just keep forgetting you haven't been there as long as Lauren. It took awhile for her to get used to my..." Macy gestured loosely with one hand, then tucked the fingers of both into the back pockets of her green fatigues. "My need for noise, I guess you could say."

"You *need* that noise?" he asked, when the question he really wanted answered was how she could possibly forget how long he'd been living in the loft when he'd been there a matter of days.

Again came the scrunched-up nose. "It's not the noise as much as the interaction. The...company."

The company. Now this he'd been wondering about. This thing she had for surrounding herself with people— or sea life—twenty-four hours a day. "I don't see how you get anything done in that zoo."

"I was the youngest of six kids, Leo. I grew up in a zoo." She smiled when she said it, so he knew resentment wasn't an issue.

He picked up his pen, drummed the ball point against the legal pad's cardboard backing. "Still...you can't tell me the racket isn't a distraction."

This time she chuckled—a quiet sound, as if she didn't expect him to understand. "Silence is a bigger one. I've never known anything but noise. I've never had the sort of privacy and quiet time others take for granted.''

''Or demand.'' He must've sounded like the jackass he looked, stomping into the barnyard wearing nothing but those damn red boxers.

''At least your methods are effective. I can't remember a staff meeting ever ending on such a climactic note.'' She let her eyes drift shut, let her shoulders relax, let her head fall back against the door. And she did it all while wearing an expression that was nothing if not purely angelic. ''It was almost…spiritual.''

He blew out a huff and dropped the pen again. She could tease and flirt and go all dreamy-eyed until the cows came home. He was not going to let her get to him. ''Spiritual's taking it a bit far.''

''Maybe not.'' She leveled her gaze on him then, and damn it, why did she have to have those eyes that saw so much and so clearly? Saw beyond the facade he was struggling to keep in place. ''I specifically remember you telling me how good you are. Surely you've inspired a religious experience or two.''

He looked at her then and looked closely, searching for the wild child, but seeing only a woman who knew what she wanted. This wasn't Macy at play. This was more. Macy with intent. Macy on fire. Macy at her grown-up best.

Hell. The last hour spent chewing himself out? A big fat waste. Leo totally screwed over by the horse he'd rode in on. He'd be walking funny until he got this woman out of his life.

He picked up the pen one more time and righted the legal pad, adjusting his glasses and his frame of mind. ''I have to get back to work. Was there something in particular you needed?''

By now she had her arms crossed over her chest and her trademark glare of intense scrutiny turned up high. "You don't like talking about yourself much, do you?"

He didn't talk about himself. Or at least he hadn't, not to anyone the way he had to Macy. And right now he wasn't in the mood for one of her silly pop-psychology sessions. "I don't need to talk about myself. My work does it for me."

"Your work tells others about the kind of attorney you are. It doesn't say anything about Leo Redding the man."

She was wrong, but he didn't want to expend his pent-up energy on an argument. Or even on a conversation. He tossed his pen back to the desk, spun his glasses across the same surface. If she wanted a fight, he'd give her one.

He leaned back, his elbows on the chair arms, and laced his fingers across his middle. "You want to know about Leo the man? Bring your ass over here."

"I am not coming over there."

One brow lifted in a dare. "Why not?"

"I think you know."

The other brow called her a chicken and arched even higher. "Afraid of getting naked?"

"No. I'm not afraid of getting naked." She stepped away from the door, stood, feet apart, in the center of his office and whipped her camouflage tank top over her head. She dropped it to the floor.

"And, no. I'm not afraid of you, either." Balancing flamingo-style, first on one foot, then the other, she made quick work of bootlaces and socks. "But there is one thing that scares me."

Leo thought he'd swallowed his tongue, because he couldn't find it to speak. "Hmm?"

Buckles and zippers undone, she shimmied out of her fatigues. "I am afraid, if you ask, I won't be able to tell you no."

Earlier she'd been bare beneath her top. Now she was wearing the leopard-print bra, what there was of it, which on Macy wasn't a hell of a lot. But it was still more than enough to pique the interest he kept in his pants. He didn't know whether to groan or growl or grovel. "So I won't ask."

"Good," she said, and produced a smile the likes of which he'd never before seen—an angel and a devil in one wicked sweetheart of a grin. "Because I don't want to blame anyone but myself for what I'm about to do."

His mind pictured dozens of possibilities.

His body only cared about one.

He kept his legs spread, kept his hands laced over his belly. She took a step forward, took another, took one more, slid a bra strap from one shoulder while she walked. She drew closer, reached for strap number two, worked it and worked it until his lower body screamed at him to get rid of his shorts.

Damn sexy woman. Damn leopard-print lingerie. Not good for anything but stripping away, which he was going to do if she didn't.

She stopped at the edge of his desk and looked down. He swiveled his chair to the side and looked up. A tense moment of nothing but edgy anticipation simmered in the boxy space keeping them apart.

The wait was making him crazy. His heart pounded, his blood rushed hot, his inner caveman grunted. He was seconds away from grabbing her hair and dragging her down to his grotto when she saved him from his primitive Neanderthal urgings by dropping to her knees between his legs.

Her hands stroked their way beneath his boxers. Her short nails softly scraped the skin of his thighs. He wanted nothing more than to arch his hips upward, but he held back...back to waiting, back to grunting...while Macy trailed her fingertips over the center of his groin, measuring his length, finding the ridge between shaft and head and drawing circles there until he shuddered.

"You like?"

"You have to ask?" He ground out the question, aching to strip, himself first and then her, to hook his fingers in those dangling straps and take her bra the rest of the way down, to rid her of the patch of leopard print between her legs, to lift her onto his lip and let her ride his wild animal.

She chuckled. "I thought I should. I wouldn't want to step on your toes. Again."

Again? Oh, right. "Feet. You were dancing on my feet."

"That wasn't the first time, you know. That you supported my weight."

"There's not a lot of you to support, Macy."

She shrugged carelessly, her hair brushing her shoulder on one side as she tilted her head. Her shoulder straps sagged lower and Leo moved his hand from his belly to the arms of his chair. The leather armrests would never be the same.

With a heavy-lidded look from beneath long sultry lashes, she said, "I wasn't sure if you remembered. That other time you held me. In the shower."

Who in the hell was she kidding? And why the hell was she talking? "You think I'd forget something like that?"

"I would hope you wouldn't. But you haven't mentioned it since."

Women. Had to talk. Had to analyze. Had to make a man work for a blow job. "I mentioned it while we were dancing."

"No. I mentioned it while we were dancing." She leaned forward, parted her lips and blew a stream of hot damp breath from the base of his cock to the head.

Leo's eyes rolled neatly back before he managed to squeeze them shut. When he found the control to open them, he looked down into Macy's waiting eyes and knew she wasn't ready to let the conversation go.

"I thought maybe you wanted to forget it ever happened. That time, and the time when we were dancing. Since you haven't had much to say. Then. Or since."

"Can we save the talking about not talking for another time?"

Her hand delved between his legs. "Sure."

"Good, because right now I can think of a dozen better uses for your mouth." He shifted in his chair, allowing her the access she was seeking. The space he was growing desperate for her to take advantage of.

"Hmm." She leaned down and hummed the same sound where her previous wash of warm breath still lingered. Then, just when he thought his dream would come true, she was back to talking.

"The thing is, Leo. Both of those times? In the shower and when we danced? Things got a little rushed."

"You seemed to have fun at the time." He refused to give in to the tug of performance anxiety. He knew Macy had had fun both times.

"Oh. I did have fun." She sat back on her heels, cocked her head to one side. "But I got to thinking that you were probably right. And that there's a lot to be said for appetizers."

He'd feed her as much as she wanted to eat. "So what are you waiting for? A menu?"

"Maybe an invitation."

He lifted his hips just enough to shuck off his jerseys and his drawers. "Consider yourself invited."

11

THE NEW OFFICES of Thomas, Williams & Whyte, Attorneys-at-law, occupied an entire floor of prime downtown real estate. One story up, the partners had leased space and outfitted an efficiency apartment.

The suite was available to any of the firm's attorneys whose cases kept them working long into the night. The kitchen and shower facilities had seen a fair amount of use since the move to the new location. The bedroom, less action. At least as far as Leo knew. Which is what he'd told Macy when he'd piggybacked her upstairs.

After he'd regained his strength from the incredible work she'd done with her mouth, if she did say so herself.

The feel of his abs at work beneath her bare legs had made the trip up the staircase to the bedroom worth the awkward effort. The elevator between floors they'd avoided. Leo couldn't be sure he was the only one putting in an evening's overtime. He'd had the courtesy, too, to pick up the clothes she'd discarded once he'd righted his own pair of shorts.

Macy kind of liked him better in the altogether. He had an awesome body. Not that he was built differently than her previous lovers. But he was built better. From her female perspective, anyway. Thick where thickness counted. Tilted and angled where tilt and angle made a difference. But more than anything, it was his sensitivity that set him apart.

And not in the way he saw to her comfort and her pleasure—though both, she'd learned, he considered high priority. No, this was about the way he jumped at her touch. The way he twitched from the pressure of her fingers, shuddered from the light butterfly flicks of her tongue.

Not to mention the way he'd nearly torn the arms from his office chair when she'd explored between his legs, zeroing in on the strip of skin where thigh met groin. When she'd scraped a blunt nail over the spot, when she'd drawn on the skin with her lips and lightly nipped, his groans had deepened, rolling up from his belly in a visceral wave.

She'd liked the response so much that she tried it again now, with Leo flat on his back, knees raised and spread. She pushed against the back of his thighs and opened his legs wider. It spoke of his level of trust that he allowed her free access to his most intimate and tender and awe-inspiring body parts.

She never wanted another woman to know what she knew about Leo. She wanted him for herself. A playground designed for her recreation. A treasure chest fulfilling her fantasies. A prized possession procured for her pleasure. Except Leo Redding was not a boy toy. And the fun and games were no longer quite so free of care and consequence.

"Uh, Macy?"

"Hmm?" Her mouth was too busy to do any real talking.

"It's probably a good idea if you stop." Leo sucked in a long hissing breath.

She hated to, truly she did. She enjoyed making him

squirm. Raising her head bare inches, she asked, "You sure?"

"Yes. I'm sure. Oh. Good. Stop. Now. Macy."

The next best thing to rendering him speechless, his short, choppy, breathless words were their own reward. Besides, she wasn't quite ready to finish him yet.

Leaving him thoroughly and intimately kissed, she bounced around in the bed and ended up sitting crossed-legged near the end. "Your wish is my command."

"Thank you," he choked out, levering himself up farther against the headboard.

"You're welcome." Macy slid off the foot of the bed, wrapping up toga-style in the sheet and leaving Leo bare. She couldn't think of anything she'd rather see than Leo bare. "The popcorn's getting cold."

She reached for the bag she'd popped earlier and, at the end of Leo's grand tour, set on the Swedish armoire. The tour had stopped in the bedroom, where they'd both agreed that the presence of a bed demanded total nudity and more sex.

And, well, she wasn't to be held solely responsible for the turn things had taken from there.

Plopping back onto the bed, she lost her grip on the sheet and decided to hell with it. If Leo could boldly lounge in all his naked glory, she wasn't going to go virginal over showing a bit of pink skin.

"Now. Back to the scavenger hunt." She settled the bag of popcorn in the bowl of her crossed legs. Leo would have to come close if he wanted to snack. "I still have most of my list left and it's barely a week until game night."

She didn't mention that she hadn't started planning for the next gIRL gAMES column. Inspiration was sure to strike in the next few days. Then again...inspiration was striking now.

She had both prime man and prime opportunity, and surely she could come up with something kinky and fun. Leo's breathing had calmed and his erection had moved from the batter's box back to the on-deck circle. A lick of her lips and he'd be ready to swing. Naked bedroom baseball. Sydney would croak.

Leo scooted down to lie flat on his back, using half of the sheet Macy had dropped to cover his lap. Then he crossed both arms behind his head and studied her from the comfort of his makeshift throne.

"So, what do you need to know?"

Mouth full of popcorn, she mumbled, "About baseball?"

"Baseball? No. Earth to Macy. What's left on your scavenger hunt list?"

Wow. "Just like that?"

"Why not? I don't think I have a lot left to hide." His quick glance swept the length of his prone body, then her naked top half.

Macy suffered an unexpected twinge of self-consciousness. Unexpected because together they'd taken their sex play where she'd never taken any relationship that had yet to be defined. And nervousness had chosen now to lift its head?

"Okay, then." She hitched up the edge of the sheet and tucked it beneath both armpits. Then, tossing back a handful of popcorn, she considered her subject material from all available angles while she munched.

The corner of the sheet at Leo's hip drew her attention. "How'd you get that scar?"

Leo tucked his chin to his chest and looked at the

faded railroad of stitching making tracks down his hip. "Adolescent immortality."

"Hmm. A bicycle. No, a skateboard. You seem more the skateboarding type." Macy reached out and measured the scar with the span of her fingers. Then she chugged her fingertips down the length, making "choo-choo" noises along the way.

"What exactly is the skateboarding type?"

"Willing to risk life and limb for fun."

Leo arched an arrogant brow, which only encouraged Macy's playful nature. She caught the edge of the sheet in the crook of an index finger caboose and tugged until she exposed his thatch of dark hair and a tempting hint of the loose skin that would tighten so easily at her touch.

She loved the way a man's skin could be as soft and pink as a woman's. The way it took no more than a kiss, or a light brush of hand or breast, to stir his interest and his blood. And then, oh, but she loved the differences.

"Are you having fun down there?"

Macy smiled at Leo's interruption of what was a curiously distracting exploration. "When was the first time you had sex?"

"Alone or with a woman?"

She flung the sheet back up over his lap, then gave him her best imitation of holier-than-thou. "Very funny."

Leo considered her intently, his eyes, free from the barrier of lenses and frames, bright on her face. She felt the heat of a rising blush and decided enough was enough. She didn't like the fact that, with only a look, he made her squirm.

And so she backhanded him. Only lightly and only on the thigh. "Stop doing that."

"What? Looking at you?"

"It's the way you look at me. It's too...I don't know. Intense." Too searching and serious and frighteningly close to seeing beneath her skin. "What are you looking for, anyway?"

He shoved another pillow between his back and the headboard and settled in to get serious. "You don't want intense? We're naked, in bed, and you don't want intense?"

What should she tell him?

That intense resonated with the suggestion of commitment? That she was having too much fun to analyze where this *thing* was going? That the contract of a relationship scared her to death?

She wasn't ready. Didn't know if she'd ever be ready. Not for the stress of balancing two careers. For the battle of quality versus quantity time with family. For the struggle of making ends meet when ends had been at polar opposites for longer than either partner could remember.

"Macy?"

Leo's tone was soft, but it brought her attention up sharply. Oh, good melancholy grief. Zoning out over unrealized fears when she had a gorgeous naked man waiting for her to pounce? What was she thinking?

Lifting a saucy brow, she gave three quick tugs to the corner of the sheet. She liked it a lot that he didn't stop her. "I want intense. Just not when you look at me."

"So...I can touch, but I can't look? Is that it?"

She pretended to contemplate his question, when all she wanted to do was get out from under his scrutiny and back to the fun and sex games. This business of being grown-up was way too much pressure.

Leo continued to stare, then shook his head as if rid-

ding himself of a daze. "You have to be the most con-
tradictory woman I've ever known."

"Glad you noticed." She reached for another piece
of popcorn. "The woman part, anyway."

"Why wouldn't I notice? I do have two working
eyes."

"That hasn't stopped you from calling me a child."

"I don't remember calling you a child."

"You've accused me of playing around too much."

He shifted his hips beneath what was left of the sheet.
"And here I was thinking you're not playing around
enough."

"You don't say."

"I do say."

"Well," she began, picking through the popped corn
for the few barely burst kernels. "Playing around is a
lot more fun when I have something to play with."

Leo flexed mysterious male muscles so that the sheet
in his lap popped up and down and did his talking for
him.

"Very cute. You and your built-in plaything." She
tossed a single piece of popcorn toward his face.

He caught it, chameleonlike. "Glad you enjoyed it."

"I have been enjoying it. Faking is not a specialty of
mine." She tossed another popped kernel. He missed,
and missed the next two as well. "Tongue out of prac-
tice?"

"Mine or yours?"

This time she tossed an entire handful, one rapid-fire
piece at a time. He dodged and ducked, eyes and mouth
both closed. Her one-sided food fight quickly ran its
course, though Leo waited a few seconds, peeking out
to see if the coast was clear before asking, "Are you
finished?"

Her bag was almost empty, and even she didn't relish the thought of rolling between sheets littered with salt and popcorn tidbits. She glanced from the bag to the mess with twenty-twenty hindsight. "I suppose so."

"You plan to clean this up, I hope."

What a crank, she thought, and frowned...though he really was cute, naked, rumpled and now littered with edible munchies. Suddenly, "clean up" sounded like dirty work of the very best kind.

She heaved a sigh, as if falsely put upon. "I guess I'll have to. I don't see you doing anything about it."

Leo did nothing and said nothing. He just sat back, all arrogant, cocky male beast, waiting to be both serviced and served.

Macy refused to analyze why she wanted to do both. It was a purely primal tug—it had to be—pulling at the threads of arousal he tightened with nothing more than a look. Oh, but she was asking for trouble, assuming she had the strength of resolve to keep this casual and all about fun.

Keeping the sheet between male skin and female, she scrambled onto her knees and crawled forward, making a huge production out of an effortless endeavor. Anticipation warmed her belly before drifting lower with breath-stealing heat, tickled her toes before working upward to tease the tender skin between her thighs.

The first piece of popcorn she found lodged in the bend of Leo's elbow. She kissed it away, making sure not to touch his skin with lips or tongue or even with teeth. The next piece she vacuumed from the center of his chest with her mouth. The third she wet with the tip of her tongue and lifted from the pillow beneath his ear.

When she released her hold on the sheet and let it drop enough to expose her upper body, Leo shifted where he lay beneath her weight. When she brushed the points of her breasts through the swirls of hair on his chest, he growled deep in his throat.

When she moved to straddle him completely, leaned forward and touched her tongue to a flat male nipple in her quest for popcorn, he reached back and slapped her lightly on the rump.

Macy's tongue stilled where it was on his chest. Resisting a wicked urge to leave him wearing the mark of her teeth, she sat back on his thighs, enjoying the press of his erection to her belly. "No, thanks. I'm not into spanking."

"Too bad," he said, and she stuck out her tongue before he added, "How about wearing a lacy apron? Like a sexy French maid?"

"I would not wear a lacy apron even if you beg."

He let her Dr. Seuss-ish rhyme fly by without comment. "Leather crops and spiked heels out of the question?"

She shook her head. "This is the extent of my domination. Woman on top."

"Hmm. Let's see here. Nursery rhymes and jokes. Food fights and scavenger hunts." Leo pressed his lips into a thoughtful line, lifted a thoughtful brow, made a comment Macy didn't find thoughtful at all. "I think you're a fake, Macy Webb. And I think you're scared."

Anticipation chugged down the drain as swiftly as it had filled the well of her soul. "What do you mean, a fake? And what do I have to be scared of?"

He lifted his knees behind her, fencing her in between the pickets of his thighs and his arousal. "You might write about adult fun, but for some reason you don't have it in you to play anything but kid games. You want to tell me why?"

His eyes dared her. His naked eyes, beautifully clear without the obstruction of his glasses, dared her to refute his challenge, to prove him wrong. Prove that playing Peter Pan was not a destructive fantasy, that living in never-never land was not a defense designed to avoid the real world.

Okay. Maybe it was both. So what? It wasn't like she didn't have her reasons. Reasons she didn't have to share with a man who'd made no promises or offers. Who'd never suggested they prolong their scavenger hunt partnership. Who'd had the nerve to call her a kid minutes after calling her a woman.

"No, I don't want to tell you why. As a matter of fact, I don't want to tell you anything. Ever. Again." What a pig, thinking he'd figured her out! And she'd come so close to uttering the dreaded "L" word. She felt as if she'd swallowed a big fat stupid pill.

Grabbing for the edge of the dangling sheet, she wrapped up in a toga-style again and scooted to the edge of the bed. She slid onto her feet and bent down for her bra and panties...and felt a tug on the sheet. And then an even sharper tug. And then heard the sound of fabric ripping. She straightened where she stood, started to turn. The sheet ripped further.

She paused. She turned. *Rip!*

Paused. Turned. *Rip!*

She waited...waited...whipped all the way around. "Are you doing that on purpose?"

Sitting on the edge of the bed, one bare leg dangling over the side, the other bent at the knee and braced on the mattress, a torn section of sheet held in each hand, he met her gaze.

"You *are* doing that on purpose!"

His answer echoed through the room, a loud rending

of new fabric. The next thing Macy knew, the sheet she held tucked to her breasts dangled waist to floor in a half-dozen strips. She looked down at the shredded sheet, glanced back up. "You're going to pay for that, I hope?"

He still didn't answer, didn't breathe a word or sound. What he did was get to his feet and, in all his naked glory, reach out, pick her up and bodily return her to the bed.

She flopped and bounced against the pillows, still holding the intact portion of the sheet around her upper body, her legs exposed in places, covered in others, a mummy half-unraveled.

And then it came to her what Leo had planned. She saw it in the heat of his eyes, the flare of his nostrils, the determined set of mouth and jaw. In the way his arousal stiffened and rose as he moved back to sit on the bed.

He took her right ankle in his hand, wrapped one of the sheet strips twice around, then tied the loose end to the footboard railing. Her right wrist was next. He twisted the middle of another white cotton strip like a long gauze bandage just below her forearm, then looped the tail end around a spindle of the headboard and fixed it tight.

Then, getting to his feet, he walked around the foot of the bed, not bothering to look back to see if she stayed where he'd left her, to see if she went to work releasing her bonds. It was as if he knew she wouldn't move, that she'd do what he wanted because the time had come to play his game, his way.

Another minute and she was spread-eagled and bound without complaint. The unused sheet strips draped in a strangely strategic pattern across her lower body. Her top half remained loosely covered, though the way Leo now stood at the foot of the bed and studied his handiwork led her to believe he was about to adjust the sheet to maximize her exposure.

She was outwardly calm, but inwardly wild to know what he had on his mind. Nerves sizzled where the bindings snugged comfortably to her skin. The air and Leo's gaze touched flesh so provocatively exposed, teased body parts barely covered.

She wasn't even thinking of struggling against her bonds. She couldn't find a single witty remark to make. Or a smart-ass comment to toss his way. All she wanted to do was spread her legs wider and lift her hips. All she could do was wait while her own desire reached unbearable heights. All she regretted was that she'd been about to walk out on this man.

Leo moved onto the foot of the bed. The mattress dipped beneath his weight. The warmth of his body spread to cover her like a blanket of baby-fine wool, and she felt her bonds loosen. Not the bonds tying her to the bed; those she could slip free of with a simple twist of hand or foot.

No. These were the bonds providing a buffer of child-like innocence between her emotions and life's inevitable ills. She didn't need them now. Now, when she looked up at Leo, she saw him as she wanted to, through an adult's eyes. This time when they came together, this time Macy knew would be her defining moment as a woman making love to her man.

Leo had crawled up the length of her body and, when she met his gaze, moisture filled her eyes. She wanted desperately to wrap her arms around his neck, hold him close and whisper into his ear words best left unspoken.

But she couldn't do either because she was all tied

up. By the sheet, and by her certainty that he'd open his smart mouth and ruin her moment of bliss.

He knelt over her, skin brushing lightly on skin, and ran a finger the length of her nose. "I'm not sure I like that look on your face."

She squeezed her eyes shut. "Is this better?"

"No. It's not." He waited a few seconds. "Uh, Macy?"

"Go ahead. Have your way with me," she said from behind closed eyes.

"I plan to," he answered, and she shivered beneath him. "But I'm not moving a muscle until you open your eyes."

"You're going to get awfully tired of being on your hands and knees like that." His hands were wedged beneath her arms tied to the headboard. His knees rested between her thighs.

He leaned down and blew a stream of warm breath from her ear to her jawline and down her neck, then retraced the same path with the gently teasing tip of his tongue. "My game, Macy. My rules. You don't open your eyes, we don't play."

Ripples of arousing expectation left her breathless. She shuddered because she couldn't help herself. His words and his tongue and his demanding expectations made for a maddening male temptation.

She opened one eye.

He was waiting; looking down at her and waiting. "The other one, too."

She opened it. "Happy now?"

A wicked grin lifted the corners of his mouth. "A man always likes a woman who follows directions."

I'll follow you anywhere, she wanted to say, but managed to hold her tongue. "Now what?"

"Now I show you how I like to play."

"You shredded a sheet for that?"

"I had to be sure I had your attention. I want you here with me. I didn't want you walking away."

He wanted her with him. Did he mean now? For the moment? In this bed that belonged to neither of them? Or did he want to make their confidential liaison public? And permanent?

She made an attempt to lift both arms, then legs. "You made your point. I'm not going anywhere."

"Good," he said, and sat back on his heels. He took hold of both her ankles and slid her feet up the bed, toward her hips, bending her knees until he hit the end of her tether.

With the loose strips of sheet, one in each hand, he wrapped her thighs like barber poles, leaving much of her legs bared to his intentions, leaving his intentions in question. He had yet to move the sections of sheet draped front and center.

His smile should have scared her senseless and did— that arrogant way he had of smiling with his eyes, leaving his mouth free to speak, to tease. Or to do as he was now doing—running his tongue over the strips of inner thigh left exposed, slicking over the barest edges of the swollen folds of her sex.

If she'd been wearing any panties, by now she'd be in need of a refresher pair. Leo's mouth mated with her skin, one leg then the other, never quite making contact where she wanted contact, skirting the center of her body with his tongue, which swirled and flicked and licked her flesh with long hard strokes, his lips drawing, sucking....

Yes, yes. That was what she wanted. Just like that, there, closer, closer, please and deeper, yes, that's it, yes, right there, oh, right there. He followed her mental directions, and she worked to scoot her hips closer and lift them to better his access. She wanted to hold his head, to pull him closer, but her hands were tied and, damn it, she whimpered.

Leo looked up then, his eyes brightly wicked and amused. "Having fun yet?"

"Beyond bearable belief," she admitted, because she no longer wished to hold back sensation or her enjoyment of this man's magic.

"Good. Then my job here is done."

Macy wanted to beat him to a pulp. She wanted to scream. She wanted to come. Repeatedly. They had the time. Why was he making her wait? "You quit now and you're fired."

"Hmm. I've never been fired from this position." He cut off her claim of a first time for everything and stripped away the sheet from the top half of her body. Then he lowered his entire length and just enough of his weight to make her appreciate both his size and his restraint.

But he didn't do anything else. He just looked down into her face. His elbows, braced above her shoulders, supported most of his weight. His erection teased her, resting between her thighs with a patience Macy hated him for.

"If this is your idea of play, I have to say I'm not terribly impressed."

"Then let me impress you." He released the bonds holding one of her wrists and guided her hand between their bodies to wrap around his thick length. He kept his fingers around hers, stroking his sex within their joined grip. His release of lubricating fluid enhanced the motion, making for a slick simulation of what was to come.

Macy let him control the pressure, the speed, and refused to move her eyes. His face was a study in male arousal, his eyes brightly dazed, his lips parted, his breathing heavy and rough, tortured from his chest pressed hard to one side of hers.

"Okay. I'm sufficiently impressed."

He shook his head. "No. You need further impressing."

"Impress me by cutting me loose." She wanted to get her hands on his body, to wrap her legs around his hips and guide him. Not that he needed direction. But the bonds were making her crazy. "Leo, please?"

He thrust hard into her hand. "Please what?"

"Please untie my other hand."

"You're doing just fine with the one." He barely managed to spit out the words before he buried his face in her neck and groaned, a deep sound that had to come all the way from between his legs because she felt the rumble in the palm of her hand.

And then, his head still tucked in the crook of her neck, Leo moved his free hand down the side of the bed, jerked at her bonds and let her go.

She pulled free and moved both hands to his backside with no care to conceal her desperation. She tugged, insisting he resettle his lower body between her legs, where she scuttled beneath him and used her guiding hands to direct him, one pressing him from behind, one between their bodies again.

She wanted him and she wanted him now and she wasn't going to wait and she didn't give a flip how hard he was working for control because she wasn't going to last long enough for control to matter. Her body was ready, wet, wanting and wildly on edge. The restraints holding her ankles heightened the tension that had her chest aching as she strained to draw a full breath.

Chuckling, he filled her until she had no more room to fill. She blew, panted, struggled to find the calm before the storm. "Why are you laughing?"

"Because it's about damn time."

"What do you mean, about damn time? You were the one making me wait."

"Only until I was sure you were ready."

"I've been ready forever and you know it." *I've been ready for you all of my life*.

"I was waiting for you to show me." And then he raised up on his elbows and cradled her head in his palms and refused to release her gaze as he began to move, driving slowly forward, backing away, pushing deep and reaching the mouth of her womb.

Oh. Oh. The first wave of shudders were cresting. She rapidly panted to hold them back. "How much more of a show do you want?"

"Fourth of July?" he growled, took a shaky breath, and added, "New Year's Eve?"

She caught him deep inside, caught her voice before it cracked, caught the air her lungs desperately needed. He was glorious. He was hard and he filled her to bursting and he knew exactly where to press and where to stroke and how best to unmercifully tease.

"So, you want fireworks?"

"I want your fireworks."

She couldn't deny him a thing.

WHEN THE LOFT'S ELEVATOR ground to a stop and the door creaked and groaned open, Macy had just decided to invite Leo to cross the threshold into her room, to sleep in her bed for the rest of the night.

212
All Tied Up

But one step into the loft, with Macy close behind, Leo nearly tripped over the suitcases in the entryway, disturbing a distraught Lauren, who'd curled into a ball on the sofa. He blew out a long breath and stared at his feet, one hand at his hip, while the other ushered Macy past him and into the room.

She caught the barest glimpse of his expression in the dim light coming through the balcony doors. But it was enough. Oh, yes, it was enough. Frustration. Resentment. Annoyance. Regret. It was all there.

She didn't need a degree in psychology to know the camel's back had cracked beneath this latest disruption of what little routine Leo had realized here in never-never land.

It was all too much, this manic panic world of hers, and she withdrew her invitation because she knew. She knew. In her heart of hearts, she knew.

Leo was ready to go.

12

"MACY?" Lauren sang out from the loft's main room. "I'm sorry. I really didn't mean to run him off."

"Hey, who's my roommate anyway, huh?" Macy called back from where she stood in the kitchen, freezer door open, mocha-java swirl in one hand, chocolate–chocolate chip in the other, wondering whether one flavor would provide more seratonin-induced euphoria than the other.

Wondering, as well, if the frigid blast of air hitting her in the face was half as frosty as Leo's sudden exit. Or as arctic as the chilly look in his eyes when he'd announced his decision to move and move *now* into his condo, which had been ready for the past two days. Or as glacial as the cold shoulder he'd turned her way, making his intentions to walk out of her life perfectly ice-crystal clear.

Finding Lauren waiting when Macy and Leo had arrived back at the loft had come as a surprise to both of the lovers. Macy knew they looked like they'd been doing exactly what they'd been doing, having arrived home freshly shampooed and blow dried—an obvious sign of fooling around.

They'd both taken advantage of the apartment's shower, Leo offering Macy first run at the facilities while he repaired the damage they'd done to the bed. Once she was wet, her hair lathered up, and enjoying the beat of warm water on her skin, he'd slid back the curtain and joined her beneath the spray.

They'd spent the time in an oh-so-sexy soaping, yet hadn't lingered—whether Leo was in a hurry to get out of there before they were caught in the act or anxious to get her back to the loft and into bed proper, Macy didn't know.

Obviously he'd only been in a hurry to get the hell outta Dodge. All that stupid blather and hands-on education in adult fun had been another one of his attempts at one-upmanship.

Showing her that he was a better strategist than she could ever be. Making clear that their involvement was all about the game and nothing more. He hadn't even asked Lauren if she was all right, the insensitive jerk.

Standing here trying to figure out how she'd been duped into thinking she could compete on any sort of level playing field with Leo Redding was proving to be less than productive. The only thing Macy had to show for her obsessing was a frostbitten nose. Never mind the icicles with dagger points stabbing at her heart.

Why was she putting herself through all this misery? Tonight called for both flavors of ice cream. Two spoons and two pints in hand, she padded in her red-footed fireman pajamas back to the living room, offering Lauren first choice of the comfort food. "You choose."

Sitting in one corner of the sofa with a puffy crazy quilt tucked around her raised knees, Lauren sighed and held out a hand. "Does it really matter?"

"Nope, so let's go halfsies." Macy handed over the mocha java, hoarding the first of the chocolate. She settled onto the cushion next to Lauren's and appropriated the quilt's loose end.

"This really does suck," Lauren said, jabbing her spoon into the rock solid slab.

"Here, then. You take the chocolate." Maybe it wasn't the flavor, after all, Macy thought, watching Lauren jab, jab, jab. "You want me to soften it up in the microwave?"

"No." One more jab and the spoon bowed at a ninety degree angle. Lauren used the volcanic rock of the mocha java's flat surface to straighten out the bend. "I mean it sucks that two sexy, intelligent women would actually resort to drowning their sorrows in food."

"Speak for yourself. I have no sorrows." Having learned Lauren's lesson, Macy dragged the edge of the spoon across the solid chocolate, scraping off an edible ribbon. "But I would like to drown Leo, and Anton. For acting like such...men."

Lauren licked the back of her spoon after rubbing it over the ice cream's frozen surface. "Anton's too good of a swimmer. He's too good of an everything. I can't measure up."

"Why should you have to measure up? Why can't you be yourself?" Macy couldn't even rouse the enthusiasm to say, "I told you so." Because she hadn't really.

And even if she had, she obviously knew nothing about relationships and should've kept her mouth shut. The hand holding a spoonful of ice cream stopped halfway to her wide-open mouth. Had she and Leo even had a relationship?

"If you drop chocolate on my quilt, I'll smack you."

Macy shook her head and made quick work of the bite. "You can't. Smacking is against the rules."

"Obviously, I don't do well with rules or I would have made sure I *knew* Anton before I moved in. And who said men got to call all the shots, anyway? Are they special just because they have a penis?''

Macy raised a brow at the rhetorical question and waited for Lauren to come to her senses.

"I know. I know." Jab, jab, jab. "But it isn't fair."

"All is fair in love and scavenger hunts."

"Your damn scavenger hunt is the root of all evil." Lauren used her spoon to emphasize her point.

"I didn't know that then. I do now." Macy closed her mouth around a huge bite of chocolate and sighed. She didn't have a clue what she was going to do about the scavenger hunt and her column. She supposed she'd write it as planned, though she doubted she could dredge up either the energy or the enthusiasm.

"So, what did you find out about Leo?"

Besides the fact that he uses his mouth better than any man should be allowed? "His first pet was an Irish setter named Bandit. He has a scar on his hip from a skateboarding accident. He doesn't know how to play for the sake of fun. He only plays to win."

"All of that was on your list?"

"Not the last part."

"Did he win?"

"What was there to win?"

"Your heart."

This time the jab, jab, jab was Macy's. "My heart hasn't been involved in a relationship for over a year. I'll be fine. Let's talk about you."

Lauren pulled her spoon from her mouth, dragging it down her tongue in a long, slow, licking motion. "It's not Anton at all. It's totally me. One hundred percent."

Macy gave a vehement shake of her head. "No way. I know you and I know Anton and I know the two of you as a couple. Whatever's going on, he has to share the responsibility.''

''A couple of weeks ago, I would've agreed. But your scavenger hunt changed everything.'' As Macy watched, Lauren wiped her mouth on the long sleeve of her pink thermal top.

Lauren was using her top for a napkin. The world was coming to an end—and so was Macy's scavenger hunt. ''Remind me not to waste any more time on the idea. I am so going to scrap this column. Oh!''

''What?'' Lauren's eyes widened. ''What's wrong?''

''Have you talked to Sydney? Or to Chloe or Mel?''

''All of them at work. Why?''

''Are they all out to kill me? Have I ruined all five of our lives?'' Oh, good panic attack grief.

''Get a grip, Mace.'' Lauren shoved a foot against Macy's hip. ''You haven't ruined anyone's life. In fact, I owe you a big thanks.''

''Oh, right.'' She slumped even further down into the sofa. ''How can you even say that with what I've put you through?''

''What I'm trying to explain before you get all Ally McBeal on me is that I needed what you put me through.'' Lauren closed her eyes, opened them and took a deep, cleansing breath. ''When I was working to discover those things about Anton, I realized there were more than a few things I didn't know about myself.''

''Including the one certain quality driving you to commit?'' That particular list item had been a stroke of genius.

''Exactly. Panic isn't a very logical reason. Emotional, yes. But totally irrational.''

''What did you have to panic about?''

Lauren looked at Macy from beneath humbly lowered lashes. "Sex, if you really must know."

"Hmm. I thought I must. But now I think I mustn't."

"Ha!" Blowing a messy ice cream raspberry, Lauren licked her lips and added, "Even as often as you and I talk about men and sex, we've never talked about why we are the way we are."

Yes. Oh, yes. Macy did understand, after all. "You mean why I would let a man like Leo Redding, who is about as wrong for me as a man can get, tie me to a bed when I don't believe in sex being done *to* and not *with* another person?"

"Yes. That's it. And why—wait a minute." One hand went up like a stop sign. "Leo tied you to a bed?"

Macy nodded.

"And?"

"And it was fireworks."

Lauren tapped her spoon to her mouth as she thought. "Was that really because of the way you feel about sex? Or because of the way you feel about Leo?"

"I don't feel any way about Leo. I can't. You saw how he walked out of here. Why would I feel anything for a man that callous?"

"Because love doesn't make any sense," replied Lauren the Oracle of Love.

Macy was not going to think about Leo and love at the same time. "Do you still love Anton?"

"The question is did I ever love Anton? Or did I love the sex?" She lifted both shoulders in a shrug. "He let me do anything I wanted. He's strong and secure and my aggressive bedroom nature never threatened him. At least until he realized I've always had this, uh, problem. And that it wasn't only my response to him."

What a pair she and Lauren made, Macy thought,

reaching the halfway point of the chocolate–chocolate chip. She took one last bite, then shoved her spoon into the carton. "So, what are you going to do now?"

"I'm going to come home, if it's okay with you."

"Of course it's okay with me." As if Lauren should have to ask. "But what are you going to do about Anton?"

"Are we still together, you mean?"

"Yeah. I guess that's what I was wondering."

"Why? You want to try your luck with him?"

This time it was Macy who shoved her foot against Lauren's hip, then shoved again for good measure. "With Anton? Me? Are you kidding? Why would I break my own best-friend rules?"

"I guess that means you'll kick my butt if I go after Leo?" Lauren asked, fighting a teasing grin of evil proportions.

That was all it took. Lauren's one simple question. And Macy's couldn't fight her feelings anymore.

She was in love with Leo Redding.

The thought of Lauren with Leo, of any woman with Leo…Macy wasn't sure which was stronger—her desire to scratch out Lauren's eyes, or the need to go after Leo and fight for what was hers.

"Macy?"

Macy turned to her best friend. "Yeah. I think I would have to kick your butt."

Lauren tossed her head back and laughed maniacally. "I knew it. You've fallen in love with the man."

Macy nearly shook her head off her neck. "Don't say that."

"Why not? It's so obviously the truth."

"I don't want to love him. He's all wrong for me."

Lauren poked a pestering finger into Macy's shoulder.

"He's all right for you, or else kicking my butt would be the last thing on your mind."

"Oh, really, Miss Know-It-All." Macy narrowed her eyes. "And why is that?"

"Get real. You're about the size of a munchkin."

"A munchkin? I'll show you a munchkin." Macy launched herself the length of the sofa, ice cream and all. Lauren screeched, her spoon flying, her mocha-java swirl ending up a cold flattened mess between her chest and Macy's.

The two rolled off the sofa and onto the floor, where the hardwood suffered the brunt of the chocolate–chocolate chip. The floor *and* Macy's hair. Lauren giggled and slid a glob of ice cream all over Macy's shirt.

Macy was not about to be outdone in a cat fight. She grappled with Lauren, rolling into the coffee table, tumbling back to bump her head on the bottom of the sofa frame.

"Ouch."

She yelped and Lauren, blond hair a tangled mess, laughed and said, "Is that all you've got, Munchkin?"

"No. Actually I have this," Macy answered, her legs caught beneath Lauren's but her right hand free and full of chocolate–chocolate chip.

Lauren sputtered and spit and blew through the mess of melted milk product Macy mashed into her face. "Okay, okay. You win. You're not a munchkin."

Dripping from wrist to elbow, another scoop at the ready, Macy asked, "Is that an apology? Or are you just trying to avoid my throwing arm?"

"Both," Lauren admitted, and sat back, winded, messy and smeared with ice cream from forehead to chin.

Macy sat up, too, grimacing. If she looked half as bad as Lauren... *If only Leo could see me now.*

Lauren sighed. "I can't believe I'm saying this, but I've missed having fun with you."

"Uh-huh. Like my kind of fun can even compare to the fun you have with Anton."

"I guess that's one of the only nice things about condoms. Less of a mess to clean up after."

Macy wrinkled her nose. "Speaking of condoms, I owe you."

"Don't worry about it. What's a bit of rubber between friends?"

"Uh, safe sex?"

"Yeah, well. There is that, I guess." Lauren pulled off her thermal top and used it to wipe her face.

"You'd better get that into the wash." Macy nodded toward the ball of crumpled cotton. "Or you're going to have a huge stain on your hands."

"Better than having a huge stain on my chest."

Macy followed the direction of Lauren's gaze down her own smeared front. Rolling her eyes, she shrugged out of her red flannel pajama top.

The two women sat there, wearing only their bottoms, splattered with ice cream and sharing a rare friendship and a frustration with men.

Lauren was the first to speak. "So, what to do we do now?"

"I don't know about you, but I'm going to take a shower and get rid of this sticky gunk."

"I mean, what are we going to do about our lives? Why do they have to be so complicated?"

"Life isn't a bit complicated if you refuse to grow up."

"You can't refuse forever."

"Wrong. I can. I plan to. And to hell with the uptight Leo Reddings of the world."

"MR. REDDING? I have a Macy Webb to see you?"

Leo waited for the smoky wreckage of the dropped bomb to clear before he glanced up from the corporate dissolution he was drafting. Macy was here. At his office. In public and in broad daylight. What could she possibly want?

Besides his hide.

He stared over the rims of his glasses at the response button on his speakerphone, wondering if he could have imagined the intercom call. But he knew that he hadn't because it wasn't his lunch of spinach, jack cheese and black bean quesadillas churning in his stomach like a wild bull gone mad. No, it was the explanations and truths, the apologies he owed her scrambling for coherence in a madcap dash.

"Send her in, Ruth."

He placed his pencil in the center of his legal pad and sat back in his chair. The same chair he'd sat in three nights ago with his bottom half buck naked and Macy and her mouth between his legs. Not the image he needed to have on his mind while he waited to see her.

He hadn't seen her since he'd left the loft the night they'd returned home from the firm's apartment, shredded sheet balled up and held beneath his arm, to find Lauren had moved back. Without warning. Reminding Leo that Macy's life was a never-ending series of unexpected events, a constant flurry of whims and spurs of the moment, having the effect of a big wet blanket thrown on his fire. The blanket was a good thing in the long run. Made sure he thought with his thinking head.

He'd had to get out of there before saying any of a

dozen things he knew he'd regret. Like he'd had it up to his eyeballs with the constant interruptions, the total chaos and lack of order, and when did she plan to grow up and settle into a civilized adult routine?

But before he'd opened his mouth, he'd realized how much he would sound like a pompous pig—and unlike a civilized adult. That self-analysis had been damn hard to swallow, so he'd pulled back, his mental gears seizing up, his emotional gears freezing. And then he'd left.

But the time away from her didn't mean thoughts of Macy hadn't crossed his mind. They had. Repeatedly. Constantly. He was still working to figure out why.

Correction, Counselor. You don't want to admit to the why.

He'd spent the two days prior to moving out of her place consulting with an interior design firm recommended by Anton, and arranging to have the things the consultant considered worth keeping transferred from storage into the condo.

He didn't know why he hadn't told Macy his place was complete. It wasn't finished, but it was livable. Maybe he hadn't wanted to hear her tell him he'd worn out his welcome. Maybe he'd wanted to leave in his own time, on his own terms.

So why hadn't he? Left when and how he'd wanted? Packed his belongings and thanked her for the hospitality? What reason could he possibly have had for sticking around, living out of a suitcase, bunking in a borrowed bedroom, surrendering his privacy to the resident of the loft's life-size aquarium?

The minute she opened the door and stepped into his office, he knew. He knew. Hell, yes, he knew.

"Hello," she said, and closed the door behind her. "I

hope you don't mind me dropping by. I'll only stay a minute.''

"Stay as long as you like.'' He gestured to the set of navy leather wing chairs facing his desk. "I need to take a break. And it's nice to see a friendly face.''

"Is that what I am?'' She tilted her head to one side. "A friendly face?''

She was more than that. And she was here. And the ton of bricks between his shoulder blades weighed no more than a feather now that he'd seen her face. And now that he'd seen the rest of her? Looking nothing like his Macy? Just the icing on the cake of the forever fantasy he no longer denied.

She wore a black leather skirt, straight, slim and knee length, and a top in stark white, sleeveless, with antique silver buttons from the shirt collar to the hem riding her waist. She carried a black lace shawl, a black leather clutch.

And though she wore black pumps that he was sure were the height of fashion but looked uncomfortable as hell, she wore no stockings. Her bare legs were the sexiest thing he'd ever seen. He couldn't take his eyes off her body as she walked, the way the leather hugged her hips and her thighs strained the skirt's confines as she placed one foot in front of the other on her way from the door to his desk.

She sat in the chair he'd offered, crossing one leg over the other, her heels giving the impression that her legs went on forever, when he knew exactly how short they were and how far they reached around his hips and how she had to lift herself up to dig her heels into his backside and how he'd never known another woman so hungry.... For his body, yes. But more so for his company, both in silence and conversation.

He looked up and met her gaze and hoped her smile wasn't at his expense. If it was, then his poker face had gone the way of the dodo. What had they been talking about, anyway? "You're smiling. I'd say that qualifies as friendly."

One brow lifted over her lightly accented eyes and she reached up to pat and tuck at the hair clipped in an untamed twist at the back of her head. "I could be an enemy bearing gifts."

He'd called her the enemy once. Before he'd spent any time in her company. When he'd thought she had no brain and no business sense. When he'd thought she lacked the aggressive nature to go after what she wanted, the balls to drive a hard bargain.

"Are you? Bearing gifts?"

"As a matter of fact, I am." She opened her clutch, pulled out a one-pound bar of Ghiradelli chocolate, leaned forward and set it in the middle of his desk.

Leo stared at the gold foil wrapping, took off his glasses and rubbed his eyes, hoping he'd see what he was obviously missing. Always with the surprises, this one, which pleased him no end. "Belated Valentine's Day?"

She laughed, a light little trill of a sound. "I didn't even think about it being February."

He returned his glasses to his face. "Nothing says 'welcome to the neighborhood' like chocolate?"

She shook her head. Loose tendrils of hair escaped her clip to tumble into her face. "I say my welcomes with popcorn."

She hadn't taken what they'd done together that lightly. He knew she hadn't. The same way he knew why she joked about things he considered significant. Her jokes, her pajamas, her bedroom under the sea—

insulators, keeping her safe from whatever it was that threatened her out here in the big bad world.

Hotshot lawyer, he'd finally figured that much out.

He picked up the candy, made a pretense of studying both sides of the wrapper, then looked into her eyes and made sure he had her attention. "Thank you. For the chocolate. And for the welcome."

Her discomfort became obvious in the way she repeatedly smoothed the lines of her skirt that didn't need smoothing, the way she ended up wrapping all ten fidgety fingers around the top of her clutch.

"The chocolate is for game night. It's tomorrow. If you want to come. Maybe you've won the sailing trip." She gave a small shrug of one shoulder, a hesitant move, almost as if she dreaded his answer to her invitation and to her unasked question about his scavenger hunt success.

The latter he wasn't quite ready to reveal. The trip was no longer his goal. As far as attending game night... "What time?"

"I try to get started by eight."

He nodded, considering. "And your newest game involves chocolate?"

She laughed again. "Actually, the chocolate is the dessert. It's probably going to be a quick evening. I haven't quite gotten the details worked out on my next game idea."

Leo lifted a brow at that. If nothing else, Macy had always taken care of her gIRL-gEAR business. "I figured with Lauren back, you'd have been spending all kinds of time brainstorming."

"Oh, we have been. Just not about work."

Macy lifted the corner of her mouth, and Leo knew

he didn't want to ask because he didn't want to hear how often he'd been the subject of their dialogue.

"I'll see what I can do. And thanks—" he gestured with the chocolate "—for dessert."

"You're welcome." This time she worked at smoothing the hem of her blouse and wrapping her fingers in the long end of the dainty silver chain she wore at her waist. "There was one other thing."

"Another gift?"

"If you want to look at it that way. It's more about your list for the scavenger hunt."

"Oh?" He had absolutely no idea where this was going.

"This is technically cheating. And it could make the difference in whether or not you win, but..." She bit at her lip, then released it, shook back her hair and lifted her chin. "Do you remember teasing me about the dirty little secret I've never even shared with my best friend?"

He did and he said so.

"Well, it's not so dirty. And it's not so little."

"I'm fine with the list, Macy. You don't have to tell me."

She got to her feet, started to pace, first the small strip of space between the chairs and his desk. But she obviously had a lot on her mind because she moved to pace from wall to wall, bookshelf to bookshelf.

"Did I tell you I was the youngest of six kids?" she finally asked, and Leo sat back for the tale.

"My parents were great. My brothers and sisters were great. What am I saying?" she asked with a little laugh. "They're all still great."

So far, so good, Leo thought, but still he waited.

"I know you'll find this hard to believe, but growing up? I was an incredible cutup." She'd stopped in front of one bookshelf to run her finger over the spines of the leather-bound volumes, frowning. "Some heavy-duty stuff you've got here."

He didn't want to give her too much of a reply, hoping if he said less, she'd say more. Because, in all the hours they'd spent talking, in all their scavenger hunt discovery, Macy had revealed few details of her life before gIRL-gEAR. He, on the other hand, had spilled his guts about everything from losing his mother to his dog.

He'd been unnerved by how distractingly comfortable he'd felt around her, and as a result he was critical of the way she lived her life instead of curious about it. It was a wonder she'd offered him the chocolate, much less the invitation to come over and play. "That heavy-duty stuff is required reading for all us esquire types. Designed to curtail our cutting up."

She gave a snort worth a thousand words and continued browsing. "My mom did her curtailing with her eyes. She could stare a hole right through any excuse we gave her or set fire to any backtalk with just one look. But she was always there when we needed her, you know?"

No, he didn't know. But he was glad Macy did. "And your dad? He was around?"

"Oh, yeah. All the time." Her eyes brightened for emphasis. "He worked a lot, selling parts for rigs and pipelines. Then, after the oil boom busted, he sold whatever he could. Cars. Insurance. Medical supplies. He did okay, but my mom had to go to work. Which meant the six of us kids had to pitch in." Macy's mouth pinched up in a grimace. "Trust me. We were not used to pitching."

Leo smiled. "Spoiled?"

"You can't even imagine."

He could, but he kept it to himself.

"I was young, seven or eight I guess, when things started going bad financially for my folks. They never fought over money. But a part of me wanted them to." She walked back to her chair, standing behind it, running her palms across the curved back, down the sides and up again. "Fighting would've been so much better than silence."

Leo didn't think that sounded so bad, but then he wasn't Macy. His father issuing orders, his mother refusing to acknowledge the militant commands, had been all young Leo had known. He'd welcomed the quiet when she'd finally left, until he came to realize that he'd never see her again.

The fact that his father hadn't had much to say afterward he'd counted as a blessing. Except his father hadn't had much to say since, leaving Leo wondering what had been the point of his parents' relationship when they were as unhappy apart as they had been together. As suitable mates, they'd failed miserably. As role models, they'd fared better, and he'd learned a valuable lesson in compatibility.

"I'd never known two people could love each other that much," Macy was saying as Leo realized he'd done the unthinkable and let his heart overrule his mind. "Neither would say anything for fear of hurting the other or adding more stress to the buckets of the stuff each one carried. It was like…"

Her hands slowed, stopping as they came together in the center of the chair's back. "I don't know. Like by ignoring their problems they wouldn't exist, you know? Like they'd be letting the other hold on to the fantasy of our old life."

The Webbs had seen their share of rough times, as

had the Reddings. Leo didn't deny either, but he didn't get why Macy was making her story out to be *The Grapes Of Wrath*. ''But you said they were doing great now?''

''Yeah. Everything's good now. But for a while...'' She let the sentence trail off and gave a tiny shake of her head. Her eyes clouded over. ''It really was tough on all of us. My dad, especially. He just...closed up. And it hit me hard. I'd always been Daddy's little girl because I was the youngest and, face it, I am the proverbial poster child for small.''

She did self-deprecation well, Leo thought, watching as she went back into motion, moving behind the twin to the visitor's chair and measuring the width of the curved back with the spread of her fingers.

''He was my fun guy. The one who had time to play games with me when everyone else was too busy with their own lives, work, school, dating...all that stuff. But he just wasn't there anymore. Mentally, emotionally. His depression nearly killed me. It came closer to killing him.'' She grew still, standing there unmoving, unemotional, uninvolved in the moment and living in another time.

A whisper of unease swept through Leo. He didn't want to hear this, couldn't bear to see her like this. ''Macy—''

''I stopped him, you know. From pulling the trigger.'' Her mouth remained grim. ''I walked into his office with my Monopoly board under my arm and he had a gun to his head. He never had been very good about locking doors.''

Oh, no. No, Leo thought. His pulse beat in his temples. His skin grew clammy and the leather chair suffocatingly humid and hot. He didn't know what to say, wouldn't have been able to form the words if he had. And yet Macy appeared to be relating the story of a birthday-party disaster. Not that of a moment that altered her life.

She frowned and went on. "I'm pretty sure it was for the life insurance, which never pays out in suicide, anyway, but then how clearheaded could he have been, unlocked door, gun to his head, kids all over the house?"

And one small, very frightened kid in the same room. Leo swallowed his nausea. "You talked him out of it?"

Shaking her head, Macy stared beyond Leo's bare office window to the unusually bright February sky and the past. "I didn't know what to say. Obviously, he didn't either, because all he did was take the gun and put it away in his desk. Then I set up the Monopoly board and we played."

"We played until my mom came home from work and my sister called us to dinner. Then we played until it was time for me to go to bed. Since he wasn't working much those days, we played every day when I got home from school. That way I knew he was safe. We'd close the door and talk for hours."

She smiled then, a softening of both lips and expression. "Well, he did most of the talking. I listened. It seemed to…relax him. After a few weeks, he started to laugh again."

Leo couldn't help but believe that Macy's father hadn't worked much those days because of his state of mind rather than any slump in any business. "Did he talk to you about the gun?"

"Nope. Never. Strange, isn't it? The very reason we were there every day playing games, and we never talked about it." Macy's smile grew wistful, melancholy even.

"We've talked about it since, but don't forget—when it happened, I was just a little kid."

"A little kid, maybe. But not an innocent bystander." And that made Leo angry with a man he didn't even know for exposing his woman—yes, Leo Redding's woman—to the unimaginable. "No one else found out what happened?"

She straightened, smoothed both palms over her hair. "I think he finally told my mother. But this was later. Months, I guess. Maybe a year? I was still coming home from school and waiting for him to get home so we could play. He was back to long hours, and a lot of days I'd fall asleep in his office chair, waiting."

"And worrying if he didn't show," Leo stated. Small in stature, huge in heart, his Macy was.

"Yes. I worried. I knew he was…better, for lack of a more clinical term. I could see it in his face. But to wake up alone in that room? To hear nothing but my own breathing?"

She paused, her deep breath tightening Leo's own chest.

"I knew where he kept the key to the gun drawer. So I'd check. Every day, I'd check. One day he caught me."

Leo couldn't have moved if a stick of dynamite had sizzled beneath his seat.

"That was the only time I ever saw my father cry." Macy wrapped both arms around her middle and held herself tightly. "He pulled me up into his lap in that huge leather chair and he hugged me. His tears ran from his cheeks to mine and we cried together. The next day he took me with him to sell the gun."

Leo blinked. What had he missed? "And that was it?"

Macy gave a little shrug. "That was it."

"That was asking a lot from a kid, don't you think?"

A kid who equated playing games with emotional safety. A woman who, despite having studied psychology, still did.

"I never said it made any sense."

Leo pushed up his glasses and dragged both hands down his face. Why hadn't he seen any of this side of Macy, her strength, her practicality, while they'd lived under the same roof? Or while he'd had her in his bed? All this time he'd had no idea who he was dealing with.

Or who he loved.

She picked up her clutch purse from the abandoned chair, wrapped the lace shawl around her shoulders, prepared to go. "Anyway. That wasn't really about the scavenger hunt, but you probably figured that out. I like you a lot, Leo. No. I more than like you. But I don't want to go there just yet.

"I could probably change who I am, but I don't want to. I'm happy being me, which is more than a lot of people can say. If that doesn't work for you...well..." She nodded toward his desk. "There's a lot to be said for chocolate."

13

"Yo, MACY. Not much in the mood for fun and games tonight, are we?"

Macy downed at least a quarter of the first of the many strawberry-kiwi wine coolers she knew she was going to need to make it through game night before giving Eric Haydon the time of day.

"What makes you say that? It's game night, isn't it? Of course I'm in the mood for fun and games."

Eric wrapped a hand around the bottle Macy held by the neck and pried it from her death grip. "I told you last month. I can judge your game nights by the feed bag you strap on. C'mon. Look at this spread. Booze and chocolate?"

Sitting to Eric's left, Macy stared down the length of the table set with platters of orange slices and bananas and what berries she'd been able to find, pound cake and banana bread and jumbo marshmallows, bottles of cherry brandy and amaretto and Grand Marnier, a carafe of coffee, a pitcher of cream, and twelve individual fondue pots, gentle heat from burning tea lights keeping the melted chocolate soft and warm for dipping.

At least eleven of the pots had the melted chocolate soft and warm for dipping. Leo had probably eaten the bar she'd delivered yesterday afternoon, never mind about dessert for game night. He'd probably been giving her lip service when he'd told her he'd try to drop by.

He'd probably decided she was a total nutcase and not worth the time of day or night.

But the rest of her usual crew, the friends she could count on to accept her for the Peter Pan she was and love her anyway, weren't the least bit shy about dipping in. Including Kinsey and Doug, who'd shown up expecting to get started on a new game and weren't particularly disappointed to find a wrap party of last month's scavenger hunt under way.

Bottom line, Macy didn't understand Eric's problem. "I was in the mood for dessert. So sue me."

Eric arched devilish blond brows over eyes too sparkling blue for a woman's peace of mind. The fact that she even noticed gave Macy hope that walking out of Leo's office hadn't been the end of her life. Then again, no eyes had ever come close to doing for her what Leo's did, and so she pouted.

"Looking at your face," Eric said, "I'd say what you're in the mood for is a pity party."

"Like I said, sue me," Macy groused, and skewered banana, banana bread and another chunk of banana bread. Then she groused because the guilt of emotional overeating didn't pack the same punch, what with her industrial-strength metabolism waiting in the wings.

Chocolate dripping and pooling onto her plate, she opened wide and inhaled the entire mouthful, listening to the chatter down the length of the table while she chewed.

Her guinea pigs were busy sharing their findings. Eric and Chloe, in fact, were doing their best to out–embarrass each other with tales of discovering ticklish spots and erogenous zones with not a stitch of clothing removed—or so they claimed. Macy had a feeling that if they hadn't already, they'd be tumbling into bed any day now. Who knew if or when they'd finally tumble out?

The table talk turned to nudity then, which got Ray into more than a bit of trouble. He quickly shut his mouth after revealing that Sydney avoided tan lines by sunbathing in the buff. Macy didn't think tan lines had been a question on anyone's list, but she didn't have the energy to put Ray, or better yet, put Sydney, on the spot.

Either Ray had invested a lot of effort in the game or the man was incredibly and eerily observant, because there wasn't an item on his scavenger hunt list that he hadn't nailed to guarantee his win. Which came as a complete shock to Sydney, who denied having revealed more than half of the items and demanded to know Ray's secret, and his source.

And then suddenly Ray was everyone's best friend as the rest of the group jockeyed for invitations to come along on his cruise. Ray made no promises and accepted the onslaught of attention with good grace and a grain of salt. And then the attention shifted from what Ray knew about Sydney to what Sydney knew about Ray.

Sydney hesitated to share, almost as if she didn't want Ray to know she hadn't equaled his effort. Or that she *had* but was reluctant to reveal her shared interest. And Macy was sure it was interest. The tension between the two was thicker than the chocolate and hot enough to suck the fire from every burning candle in the room.

At least she hadn't ruined *everyone's* life, Macy thought, swirling the tip of her tongue through the chocolate coating the marshmallow she held. Though the story of Jess and his chest-shaving scar would no doubt haunt him until his dying day. Judging by the look in his eye, however, Macy had a feeling Melanie would be forced to ante up a little payback.

And indeed, she was relating her own experience as a high-school freshman in a new town where, as Mel Craine, hair cut short and breasts bound, she tried out for and made the junior varsity football team before the school year started and her ruse blew up in her face.

But it was when Anton, whose fondue pot was filled less with chocolate than it was with cherry brandy, interrupted Mel's high-school story to let everyone know that Lauren had been voted the girl most of her male classmates wanted to sleep with, that the party finally pooped. Macy had a mind to let him sleep it off in the alley behind the warehouse, but Lauren was quick to his rescue.

Ray and Jess flanked Anton as the entire group headed as one to the loft's parking garage, where the guys belted Anton into the passenger seat of his Jag and Lauren insisted on seeing him home. Anton mellowed at that, and apologized, and the group dispersed with promises to be back next month, Sydney threatening bodily harm if Macy didn't get her column pulled together by deadline.

Macy had never been so glad to see a game night come to an end. She would've breathed deeply to settle her frazzled nerves, but the garage was too full of exhaust fumes and her stomach too full of chocolate—not a good combination.

So she leaned against the side of the Jaguar while Lauren stood in the wedge of the driver's open door, screwed up her nose and pulled a face.

"I'm sorry tonight turned out so sucky. Game night is usually such a blast."

Macy heaved a big sigh. "It wasn't all that sucky. I just wasn't in the mood. But it was fun to see Ray win."

"And to see Sydney's sangfroid."

"You think they could..." Macy let the thought trail off.

Lauren picked it up with a shrug. "Yeah. I do. Though with the way things are between Sydney and her father, I'd hate to think she'd use Ray to get back at Nolan."

"You think she would?"

"Maybe not consciously."

"Lauren?" Anton called from inside the car.

Lauren inclined her head. "I'd better get him home. He won't be worth knowing if he loses all that booze and chocolate in the Jag."

Macy shuddered at the thought. "Listen, I know I rag on Anton, but I don't think he's worth giving up on. I want y'all to work things out."

"I know you do." Lauren smiled. "Just like I want you and Leo to get your act together."

"We don't have an act to get together." Macy warded off Lauren with an index-finger cross.

Lauren grabbed both of Macy's hands and squeezed. "You are full of so much crap and if it wasn't for your stupid rules I'd knock it out of you."

"Okay. I'm full of crap. Can I have my fingers back now before you break them off at the knuckle?"

Lauren let her go. "Listen. I was going to stay in Anton's guest room, but he'll be fine. A few hours of sleep and he'll be back to his usual belligerent self. Let me get him settled in and I'll catch a cab back and help you clean up. We can talk."

"No. You stay. He may want you there when he wakes up and realizes what an ass he was tonight."

Lauren hesitated. "I would like to stay in case he needs me.... Are you sure you'll be okay?"

Macy shook her head, shooed Lauren into the car.

"Are you kidding? With all that chocolate and alcohol waiting upstairs? And no man to ruin it for me? I'll be peachy. Just peachy."

THE WHIR OF THE ELEVATOR caught Macy contemplating the long table of leftover chocolate. No, no, no. She would not drown her sorrows in the remaining Ghiradelli. She would not lick the fondue pots clean.

She would not give Eric Haydon the satisfaction of having called her on the pity party. She would not waste another minute whining to herself or to Lauren about that other man, that esquire, who didn't deserve the time of day.

And she would not let her best friend spend the rest of the evening baby-Macy-sitting, when Lauren had issues to work on with Anton.

Intending to head Lauren off before she stepped a single foot into the loft, Macy moved from the table to the elevator. But when the big boxy car ground to a stop, when the gate rattled and creaked open, Lauren was the last thing on Macy's mind.

Because standing inside the metal cage stood Leo Redding.

He leaned against the back wall, feet crossed at the ankle, head down in a study of the floor. Macy felt a strange mix of emotion—elation, annoyance, a forced indifference—and then he looked up.

And the tingle of hope curling her fingers around a fondue fork, her toes inside her leather clogs, centered in the pit of her belly and exploded in the direction of her heart.

He stepped out of the elevator, into the loft. The gate creaked and rattled closed. Macy stood still, fists at her hips, waiting. Leo reached back and hit the switch, sending the car to the ground four stories below.

She took a step in reverse, her rear end coming into contact with the back of the red-and-yellow plaid chair. She parked her butt on the edge and made an attempt to give him a dismissive once-over, but he made the pots of chocolate look like so many rainy-day puddles of mud.

Oh, good Cupid grief. Who was she kidding? She was head over heels in love.

"You're too late. The party's over." A double entendre if she'd ever uttered one.

Leo frowned, patted at his navy blazer, reached inside the breast pocket and pulled out the chocolate bar. He looked up from the candy and into her eyes. "Am I too late for dessert?"

Macy fought the urge to present herself as dinner, dessert and the evening's entertainment. "I'm not sure there's much left to dip but oranges. Maybe a few crumbs of pound cake. There's plenty of booze."

"Booze and chocolate," he said, and smiled. "Sounds like my kind of party."

Oh, why hadn't she left well enough alone, way back when? His smiles now came too easily and often. "Tell that to Eric. He was complaining that I wasn't serving fun food."

One brow went up. "Since when did you start listening to Eric Haydon?"

"Oh, that would be...never. I do my best to tune him out." Pushing off from her perch, she stood and held out her hand because it was the only safe move she could think to make. "So? Do you want dessert or not?"

He surrendered the pound of candy and followed where she led—which wasn't far, only half the width of the loft away to the table. Once there, Macy found the lone unused fondue pot. She found her lighter, as well.

She settled into the closest chair before unwrapping the chocolate bar and breaking it into chunks, dropping each one into the ceramic bowl with a clunk that echoed in her belly. Then she lit the tea light.

Leo eased down into the chair across the table as the candle flamed. "So? Who won?"

"Won?" she asked, trying to figure out the dynamics of entertaining a man one had slept with before one's emotions were involved, when sleeping with the same man now was both out of the question and the thing one wanted more than life itself.

"The scavenger hunt."

"Oh, right." Duh. "Ray won, much to Sydney's dismay."

"He did good on his list, then?" Leo asked, crossing his arms and leaning his chair back on two legs.

Macy nodded, smiling, staring down into the pot of fondue. "One hundred percent right on."

"And Sydney?"

"Hard to tell. She didn't have much to say after finding out she'd been so thoroughly made."

"Hmm." The chair came down. Leo leaned forward, joined Macy in a study of the melting candy. "What about Lauren and Anton? They still toughing it out?"

Macy offered a one-shouldered shrug. "He got drunk. She drove him home. Just another day in paradise. But they're working on it."

"Lauren's got a good head on her shoulders. And Anton's no slouch. They'll get it together."

"Hope so." That was about all Macy could manage to say, wondering as she was if she was sitting across from the same man who hadn't expressed two words of concern about Lauren and Anton in the past.

"What about Eric? And Jess? Did they make much of a dent in their lists?" Leo inclined his head toward the pink and blue papers haphazardly scattered at the far end of the table. "Or did Chloe and Mel run 'em over?"

Okay. This was getting weird. Especially since soccer was Leo's only connection to any of Macy's men, and the women he only knew as clients. What was his sudden interest? "Jess got Melanie back in a big way for the chest-shaving story. And who knows about Eric and Chloe? Those two deserve each other and all the trouble they can cause."

Chuckling, Leo found a clean mug and poured coffee and amaretto in equal parts, then added cream. He stirred the brew with a fondue fork. "Guess everyone left with a lot of cold beer stories to share."

Macy wasn't sure if he was making a dig or an apology. She wasn't sure where anything he said was coming from. Or why he seemed so...mellow. "You missed a good time."

Cradling the mug between his large hands, he sipped, swallowed, sucked air through clenched teeth and shuddered. "I did think about coming for the party."

"But decided instead to perfect your fashionably late arrival?" She skewered a marshmallow with the fondue fork and tested the consistency of the softening chocolate.

"What I decided—" he set his mug firmly on the table "—was that I'd rather give you my list in private."

Oh, boy, Macy thought. This was it. The big kiss-off. She swirled the marshmallow in a nervous figure eight. "Well, if you're waiting for an invitation...then consider yourself invited."

His mouth quirked and he leaned back, lifted his hips, dug into the back pocket of his khaki slacks and produced the sheet of blue paper. He took his time smoothing and unfolding the list, finally spreading it out on the table for Macy to see.

What she saw was nothing. The list was blank except for the printed questions. She stopped stirring the chocolate and stared, blinking, thinking, then slowly lifted her gaze to meet his. "I know I'm pointing out the obvious, Leo, but all you're giving me is a blank sheet of paper. The same one I gave you."

Slowly, he shook his head, his hand flat on the paper on the table. He flexed his fingers once, twice, and then he said, "No, Macy. I'm giving you more."

He turned the paper facedown. And there, on the back of the blue page, written in black ink and block letters, were three words. Three words that had her eyes blurring and her ears ringing and her pulse bursting in her veins. If this was a dream, she never wanted to wake up.

She pulled in a deep breath and swore she'd hate herself forever if she cried. Her voice was level and low when she asked, "This isn't because of my tragic childhood reenactment yesterday, is it?"

He shook his head, but she cut him off anyway. "Because if it is—"

"Trust me." He reached across the table to still her trembling hand, which rattled the fondue fork against the side of the pot. "It's not. I knew how I felt before you walked through my door."

"But you didn't say anything." This time all she could do was whisper. "Why didn't you say anything then?"

The smile he offered was tender and sweet. "Because

I didn't want you to think what you just thought. That I was reacting to what you'd come to tell me.''

She didn't know how to respond. From totally out of left field, he'd said the very thing she would've died to hear him say. Well, he hadn't said it. He'd written it. As if she was going to quibble.

''But you left. We made love and you left.'' This was what she didn't understand. ''Lauren had come back and you'd already been run off once that night and I don't even know the meaning of peace and quiet and what kind of successful, driven attorney wants to live in a madhouse?''

''Is that a lawyer joke? Or just a really long run-on sentence?''

She shook her head. She nodded. She wanted to laugh. But her breath caught and she could do little more than sniff back the emotion puffing up in her throat like a hot air balloon. She had so much to say, so many things to ask. But her big fat mouth wasn't working, damn it.

Leo stood, came around the table and pulled her out of her chair and to her feet. He cradled her face in his hands, brushed his thumbs over the tears clinging to her lashes.

''I left because I didn't know what else to do. Lauren needed you.'' He paused, hesitated, finally said, ''And what I needed could wait.''

She moved her hands to his chest, beneath his blazer, feeling the warmth of his skin, the hard beat of his heart through his white oxford shirt that wasn't stuffed or the least bit stiff. How could she ever have thought otherwise? ''What was it that you needed?''

''I needed you to kiss me.'' He pressed his fingers to her lips when she opened her mouth to interrupt. ''Not because of any dare or any game. Not because it was what I wanted." He ran the barest tip of a thumb over her lower lip. "I needed to know you wanted me then as much as you'd wanted me in bed."

Closing her eyes and clutching the lapels of his blazer, Macy buried her face in Leo's chest and breathed in the scents of his clothing and his skin and his soap, and knew nothing in the world could possibly smell as sweet as love.

She used her tongue to part the lapels of his shirt and kissed his breastbone, sighing into his damp skin. "I love you, Leo Redding."

"I love you, Macy Webb."

For several long moments he stood quiet and still, stroking his hand over her hair. Macy refused to move. This moment was too fairy-tale perfect and she didn't want it to end.

Of course, Leo, being Mr. Practical, had to bring her back to the real world. "So, how'd you do on your list?"

"I did okay." She did better than okay. She'd won the biggest prize of all. And, no matter what Leo said, size did matter.

"Are you going to show it to me?"

Macy opened her eyes, bit her tongue on the comeback his comment deserved, but didn't move another single muscle. She was too comfortable, and moving would mean she had to let go when she never ever wanted to let go.

"Macy? Your list?"

She looked down at the table. At the warm liquid chocolate. And at the marshmallow that would serve quite well as a sponge brush for painting...

"It's in the bedroom." She grabbed him by the tie with one hand, took hold of the fondue pot's handle with the other. "C'mon. I'll spell it out for you. But you'll have to get naked."

Both brows went up over his pewter rims. "Naked?"

She licked her lips. "Yep. Chocolate is hell on white dress shirts."

*You haven't seen the last of gIRL-gEAR!
In March, Alison Kent returns with another
three-alarm Blaze that's sure to keep
you turning pages.*

*Chloe and Eric strike up a deal when she has to
correct her man-crazy image. He'll be her perfect
escort at three high-profile functions; in return,
she'll grant him three wishes...
within reason...as long as there's*

NO STRINGS ATTACHED

Here's an excerpt...

1

"THINK ABOUT IT, ERIC. Three dates. That's all it is." Chloe counted them off on her fingers; one, two, three. "Three nights spent in my company, schmoozing with the media. With designers. Supermodels."

She'd called him Eric, he noted. Not sugar. "Supermodels?"

"I'd do the same for you."

Oh she would, would she? "I tell you what. I'll make you a deal."

He had to give her credit. She didn't turn him down immediately the way he'd said flat out, "No," before hearing the dirty details of her idea. She had an open mind.

A desperate open mind?

Willing to go to any lengths to save her career?

Hmm. He could see himself playing the devil to her Faust.

"What? What's the deal?"

"You get your three dates." He did the finger thing; one, two, three. "And I get my three—"

"No." She shook her head so forcefully, wisps of her blond hair caught on her lips, leaving her decidedly disheveled.

Eric liked the look. "What kind of double standard is this? I'm not allowed to say no, but you can turn me down flat without hearing me out?"

"I don't want to hear you out. Not if it's going to be about sex."

He hung his head and did his best to look puppy-dog pitiful instead of guilty as hell. "After all that talk about friends being there for each other? You've gone and hurt my feelings, Chloe."

"You're saying your deal-making efforts aren't intended to get me into bed?"

He looked up in time to catch the imperial lift of her brow. "What? And ruin this beautiful friendship?"

He wasn't about to admit what the picture of her tousled hair was doing for his imagination. Just get her out of her shoes and shorts and, yeah, he could see Chloe Zuniga in his bed, wearing nothing but her socks and that jersey hanging over her thighs and curvy bare ass.

"Okay." Her chin went up. She shook back her hair. "What three *non-sexual* things do you want in exchange for your escort services?"

"We're going to do this, then?"

"Well, it depends on what you want."

Nope. He wasn't going anywhere near that one, either; there wasn't a long enough pole. "Don't worry. I'll think of something."

"So, you don't even know what you want? This is just an open-ended deal? I'm expected to be at your beck and call while you get off on stringing me along?" At each question asked, her voice had risen. Her final query was nothing if not a screech.

"I suppose we can set a time limit."

"Damn straight we're going to set a time limit. I'd be a thousand kinds of fool to leave myself open to the warped working of your imagination."

Ah. Now this was the Chloe he knew and...definitely

didn't love. Admittedly had the hots for. "Okay, then. What? A month? Six weeks?"

She'd pulled a mini Day-Timer from her mini knapsack. "The date of my third event is the middle of May, so let's wrap up this deal by Memorial Day."

He thought of everything he had on his calendar between now and then. A huge grin started at the edge of his mouth and spread until he thought his face would split.

"What the hell are you so happy about?" Chloe groused, hoisting her small leather backpack onto one shoulder.

"Just thinking how I've always wanted a genie to grant me three wishes. And here you are."

Who needs Cupid when you've got kids?

Sealed with a Kiss

A delightful collection from *New York Times* Bestselling Author

DEBBIE MACOMBER

JUDITH BOWEN

HELEN BROOKS

Romance and laughter abound as the matchmaking efforts of some *very* persistent children bring true love to their parents.

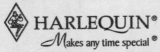

HARLEQUIN®
Makes any time special ®

Available in January 2002…just in time for Valentine's Day!

Visit us at www.eHarlequin.com

PHSK

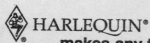

HARLEQUIN®
makes any time special—online...

eHARLEQUIN.com

shop eHarlequin

💗 Find all the new Harlequin releases at everyday great discounts.

💗 Try before you buy! Read an excerpt from the latest Harlequin novels.

💗 Write an online review and share your thoughts with others.

reading room

💗 Read our Internet exclusive daily and weekly online serials, or vote in our interactive novel.

💗 Talk to other readers about your favorite novels in our Reading Groups.

💗 Take our Choose-a-Book quiz to find the series that matches you!

authors' alcove

💗 Find out interesting tidbits and details about your favorite authors' lives, interests and writing habits.

💗 Ever dreamed of being an author? Enter our Writing Round Robin. The Winning Chapter will be published online! Or review our writing guidelines for submitting your novel.

All this and more available at
www.eHarlequin.com
on Women.com Networks

HINTB1R

Enjoy the fun and frolic of the Regency
period with a brand-new novel from
New York Times bestselling author

Stephanie Laurens

A Comfortable Wife

Antonia Mannering was a young
woman with plans—and becoming
and old maid was not one of them! So she
proposed a marriage of convenience to her
childhood friend, Lord Philip Ruthven.
Never had she expected that their hearts
would somehow find their way into
the bargain!

"All I need is her name on the cover
to make me buy the book."
—*New York Times* bestselling author
Linda Howard

*Available January 2002
at retail outlets everywhere.*

HARLEQUIN®
Makes any time special.®

Visit us at www.eHarlequin.com

PHCW

If you enjoyed what you just read,
then we've got an offer you can't resist!

Take 2 bestselling love stories FREE!
Plus get a FREE surprise gift!

Clip this page and mail it to Harlequin Reader Service®

IN U.S.A.
3010 Walden Ave.
P.O. Box 1867
Buffalo, N.Y. 14240-1867

IN CANADA
P.O. Box 609
Fort Erie, Ontario
L2A 5X3

YES! Please send me 2 free Harlequin Blaze™ novels and my free surprise gift. After receiving them, if I don't wish to receive anymore, I can return the shipping statement marked cancel. If I don't cancel, I will receive 4 brand-new novels each month, before they're available in stores! In the U.S.A., bill me at the bargain price of $3.80 plus 25¢ shipping and handling per book and applicable sales tax, if any*. In Canada, bill me at the bargain price of $4.21 plus 25¢ shipping and handling per book and applicable taxes**. That's the complete price and a savings of at least 10% off the cover prices—what a great deal! I understand that accepting the 2 free books and gift places me under no obligation ever to buy any books. I can always return a shipment and cancel at any time. Even if I never buy another book from Harlequin, the 2 free books and gift are mine to keep forever.

150 HEN DNHT
350 HEN DNHU

Name	(PLEASE PRINT)	
Address	Apt.#	
City	State/Prov.	Zip/Postal Code

* Terms and prices subject to change without notice. Sales tax applicable in N.Y.
** Canadian residents will be charged applicable provincial taxes and GST.
  All orders subject to approval. Offer limited to one per household and not valid to current Harlequin Blaze™ subscribers.
  ® are registered trademarks of Harlequin Enterprises Limited.

BLZ02

Coming in January 2002 from Silhouette Books...

THE GREAT MONTANA COWBOY AUCTION
by
ANNE McALLISTER

With a neighbor's ranch at stake, Montana-cowboy-turned-
Hollywood-heartthrob Sloan Gallagher agreed to take part
in the Great Montana Cowboy Auction organized by
Polly McMaster. Then, in order to avoid going home with an
overly enthusiastic fan, he provided the money so that Polly
could buy him and take him home for a weekend of playing
house. But Polly had other ideas....

Also in the Code of the West

Available at your favorite retail outlet.

Silhouette®
Where love comes alive™

Visit Silhouette at www.eHarlequin.com

PSGMCA